An Aria of Omens

Patrice Greenwood

Evennight Books
Cedar Crest, New Mexico

An Aria of Omens

Copyright © 2014 by Patrice Greenwood

Published by Evennight Books, Cedar Crest, New Mexico, USA, an affiliate of Book View Café Publishing Cooperative

Cover photo: Chris Krohn

Publication team: Sherwood Smith, Phyllis Irene Radford, Elisabeth Waters, Chris Krohn

ISBN: 978-1-61138-402-4

Book View Café Publishing Cooperative
P.O. Box 1624, Cedar Crest, NM 87008-1624
http://bookviewcafe.com

An Aria of Omens

Patrice Greenwood

for Ken and Marilyn

Acknowledgments

Deepest thanks to the following stalwarts for their invaluable assistance with this novel: to my publication team, Sherwood Smith, Phyllis Irene Radford, Elisabeth Waters, and Chris Krohn; to Ken and Marilyn Dusenberry, my patient consultants; and to my colleagues in Book View Café for their help with mending and polishing.

And as always, warm thanks to Mary Alice Higbie and the staff of the St. James Tearoom, for inspiring me to write this series and for making Wisteria White tea a reality.

1

I stood at the top of the stairs, my gaze following the long, oriental rug down the hall to where Violetta Benning stood by the front window. "Vi? It's time," I called softly.

With sunlight filtering through chiffon curtains and setting her lace aglow, she was an airy silhouette of shadow against white, touched by just a glint of color from her auburn curls. She looked as ethereal as a young woman of Junoesque stature could.

Turning to me as I came closer, she took a deep breath. "Thanks, Ellen. I'm ready."

Vi's vocal coach and accompanist, Wendy, rose from one of the chairs in the little sitting area I had made at that end of the hall, holding a black binder to her chest. She was a good two feet shorter than Vi and a little stout, with short brown hair, and always cheerful. She smiled as I came to join them.

"Mr. Solano is here," I added. "I thought you'd want to know."

Now that I was no longer blinded by the window, I could see Vi's face. Her green eyes widened.

"OK. Yes, thanks for warning me. Is anyone else from the Opera here?"

"No one that I recognize, but that doesn't mean much."

"It's very nice of Victor to come and support you," said Wendy. "No need to be nervous. He's on your side."

Vi nodded, then squared her shoulders and put on a smile. Her duster-length jacket of lace over a cream silk sleeveless blouse and trousers looked cool and elegant on this warm July afternoon.

"He's been wonderful," Vi agreed. "Yes, it's great of him to come."

"You've got a full house," I said. "They're all excited—and by the way, I'm so proud of you, Vi!"

She smiled and gave me a hug. "Thanks for doing this, Ellen!"

"Are you kidding? It's the event of the season. We sold out two weeks ago."

I led the way downstairs, where the smell of fresh-baked scones greeted us. A hubbub of voices came to us from the front of the tearoom. We paused outside the main parlor and I smiled at Vi, then stepped in to introduce her.

The parlor had been rearranged for the occasion, pocket doors thrown open and furniture adjusted so that everyone in the room faced the fireplace in the center of the back wall. Savories and breads had already been served, and the guests were chatting over their scones while two of my servers, Iz and Dee, moved among them with fresh pots of tea.

The girls looked lovely in their lavender dresses and white aprons, and I couldn't help thinking of how pretty Vi had looked in the same outfit on opening day. It seemed a long time since she'd left us to be an apprentice at the Santa Fe Opera, though in fact she had only started rehearsals two months ago.

All the tearoom regulars had come out for Vi's appearance. My aunt Natalia and her beau, Manny, were catching up with Vi's mother, Rhonda, and my best friend, Gina Fiorello. My neighbors, Bob and Katie Hutchins, chatted with Thomas Ingraham, the food critic from *The New Mexican*. And, inevitably, the Bird Woman was there with a bevy of her friends, wearing an enormous purple hat with crimson ostrich plumes curling over its brim.

Sitting in a place of honor, in a blue wing chair with a cup and saucer on his knee, was Mr. Victor Solano, baritone, a featured soloist at the Opera this year. In a sage linen jacket and dark trousers, brown hair waving over a classical brow, he looked gentlemanly and unremarkable, but I'd heard him sing in prior seasons and knew the power hidden in his chest. He was a big name in opera. Vi was indeed lucky to have caught his notice.

The upright Steinway that had been my mother's, freshly tuned for the occasion and glowing from a beeswax polish, stood near the fireplace. A single candle burned in the hearth, and vases of lisianthus adorned the mantel.

I went to stand by the piano and glanced around the room. Conversations began to drop away, and when it was quiet enough that I didn't need to shout, I began.

"Thank you all for coming to this very special event. Many of you have met Violetta Benning here at the tearoom. This summer she is an apprentice at the Santa Fe Opera, and today she's here to sing for us. Welcome back to the Wisteria Tearoom, Violetta!"

I made way for Vi, who showed no sign of nerves as she stood smiling, accepting the polite applause of the guests. Wendy slid unobtrusively onto the piano bench, but Vi drew everyone's attention to her at once.

"Thank you," she said as the applause faded, "and please welcome my coach, Wendy Richardson. I wouldn't be here without her."

Wendy nodded and smiled, then set her notebook on the music rack and turned the pages as another brief round of applause subsided.

"I'd like to sing for you an arietta from *Le Nozze di Figaro*, by Mozart," Vi said. "It's called 'Voi, che sapete,' and is sung by Cherubino, a young page. This is what is called a breeches role, a male character performed by a woman, which is why I'm wearing trousers today."

Leaning against the open doorway, I smiled. She looked anything but masculine, though she was indeed wearing trousers. Her hair was caught up into a bun, but a few ringlets had escaped to curl around her face. The effect was charming.

"Cherubino has just joined the military and is showing off his new uniform to the Countess Almaviva and her maid, Susanna. He asks them to explain love to him, why it makes him freeze and then burn, why it robs him of peace, even though he rather enjoys these sensations."

A chuckle went through the room, then Wendy addressed the keyboard. Vi's voice soared, a rich mezzo-soprano, filling the tearoom with wonderful music. My heart swelled with pride, both in her and in the moment of beauty, the sort of moment I had been aiming to create all along.

I hadn't heard Vi sing before, not like this. A shiver went through me as I realized she really had it; she could make a career in opera. Well, of course. The Santa Fe Opera wouldn't have taken her on as an apprentice if that weren't true. They turned away a lot of candidates every year.

Julio, my chef, came up beside me to peer through the doorway, his dark eyes big with wonder as he listened. He and Vi had struck up a friendship when we first opened, and I knew that he had missed her. We all had.

"Are the cakes ready?" I whispered to him.

He nodded, not taking his eyes off Vi. Kris, my office manager, joined us, her black lace a counterpoint to Vi's cream.

The arietta drew to a close, and the tearoom burst into applause. Flushed and smiling, Vi made a professional bow. I saw her glance flick toward Mr. Solano and her smile widen a little.

I joined her, applauding with the rest until the clamor died down. "Thank you, Violetta! That was beautiful! Before we pester you with questions, which you've so kindly agreed to answer, I'd like to announce a special treat." I turned to address the room. "Our chef, Julio Delgado, has created a dessert in Violetta's honor. It's called an Aria Cake, flavored with Assam tea and almonds, and it's making its debut at the tearoom today."

Dee and Iz brought in trays of cakes, each an elongated triangle about a finger's length, with multiple layers of cake and icing, topped with sliced almonds and candied violets. Excitement hummed through me as I watched the girls serve the cakes and my guests sample them.

Julio had invented the Aria Cake as an act of rebellion. I had asked him to make Opera Cakes for Vi's tea, and he'd flat-out refused.

Opera Cake is just glorified tiramisu, Parisian style. You don't like coffee in the tearoom. Besides, have you ever made it? It's a royal pain!

So I'd invited him to come up with something better. And he'd done it.

By replacing the coffee and chocolate with tea, he'd allowed the cake's almond flavor to shine through. The Aria Cake was lighter and, I thought, more unusual than Opera Cake. As I watched from the doorway, it seemed to me that the guests approved. Gina caught my eye, took a bite, then closed her eyes in ecstasy. Hiding a chuckle, I stepped back out into the hall.

"Congratulations, Julio. I think it's a hit."

He shrugged. "Of course." But he looked pleased.

Vi, who had paused to sip some water from a glass on the piano, returned to center stage and began taking questions. The Bird Woman's hand shot up into the air.

"Which opera are you in?"

"I'm in four of the five productions this season. I'm in the chorus in *Tosca* and *Cesar Chavez*, I'm one of the three ladies in *The Magic Flute*, and I'm singing the role of Hermia in *A Midsummer Night's Dream*. I'm also covering the Shepherd Boy in *Tosca*."

"What's that mean?" said the Bird Woman, blinking through her feathers.

"A cover is someone who learns a role so they can step in if the performer can't go on for some reason."

"Like an understudy," said Gina.

"Yes, exactly." Vi smiled at her.

"That sounds like a lot to learn," said the Bird Woman.

"Well, it is. We're kept very busy with rehearsals every day. The busiest time was right before opening night, when we were learning two productions at once. After that it got a little less hectic."

She answered a few more questions, then took another sip of water and nodded to Wendy, who turned a page in her notebook.

"I have another aria for you," said Vi. "'Crude furie' from *Serse* by George Frideric Handel. This is again a breeches role: Serse is the emperor Xerxes, and he's been plotting to marry the woman he loves, but she loves someone else and through various misadventures she winds up married to her true love.

Serse is enraged, and in this aria he calls on the Furies to inspire him with their venom. He wants the world to turn to ash and the sun to be eclipsed by the heat of his fury. I'm sure we've all had days like that."

As the guests laughed, Vi took her place and squared her shoulders. Wendy played the introduction, and Vi launched into Serse's tirade, eyes flashing. It was a longer piece, but she had the stamina for it, and she was magnificent.

> *Crude furie degl'orridi abissi*
>
> *Rise up, furies, from horrid abysses.*

If the mood of the aria was a little troubling for me, the beauty of the music and the obvious enjoyment of my guests made up for it. Vi received a standing ovation, which shortly dissolved into a cluster of people around her, eager to embrace and congratulate her.

I remained in the hall, watching Vi's success. A few of the guests began to depart, and I thanked them as they came out. The tea was breaking up.

Victor Solano drifted toward me. There was no getting near Vi, and he probably saw her frequently at the Opera's campus anyway. I thought it tactful of him to refrain from intruding on her moment in the spotlight, and gave him a smile as he came into the hall.

"Thank you for coming, Mr. Solano. I hope you enjoyed the tea."

"Very much, especially that Aria Cake." His gaze shifted to Julio standing beside me, and took in his chef's jacket over the usual loud print pants (giant music notes today). "Are you by chance the creator?"

I sensed Julio stiffen ever so slightly. "Yes," he said.

"Inspired work. Congratulations." Mr. Solano offered a hand, and after a tiny hesitation Julio shook it.

"Thank you." Julio glanced at me. "That reminds me, I have something to give Vi before she goes. Please excuse me."

He strode down the hall toward the kitchen, leaving me and

Mr. Solano with Kris between us. I turned to Mr. Solano with a smile.

"This is my office manager, Kris Overland. Kris, this is Victor Solano. He's a soloist at the Opera this year."

"Lovely to meet you," said Kris, shaking hands. "What roles are you performing?"

"I'm singing Scarpia in *Tosca*."

"And that's quite enough for one season," said Mr. Ingraham, joining us. "I look forward to it," he added, nodding to Mr. Solano.

"We've met, haven't we?" said the singer, eyes narrowing a little.

"At the Patrons Council dinner two years ago," said Mr. Ingraham. "Good of you to remember."

"I remember your face, but I confess I'm terrible with names."

"Ingraham. Thomas."

"Ah, yes."

I knew Mr. Ingraham was an opera-goer, but I hadn't known he was a Patron. That meant he gave them a chunk of change every season. I wished I could do the same—then told myself I *looked forward* to the day that I would be able to. An exercise in positive thinking.

The Bird Woman chose this moment to lead her gaggle into the hall. With a glance at Mr. Ingraham, whom I trusted to entertain Mr. Solano for a moment, I drew her toward the front door. She only came up to my shoulder, and her hat rather eclipsed her. She had a matching purple cardigan buttoned over her pink and lavender flowered dress.

"I hope you enjoyed the tea, Mrs. Olavssen."

"Yeah, it was great. Boy, that Violetta sure can belt out a tune!"

I heard a choke of masculine laughter behind me, quickly transformed into a cough. The Bird Woman glanced toward Mr. Solano, then dismissed him with a shrug and headed for the gift shop across the hall.

"Wish they'd been in English, though. I couldn't understand a word of it."

"That's why she told us the story," said one of the gaggle.

"Yeah, but it would be better in English."

To my relief, she disappeared into the gift shop, trailing her friends after her. Kris gave me a sidelong glance. "I'll see if Dee needs help," she said, and followed the ladies into the gift shop.

I rejoined the gentlemen. Mr. Solano's eyes crinkled with amusement.

"One of our regular customers," I said.

He nodded. "She's delightful. The world would be less without eccentrics. I can say that, because I am one."

"Oh, no!"

"Oh, yes. All artists are."

"But the most successful ones are revered for it," said Mr. Ingraham. "Don't run away, Ellen. I have something for you."

I had been about to go back into the parlor, but stayed. Mr. Ingraham pulled an envelope from the breast pocket of his tweed jacket and put it in my hands. "Happy birthday, a little early, from me and your aunt."

I glanced at Mr. Solano, then peeked inside the envelope. Two printed tickets nestled inside, and I squeaked as I recognized the distinctive architectural silhouette that was the SFO's logo. I pulled them out to read the details. "*Tosca!* Oh, Mr. Ingraham, thank you!"

"I hope you and your guest will join me for dinner before the performance," he said.

"You're tailgating?"

"But of course!"

"I wouldn't miss it for the world!"

I was so pleased I couldn't resist hugging him, even though I didn't know him that well. He chuckled and patted my back.

"May I bring something?" I asked. "Some Aria Cakes?"

His brows went up. "I was about to say no, but now I'll have to reconsider. Those were quite good."

I smiled at him, as pleased by this compliment as by his generous gift. When a noted food critic says your work is quite good, that's something to celebrate. Not that it was *my* work; Julio deserved the credit, but it was still an accomplishment for my tearoom.

I turned to Mr. Solano. "Now I'll get to hear you sing! I wasn't certain I'd manage it this season."

He bowed slightly. "Happy birthday, whenever it is."

"Thank you."

In truth, I'd planned to buy a ticket this season. I treated myself to an opera almost every summer, but the tickets were expensive and this year I'd been torn between wanting to see Mr. Solano in *Tosca* and Vi's solo in *A Midsummer Night's Dream*. Now I didn't have to choose; if I was lucky, I could do both.

Even better, I could bring a guest to Mr. Ingraham's party. A date, possibly. Would Tony be interested?

My heart jumped at the thought, and I shied away from it. I couldn't think about that right now. I needed quiet, and privacy, for that.

Aunt Nat and Manny came out of the parlor, Nat in a light blue cotton dress with a full skirt and puffed sleeves, complemented by a necklace of bird fetishes, the ensemble slightly fiesta-looking. Manny wore a jacket and bolo tie over light trousers. They both grinned at me.

"I see Thomas has sprung our surprise," said Nat.

I hugged her, burbling thanks. "I can't wait! I haven't tailgated in years."

"Not even at a football game?" inquired Mr. Solano, all innocence.

I shook my head, smiling. "Not a football fan."

"How un-American. To be honest, I'm not either."

By this time, most of the guests had left, and Vi and Wendy came out to join us in the hall. Vi went straight up to Mr. Solano.

"Thank you so much for coming."

He smiled. "I wouldn't have missed it. You were in fine voice."

She grinned, pink with pleasure. "Thank you."

Rhonda Benning and my girlfriend Gina ambled out together.

Gina, her dress a white print splashed with big sunflowers, complemented by a gauzy, white, broad-brimmed hat, caught me in a big, Italian hug.

"What a lovely event! Congratulations!"

"Thank you, but the kudos go to Julio, and to Vi for being the pièce de résistance."

"Oh, yes!" Gina turned to Vi. "I loved what you sang, although I half-expected something from *La Traviata*."

"Well, I turned out to be a mezzo-soprano, much to my mother's dismay."

"Not true!" said Rhonda in mock indignation. She smiled with pride, and I saw the same laughing light in her eyes that so often shone in her daughter's. Rhonda was darker than Vi, and not quite as tall, but the bones of their faces were the same.

Vi introduced her mother to Mr. Solano, and while they were chatting, Mr. Ingraham came up to me to say goodbye. "I'll call you about the details for *Tosca*."

"Yes, do. And I meant it about the cakes—I'd be glad to bring some."

"Let me look at my menu, but I have a feeling I'll be taking you up on that."

Nat and Manny left with him, and I slipped into the parlor. The last of the guests were departing. I thanked them for coming and walked them out, passing Iz in the doorway. She had a large tray for collecting china, a signal that the party was over.

Vi and her mother, Gina, Wendy, and Mr. Solano were all that were left. As I joined them, I saw Julio hovering a little way down the hall, a pastry box in his hands, watching Vi.

"Mr. Solano," I said, "is this your second season at Santa Fe or your third?"

"Fourth, actually. My first role was Escamillo in *Carmen*, nine years ago, early in my career."

Julio slipped up and touched Vi's elbow, drawing her away. From the corner of my eye I saw him give her the box. They exchanged whispered words.

"I don't think I saw that," I said. "I must have gone to

something else that year."

"My performance was not terribly memorable, but it was my first time in Santa Fe, and I was absolutely hooked. I would have come back every summer if I could."

"Well, I'm glad you're here this year."

"As am I."

Vi rejoined us. Julio had disappeared again. Mr. Solano looked Vi up and down.

"Well, fledgling. Back to the salt mines?"

She nodded, then turned to me. "Thanks so much, Ellen!"

"Thank *you*. We're the ones who benefited."

"So did she," said Mr. Solano. "It's good for her to sing out."

"You forgot to mention the apprentice showcase," Wendy said to Vi.

"Oh! Well, I'll be doing *Serse* again."

"I'd love to hear it again," I said. "The apprentice concerts are always delightful. I can mention them in the tearoom's newsletter, if you like."

"Yes, thanks!" Vi said. "I'll send you all the details."

Hugs and farewells, and she was off, with her mother and Mr. Solano in attendance. I glanced into the parlor, where Iz had already loaded her tray. I knew if I tried to help her she'd shoo me away, so I turned to Gina.

"Want more tea?"

"Thanks, but I've got a meeting with a client," she said, moving toward the front door.

I strolled along with her. "Well, thank you for coming. I know opera isn't your favorite."

"Shh! An Italian who doesn't like opera? Sacrilege!"

"You might enjoy the apprentice showcase. It's inexpensive, and if you haven't seen the opera house it's a great excuse."

"I'll think about it. I don't suppose you wear football jerseys to the tailgate?"

I laughed. "No."

"Opera costumes?"

"Not unless you're *really* eccentric."

The Bird Woman chose that moment to emerge from the gift shop, carrying a large shopping bag and blinking at us before heading for the door. I had to stifle a laugh.

"Well, you'll have to explain all the customs to me," said Gina. "Ciao, dearest. I'll call you."

"Ciao."

I watched her go, the afternoon sun electrifying her sun-flowers as she strode down the path to the street, passing the slower-moving Bird Woman with a friendly smile. I watched her get into her hot red Camaro, then went back inside.

On the way to my office, I looked into the kitchen. Julio was gathering up his things, about to head home.

"Brilliant job, Julio. Thanks."

He flashed me a smile as he slid his coffee thermos into his backpack. "It was good to see Vi. Great to hear her sing. Thanks for letting me listen in."

"Of course! I only wish you'd taken a bow."

He shook his head. He didn't much care for being fussed over in public.

"Everything all right?" I asked.

He hefted his pack onto his shoulder. "Sure. Why?"

I recalled the unease I'd sensed earlier, but it had just been for an instant, and I didn't know how to explain my concern, so I just smiled. "No reason. See you tomorrow."

He headed out the back door, and I went upstairs to my office. Tucked beneath the sloping roof of the upper floor, it was cozy and dark compared to the airy, light-filled center hallway. I turned on the stained-glass lamp and sat at my desk to admire my birthday gift.

I took the tickets out of the envelope and held them in my hands. Opera tickets had always been a treat for me.

My parents had supported the Santa Fe Opera for as long as I could remember, and from the time I was twelve (the dawn of young-ladyhood, as my mother had called it) they had consulted me each year on the choice of which opera the family should attend. My brother, three years older than I, had never been that interested. He was not musically inclined, and often bowed out of the annual excursion to SFO. Aunt Nat had come, though, as had Uncle Stephen while he was alive.

When I was little, going to the opera had been a magical evening, not only for the performance, but for the opera house and grounds, and the audience as well. In those days (long gone, alas), people dressed up to go to the opera. I remembered goggling at beautiful and astonishing attire: a gorgeous blonde in a white full-length gown with a spray of roses in her hair and a feather boa; a young man in a morning coat with a waterfall of black hair down his back, carrying a walking stick and top hat; numerous gentlemen in formal kilts for a performance of *Lucia di Lammermoor*.

Nowadays, opera-goers could be seen wearing tee-shirts and shorts. I was certain Miss Manners must share my opinion that this was a travesty.

The Santa Fe Opera performed in an open-air theatre perched on top of a hill north of Santa Fe, with a view of the Jemez Mountains behind the stage so splendid that the sets were usually constructed so as to leave it visible. Sometimes a lightning storm would add atmosphere to the performance.

I was too young to have seen the first opera house, which burned down in 1967. The Opera of my memory was the second building, with its distinctive, swooping roof extensions that failed to completely protect the center rows of the audience from rain, and gave the house its famous architectural silhouette. The front courtyard featured a long, curving flower bed planted entirely with white petunias that glowed in the dusk as the audience gathered before the performances.

I cried when that second opera house was demolished to make way for the third structure. The change had been necessary, but despite the many improvements of the new theatre (not the least of which was complete overhead protection for the audience), I still missed the old building, where my love for the opera had been formed.

That love filled my heart as I sat gazing at the tickets in my hands. What a wonderful gift from a beloved aunt and a new friend. Now that I was alone, I could think about who to invite.

Tony Aragón came into my thoughts. He'd been hovering at the edge of them since Mr. Ingraham had given me the tickets, but I wasn't sure I had the courage to ask him to join the opera party.

Would he accept? Or would he think opera was one of those activities reserved for a privileged few that did not include him? An Anglo thing?

There were plenty of Hispanics who attended the opera, but they weren't from Tony's class. He was a detective, definitely working-class, more a football guy than a fine arts guy. I could picture the narrowing of his dark eyes, the pinching of his nose in the hint of a sneer.

I wanted to share this treat with him, but I wasn't sure he would see it as a treat.

Sighing, I laid the tickets down on my desk. Detective Aragón was a perpetual question mark in my life. I liked him; he'd done me some favors.

Well all right—he'd saved my life. That was more than a favor.

And he was...very attractive. I couldn't deny that. It was one of the things that made thinking about him uncomfortable.

Footsteps in the hallway preceded Kris's entrance through the entrance that our offices shared. She looked in at me with a smile, her black hair and kohl-dark eyes making her look Cleopatra-esque.

"Bird Woman spent a hundred dollars in the gift shop."

"God bless her," I said.

"Everyone loved the event. Heard lots of good comments."

"Thanks. What did you think?"

"I thought it went very well."

"No, I mean Vi's singing. Did you like it?"

She tilted her head, thinking. "I liked the second number better."

That was no surprise. Kris had excellent taste, but she was

also a Goth, so her preferences ran toward darker themes. Her work clothes were always elegant, and the décor she had chosen for her office was, too, but the lovely print of Millais's *Ophelia* she had on the wall was still a picture of a dying woman.

She headed into her office, and I looked back at my opera tickets.

I could play it safe and invite Gina. She wasn't an opera buff, but she was always up for a party.

Coward.

I hated it when the little voice in my head talked to me like that. Especially when it was right.

I grabbed my phone, and before I could chicken out completely, I sent a text to Tony Aragón.

PLEASE DROP BY THE TEAROOM WHEN YOU GET A CHANCE.

I refuse to use shorthand when texting. I know it's faster, but I grew up with a respect for proper English. Yes, I know it's a losing battle. Still, I endeavor.

I put the phone down, then went downstairs so that I wouldn't stare at it. The girls had the parlor rearranged already, restored to its normal configuration of four smaller seating areas separated by a combination of pocket doors and strategically placed furniture. My mother's upright piano was back in its normal place against the wall.

I should get out some music and come down and play it after hours. I hadn't touched the piano since the move. Granted, it had been out of tune, but I hated to think I might lose my music from being too busy with other things.

I smiled, looking at the polished, dark wood. I'd learned to play on that piano. I wasn't great, but I could play a few pieces competently, and I so loved it.

Nothing like the soaring music that had filled the room that afternoon. Remembering Vi's wonderful voice, I smiled.

The day was ending. Apart from one couple in the Iris seating, the tearoom was empty of guests. I strolled down to the butler's pantry and found Iz arranging scones on a tray for them.

"Is there any tea brewed for staff?"

She nodded and gestured to a cozy-covered pot. Iz, a native of Tesuque Pueblo, is quiet and shy, but steady as a rock. Staying out of her way, I collected a cup and saucer and poured myself some tea—Keemun, it smelled like—then went into the kitchen.

Julio had left the place tidy, as always. Mick was in the alcove with the industrial dish-washing station, finishing up the china from the event. His long, blond hair was tied back in a ponytail and he wore a Pearl Jam tee-shirt. His face, very like his sister Dee's, was slightly flushed from the steam.

I headed for the fridge. As I'd hoped, a tray of Aria Cakes sat inside. I took it out and put a cake on a plate.

"Mick? Did you get to try an Aria Cake?"

He turned off the water and took out his earbuds. "Sorry, what?"

I held out the plate toward him. "Cake. Did you get a piece?"

"No, not yet. Thanks!"

I fetched him a fork, and another for myself, then served up my own piece of cake before putting the tray back in the fridge. Picking up my tea, I went across the hall to the dining parlor and sat in the middle of the table, looking out through the gauze-draped French doors at the back garden.

With a small sigh of satisfaction, I sipped my tea and took a bite of cake. Almond and butter and assam, sweet with a little crunch. Perfection.

Soft strains of music played over the house sound system—a Chopin nocturne. I relaxed as I listened, happy with the result of all the work that had led up to Vi's event.

This room was one of my favorites in the house. It had been the study of the original owner, Captain Dusenberry, for whom the house was built in the mid-19th century. He had also been killed in the room, as had Sylvia Carruthers, the woman without whose help I would not have been able to acquire the building for my tearoom.

Sighing, I reminded myself there was nothing I could do about the murders. In fact, they had attracted a certain amount of business from Kris's goth friends, and had made the tearoom a regular stop on a local ghost tour. I really should try to find out more about Captain Dusenberry, considering that he apparently was still around.

I took another bite of cake. I had never believed in ghosts, but I had no explanation for some of the strange things that happened in the tearoom. Lights turning on or off, music likewise. I glanced up at the chandelier over the table, but the crystals were all still, though I'd often seen a single drop swinging back and forth.

Willow Lane, the owner of Spirit Tours of Santa Fe, had assured me that Captain Dusenberry could do all of that. If he actually understood the stereo system, he was possibly more competent with electronics than I.

Tony Aragón suspected that someone had meddled with my ancient wiring. But why would anyone do that? Why go to so much trouble for a prank, when they weren't even around to witness its effects? In a fit of paranoia I had checked every corner of the dining parlor and every object and fixture in it for hidden cameras or microphones, and found nothing.

And besides, I sometimes felt Captain Dusenberry's presence. Not in a frightening way—in fact, I found it comforting. I had a benevolent, invisible roommate.

Dee stepped into the doorway, knocking on the open door. "Sorry to bother you, but Detective Aragón is here. He said you asked him to come."

"Yes, send him in."

"He's waiting on the front *portal*. He said you wouldn't want him to come in."

Oh. Yes, the gun.

We were still negotiating about the gun. I'd asked him not to bring it into the tearoom. He'd been pretty indignant.

"All right, tell him I'll be right out. Did you offer him tea?"

"Yes. He said no thanks."

"Thank you, Dee."

I stepped across to the kitchen and put another Aria Cake on a plate. Armed with this and a fork, I went down the hall to the front doors and out onto the *portal*.

Tony was sitting at one of the small tables in the shade of the wisteria vines, watching the traffic, a slight scowl on his face. The lines of his profile made me catch my breath—he really was quite handsome in a classically Latin way. He was dressed in jeans and a motorcycle jacket, open over a plain black shirt on this hot afternoon. His bike was parked on the street past the white picket fence that bordered my garden.

I sat across from him and pushed the plate of cake across the table. "Thank you for coming. Would you like to try Julio's latest creation?"

He looked surprised, and the scowl disappeared as he took off his shades and picked up the fork. "Thanks! What's up? I've only got a few minutes."

I discovered I didn't know how to phrase my invitation. I should have rehearsed. I cleared my throat.

"I was wondering if you'd like to join me...I've been given a gift of opera tickets."

He paused with a forkful of cake halfway to his mouth. "Opera? You're kidding, right?"

I shook my head, my heart sinking a little. "Do you dislike opera?"

"Don't know anything about it." He ate the cake. "Mmm! Oh, man. That's fantastic."

"Thank you." I watched him chop another bite with the fork. "Julio created it in honor of Violetta. She's an apprentice at the Santa Fe Opera this summer. You remember Vi?"

He frowned, then gave a nod and swallowed. "The tall one, right? Redhead?"

"Yes. She'll be in the opera I'm going to, *Tosca*. Mr. Ingraham and my aunt gave me two tickets, so I can bring a guest. And Mr. Ingraham has invited us to his tailgate supper beforehand."

I was babbling. I clasped my hands in my lap, trying to organize my thoughts.

Tony chewed meditatively, then focused on cutting another

bite of cake. "Yeah, I've heard of that. Opera tailgating. Candela-
bras and wine."

Candelabra, whispered my little voice. I ignored it.

"It's a lot of fun," I said. "If you've never been to the Santa Fe
Opera, it's worth going once, even if you're not an opera fan."

He scraped frosting from the plate with the edge of his fork.
"I don't have anything to wear. It's tuxedos, right?"

"Not necessarily. In recent years it's become a lot less formal."

I was fudging, because I strongly suspected that Mr.
Ingraham, and probably Manny, would dress. I also suspected
that Tony didn't own a tux.

"The suit you wore when you took me to dinner would be
fine," I added. "You'll be better dressed than a lot of the men in
the audience. Some of them won't even wear jackets."

"Yeah, but *your* friends will."

"True."

I watched him eat the last bite of cake, still without meeting
my gaze. "Why me?"

My little voice started gibbering. My heart was beating rather
fast. I took a deep breath.

"Honestly? You're the first person I thought of. I'd love it if
you'd escort me to the opera."

He set down the fork. The small click filled the awkward
silence.

"You know it's not my ..." He laughed softly. "... cup of tea."

"I know, but I thought you might enjoy the novelty."

He looked up at me, his warm brown eyes causing an
uncomfortable stir in my chest. "Tell you what. I'll go to the
opera with you if you'll go to a movie with me."

"Deal."

"You can even pick the movie. Doesn't have to be violent."

I thought about *Tosca,* in which Scarpia reveled in the
prospect of his "violent conquest" of Tosca, and in torturing her
lover. Well, it would be in Italian. Though of course, there were
the captioning screens on the backs of the seats...

Truth was, it was a dark opera and not what I would have

chosen for Tony's introduction to the art form, but it was what I had. Tickets were expensive enough that I doubted Tony would let me buy him one for a different production.

"OK," I said, and smiled. "It's the 20th. I'll let you know the details about dinner once I get them from Mr. Ingraham."

Tony's eyes narrowed. "Ingraham. The food critic?"

"Yes, you remember him?"

"Yeah." The scowl flicked back on his face. Must be remembering the murder at the tearoom on opening day. Mr. Ingraham had been at the tearoom, and Tony had interviewed him.

Was it work, then, that made Tony scowl like that?

He checked his watch. "Gotta go. Talk to you later."

We both stood, and he came around the table to kiss my cheek. "Thanks for the cake."

I blinked, recovering from the electric shock that had just gone through me. "You're welcome."

Watching him jog down my path to the street, I remembered belatedly to breathe. He swung onto his bike, started the engine with a roar, and cruised down the street toward the plaza. When he was out of sight I picked up the plate and took it back to the kitchen.

I passed the last guests in the hallway. They were leaving; the day was over. In the kitchen, I handed the plate and fork to Mick, who washed them in a flash and started packing up to go.

Dee had stayed to close up, and she and Mick teased each other—brother and sister stuff—as they walked out the back door. The tiny staff parking lot was empty except for my sedan and Mick's Mustang, which was a work in progress. Primer gray blotched it in a pinto-like pattern over at least three different colors of body paint. My private nickname for the car was "Frankenstein."

Dee turned to wave at me as they got in. I smiled and waved back, then locked the door.

Alone at last. The house was mine until five the next morning, when Julio would arrive to start baking.

The sun was still up, pouring in through the western windows. I went to the gift shop and closed out the cash register, taking the bank bag with the day's receipts up to my office where I locked it in my desk. It was warm upstairs; even though the office had no window on the west side, the adobe wall radiated heat.

I retreated downstairs, poked my nose in the fridge again and nabbed some leftover cucumber sandwiches, virtuously resisting the cakes. I'd skipped lunch in all the busy preparation for Vi's event.

The dining parlor was the coolest room in the house, being on the northeast corner of the ground floor. I sat at the table and nibbled my sandwiches, thinking over the day.

Vi's event was a lot of work, but it also gave everyone a lot of pleasure. It had filled the tearoom with guests on an afternoon that might otherwise have seen empty tables. I wasn't worried; the summer tourist season had brought an increase in business. In the fall and spring, though, when things would be slower, a few events like today's might give my bottom line a boost.

I should call Mr. Ingraham and tell him that Tony would be escorting me to his opera party. A little swell of pleasure rose in my chest at the thought.

Mr. Ingraham would remember Tony from the investigation of Sylvia Carruthers's murder. Tony had been a little aggressive about that, but it was his job. I hoped he'd feel comfortable talking to my aunt and Mr. Ingraham in a more social setting. If he didn't, it wouldn't be their fault.

I wondered what Captain Dusenberry had thought of Vi's singing. Smiling at myself, I got up and went to the French doors, then ran my hands over the wall to the left of them. A habit of mine; I knew that Captain Dusenberry had been shot in this room, and I often wondered if any bullets had lodged in the adobe wall.

If they had, they had long since been plastered and painted over. Maybe I should try to borrow a metal detector. I bet one of Tony's Civil War reenactor friends would have one.

I felt all the way to the corner. A board creaked beneath my foot, and I grimaced. The last thing I needed was to have to repair the floor.

Three gentle notes of music sent a chill through my shoulder blades. Someone was playing my piano.

I froze. The notes hadn't been loud, but I was certain I had not imagined them.

It wasn't the stereo; Dee had turned that off when she left. Of course, Captain Dusenberry could have turned it back on...

But the music didn't continue. I turned, trying to be silent, and stepped out of my shoes. Padding down the hall in my stocking feet, I strained to hear anything more. I slowed and peeped around the edge of the parlor doorway.

The room was empty, the piano closed.

I could still hear the three notes in my mind: ti, la, sol. I walked over and opened the keyboard, and played them. B, A, G.

A song? Or just a scale?

Three blind mice.

Too short a fragment to identify, really. It could be anything.

I gazed around the room. I felt as if a question had been asked, and I'd missed it, so I couldn't answer.

2

The morning of the 20th was blustery, with fits of scattered rain. Not the best weather for an outing to the Santa Fe Opera, especially a tailgate dinner. I checked the forecast online, and prayed that the showers would taper off before the evening.

It was a Friday, and the tearoom was busy all day. I stayed downstairs until almost six, then left it to Iz and Rosa to close, and hurried up to my suite to dress.

Waiting for me on a hanger hooked on my canopy bed was the dress I had chosen for the occasion: an Edwardian-style, cream-colored silk with lace insets and pearl buttons, one of my favorites. I briefly considered picking out something warmer instead, but decided that my long coat and the lap blanket I always brought to the opera would be enough protection.

The sun had emerged in the afternoon, and the upstairs was warm. I stepped out of my work dress, and in my slip redid my hair and touched up my makeup for the evening. To my Gibson-girl hairdo I added three fresh rosebuds, creamy white. I had made a matching boutonnière for Tony, to help him feel more dressed-up.

Satisfied with my hair, I slid the silk gown over my shoulders, deliciously cool against my skin. A check in my full-length mirror showed me an acceptable self: not a tall goddess, or a voluptuous vamp, but a reasonably elegant lady of medium height with soft brown hair and pleasant features. Best I could do.

I moved my billfold and a lipstick into my beaded evening bag, slid the opera glasses that my father had given me for my eighteenth birthday into the tote that held my lap blanket and a collapsible umbrella, draped my coat over my arm, and picked up Tony's boutonnière. Locking my suite behind me, I went downstairs to the kitchen.

Mick was finishing the last of the day's china. He glanced up and gave me a nod, did a double-take with a smile and a thumbs-up, then continued bopping to whatever was playing in his earbuds.

Julio had left for the day. I opened the fridge to check that the Aria Cakes I'd asked him to make for the dinner hadn't been raided by the staff. They were safe in a covered container, protected by a note in Julio's sternest black marker: "HANDS OFF – OPERA PARTY."

I left them there and stepped out into the hallway, looking out the lights around the back door at the lilac bushes outside. They were stirring, but not wind-whipped. The sky over the Sangre de Cristo mountains was filled with rather dramatic, dark, storm clouds, but it wasn't raining down here in Santa Fe. Sunlight slanting in from the west lit the face of Santa Fe Baldy. I drew a deep breath, grateful for the beauty of my world.

"For a minute I thought you were a ghost."

Startled, I turned to find Tony standing behind me. He grinned, pleased with himself for sneaking up on me.

"A Victorian ghost. Maybe Captain Dusenberry's wife."

"He was unmarried. You look very elegant!"

He wore the dark suit I remembered, which set off his shoulders quite deliciously. There was no telltale bulge in his armpit. My glance went to his hips.

"I left it at home," he said. "Off-duty."

"Thank you. I know you'd prefer to carry it."

"Didn't seem right for the opera."

I smiled. "Come in here a minute."

I drew him into the dining parlor, set down my burdens, and raised the boutonnière to his lapel. He peered down at the rosebud as I affixed it.

"Nice. Thanks."

With my hands on his lapel, I felt my pulse increasing. He lifted his chin and looked at me. I could smell his cologne, feel his warmth.

"Is your bike out front? Would you rather park it back here?"

"It'll be fine."

His voice was soft and a little husky. His eyes—lovely warm brown—were hard to look away from. Feeling shaky, I smoothed the lapel and took a step back.

"I guess we're ready, then. Would you mind carrying something for me? I'm bringing dessert."

For a second he looked disappointed, then he smiled. "Sure, especially if it's that cake."

"It is."

I fetched the tray from the fridge and gave it to Tony. Rosa was on her way out the back door.

"You look beautiful, Ellen!" she said, smiling shyly.

"Thank you. Everything set for tomorrow?"

"Yes. The front's locked."

"See you in the morning, then."

"Have a great time!" Her glance flicked from me to Tony, then she headed out the door.

We followed, leaving Mick to lock up. I glanced up at the stormy sky. To the east the clouds were clustered on the crown of the mountains; westward they were more broken up, with the sun stabbing through here and there.

"Would you mind holding that on your lap? I'm worried it will slide around on the back seat."

"No problem," Tony said.

We climbed into my car and I headed north out of town. It was a little early, but Aunt Nat had told me that Mr. Ingraham's tailgates were elaborate and took a while to set up. If the table wasn't ready by the time we got there, I could always show Tony around the opera house.

"Hope it doesn't rain on our parade," Tony said.

"Did you bring an umbrella? I forgot to remind you."

"I don't have one."

"Well, we can share mine if we need to."

"You take an umbrella to the opera?"

"Always. It's an outdoor house—I told you that, didn't I?"

"Yeah. I guess I figured they would cancel if it got rained out."

"Oh, no—the audience is covered. It can get a little windy sometimes, but we shouldn't get rained on."

I told him a couple of stories about rainy performances in the old opera house, my favorite being the time that I and the other occupants of the unlucky middle rows left our seats and came down to crouch in the front of the aisles—only to be choked by waves of stage fog rolling over us. I'd always wondered how the orchestra could stand that stuff.

"You're a big fan, eh?" Tony asked.

"Of *this* opera house, yes. I'm not an opera expert, but I've always loved coming here."

I turned off the highway onto the road that wound its way up Opera Hill. The pinon trees were dancing a little in the breeze, but it didn't look too horribly windy.

"What's your favorite opera?"

"I'm not sure I have a favorite. There are so many wonderful ones. Mozart's *Magic Flute*, of course, and the *Figaro* operas, Donizetti, Bizet, I love Verdi."

He was silent. I suspected he thought I'd just started speaking Martian.

"We're supposed to look for a white SUV," I said as we pulled into the parking lot.

There were only a couple of dozen cars so far. Bored volunteers in fluorescent vests jumped into action, waving flashlights that weren't yet needed to direct us into the lot. I spotted a big white vehicle with a white tent set up behind it.

"That must be it."

I had a brief, gestured disagreement with one of the traffic volunteers, who finally let me drive through toward the SUV. I parked next to Manny's car and got out, leaving my coat and tote for later. Going around to Tony's door, I offered to take the tray of cakes, but he shook his head.

"I've got it."

He stood without trouble. I closed his door and we walked over to the tent. In the middle of one long side, the canvas had been parted and pulled back to form a prettily-draped entrance.

Inside was a table set for six, with a linen table cloth and gleaming crystal. The opposite side of the tent was against the SUV, with a similar draped opening giving access to the various coolers and insulated trays sitting in the back of the vehicle. Mr. Ingraham and Manny, both in black tie, were setting out tea lights protected by tall, glass hurricane chimneys on the table.

"Those are pretty," I said.

Mr. Ingraham looked up. "Necessary, I'm afraid, because of the wind."

"Even inside the tent?" Tony asked.

"Oh, yes—it can be gusty, and I refuse to use those electric abominations. Here, let me take that." Mr. Ingraham relieved Tony of the tray, which he set in the back of the SUV, and turned back, offering to shake hands. "Thank you! And good evening—I'm glad you could join us."

"Tony, you remember Mr. Ingraham?" I said belatedly.

"Thomas, please," he said, smiling as he glanced at me. To Tony, he added, "I heard how that murder case ended. You did a good job, taking care of our Ellen."

"Oh. Thanks." Tony's hands moved toward his back pockets, then he changed the gesture and clasped his hands behind his back.

"Where's Nat?" I asked Manny.

He nodded toward the front of the car. "Talking with Claudia."

"Claudia's here? Oh, how lovely!" I glanced at Mr. Ingraham, wondering if he'd invited Claudia Pearson because of our acquaintance or if he had struck up a friendship with her. She had worked with Sylvia Carruthers, and had also been at the thank-you tea that had ended in Sylvia's death.

I thought about saying hello to the ladies, but decided it would be better not to abandon Tony. Instead, I turned to Mr. Ingraham.

"How can I help?"

"Everything's under control, but thank you. Would you like some champagne?"

I smiled. "I won't say no."

He bent to reach into an ice chest on the ground under the tailgate and produced a bottle of Gruet, which he wiped down with a white napkin. I picked up a flute from the table and stood ready while he eased the cork from the bottle. He filled my glass and turned to Tony.

"Some for you?"

"Sure," Tony said. He glanced at my glass, then picked up a matching flute from the place setting next to the one I had raided, and held it out.

"To a lovely evening," I said, raising my glass.

"I'll drink to that," said Manny.

By the time all six flutes were filled, the bottle was empty. Mr. Ingraham took out another, and Manny strolled toward the front of the SUV, glass in hand. He returned almost immediately with my aunt and Claudia in tow.

"How delightful you look, Ellen!" said Claudia.

"Thank you. And you look simply stunning!" I said, admiring her high-necked, sleeveless navy gown. Her silver hair was swept up in an elegant French twist, and a squash blossom necklace of needlepoint turquoise glowed against her dress.

Nat was dressed à la Santa Fe Lady, in a black velvet broomstick skirt and matching full-sleeved blouse, with a cashmere shawl woven in wide bands of blue and green. She smooched my cheek and demanded, "Where's my champagne?"

Hugs and greetings exchanged, we all gathered around the table, where Mr. Ingraham had set out a platter of pâté. He took his seat at the head, with Claudia to his right and Nat to his left. I sat at the foot, between Manny and Tony.

The light of the candles filled the tent with a warm glow. Though the sun was still up, the evening was already getting cool and the occasional breeze made me glad for the shelter, not to mention the privacy it afforded us. Usually when I tailgated it was a card table behind my sedan, at the mercy of the elements and under the curious scrutiny of the neighbors. Like Mr. Ingraham, I liked to put on a good show—I draped my card table in lace, and had candles when the weather didn't make it hopeless—but he'd outdone me by several levels with the tent.

We all knew each other, and Tony was acquainted with everyone, for which I was grateful as it must make it easier for him. No need to explain his presence or describe his job. He was shy at first, but a couple of jokes from Manny made him relax. I relaxed, too, seeing him smile.

"I love that shawl, Nat," I said to my aunt. "It reminds me of the one I wore when I was an usher."

"Thank you! It's a gift from my beau," she said, leaning over to kiss Manny's cheek.

"You were an usher at the opera?" Mr. Ingraham asked.

"Yes, when I was in high school."

"Then you've seen *Tosca* before?"

"No, this is my first time, actually. I think the last time it was performed here was the year before I started ushering."

"Too bad. I was wondering if you might have any stories of disasters."

"Disasters?"

"Yes—*Tosca* is the 'Scottish play' of opera. Didn't you know?"

"No!"

Tony shot me a bewildered glance.

"The Scottish play is *Macbeth*," I explained. "Theater people call it that because they're superstitious. Saying the title out loud is supposed to be bad luck."

"Uh-huh."

"The whole play is considered bad luck," said Mr. Ingraham. "Bad things happen during productions."

"Then why do they do it?" Tony asked.

"Because it's Shakespeare," said Claudia.

"And the opera equivalent is *Tosca*, though they're not silly about the title," said Mr. Ingraham. "Tales abound of catastrophes during production. Maria Callas's wig caught fire onstage during a performance."

Nat gasped. "Was she hurt?"

"Not badly. She's not the only one; at least one other soprano's hair caught fire when she was singing *Tosca*. And of course, in the original play, Sarah Bernhardt broke her leg jumping off the balcony at the end. Some of the operatic Toscas have been injured that way too."

"You'd think they would be careful to make it safe," said Claudia. "Coloraturas don't grow on trees."

Mr. Ingraham continued to regale us with tales of the *Tosca* curse. Gradually the conversation flowed to opera in general, then to Santa Fe politics and what the tourists were up to this year. Claudia was excited about a new project at the Preservation Trust, a house designed by John Gaw Meem that the Trust was arranging to buy. She seemed to be handling the burden of running the Trust fairly well.

When the pâté had faded away, Mr. Ingraham unswathed a Dutch oven and served up steaming coq au vin. This was accompanied by a petal-soft Bordeaux and followed by a salad of baby greens and roasted beets, and finally a platter of cheeses.

When the Bordeaux was gone and the cheeses severely depleted, our host set a cut crystal decanter by his place, then brought out the tray of Aria Cakes and presented them with a flourish, announcing that I had provided the finale.

"Oh, good!" said Claudia. "I love these!"

"I've chosen a white port to go with them. Let me know what you think, Ellen."

I took a bite of cake and then sipped from the cordial glass he filled for me. The wine was lighter than I'd expected, with a floral hint that went nicely with the cake. "Mm, lovely!"

Tony sniffed at the port, frowning. I leaned toward him. "It's a sweet wine, a bit strong. If you don't like it that's all right."

He shot me a sidelong glance, sipped cautiously, then set the glass down. His face showed nothing, but he didn't try it again.

Ah, well. An acquired taste.

The sun was setting by the time we had finished the last of the cakes. Mr. Ingraham topped up my glass of port and I carried it outside the tent to admire the splashes of peach, orange, and crimson in the cloud-troubled sky. Tony came with me, and since

I didn't have my coat I stood close to him, using him for a wind break.

The breeze smelled of hot wax and grilled salmon. Other tailgaters were still enjoying their dinners. The parking lot had filled up considerably; at least a dozen other parties were dining al fresco, and on several tables wineglasses glinted in the sunset light. A couple of groups had even set up awnings, though Mr. Ingraham had the only true tent.

A rumble made me glance behind us at the mountains. Definitely some storm-action there, but since the usual weather track was west-to-east, I wasn't too worried about rain.

"Great views," Tony said.

"Aren't they? It's magical up here, especially in the twilight."

"Mm."

I turned to look at him. Sharp jaw shadowed by the fading light, dusky-dark hair and his shoulders trim in the suit coat. He looked delicious.

"Having fun so far?"

He gave a nod. "The food was great."

"High praise."

"Hey, I'm not good at flowery talk. You know that."

"True."

I looked back at the sunset, feeling content. Took another sip of port, then caught my breath as Tony slid an arm around my waist. I leaned against him, soaking in the warmth of his body. His head rested against mine.

"Hm." His voice resonated through my skull. "The evening just got more interesting."

A little too interesting, especially since we had an audience. I finished my port, letting the last mouthful sear itself into my senses, making me blink, then turned to face him, sliding out of his clasp.

"We should go back."

He looked disappointed, but smiled and with a formal little bow offered me his arm. I took it, soaking up more of his heat. I'd be needing my coat shortly.

Manny and Mr. Ingraham had the remains of the feast packed away and were breaking down the table. Again, my offer of help was refused.

"If you and Tony would escort the ladies in," he said, relieving me of my glass, "we'll be after you in a jiffy."

"All right. Thank you for an exquisite dinner."

Mr. Ingraham bowed slightly, an upturned corner of his mouth beneath the salted mustache betraying his pleasure. I collected my coat, beaded bag, and humble tote of weather gear from the car.

"A jiffy?" Tony whispered hotly in my ear, making me shiver. I threw him a repressive glance but ruined it by smiling.

Tony offered an arm each to Claudia and Nat, a deferential gesture of which I approved, and the four of us headed for the opera house. We joined a short line of people already filing through the gate. I dug our tickets out of my purse and we passed through the courtyard into the theatre.

We found our seats—very good ones, orchestra center—and I put my tote beneath mine. "Since we have a little time, I could give you a tour of the grounds," I said to Tony.

"Sure," he said, then glanced at Nat who was settling into her seat.

"You go ahead," she said. "We'll stay to welcome the men-folk."

I bent down to smooch her cheek, then stepped out into the aisle with Tony and led him down to view the orchestra pit. The stage was set with minimalist Italian-looking pillars framing the westward view: the last of the sunset glowing over the Jemez. A table that suggested an altar stood in the middle of the stage. I recalled that *Tosca* opened in a church.

"See the water here?" I said, indicating the gently restless, yard-wide band that curved around the orchestra pit. "That's in honor of the first theatre. It had a pool between the orchestra and the audience. Something about the acoustic quality of water— I'm not sure exactly what."

"I see why they call it a pit," Tony said, peering at the

musicians who were beginning to gather beneath the lip of the stage.

"Let's go look at the terrace."

I led him up the aisle and over to the Stravinsky Terrace, where the views to the north were darkened by clouds. A few planters held token petunias. The snack bar was doing a brisk business in hot beverages, and beverages of a different warming nature. Patrons with cups strolled the terrace.

Tony paused to look at the bust of Stravinsky set in a place of honor at one side of the terrace. "That *the* Stravinsky?"

"It is."

"He conducted here?"

"He raised money for rebuilding after the first theatre burned down. I think he may have conducted something for that, but it probably would have been in town. Anyway, the second theatre wouldn't have been built without his help."

"Huh."

We ambled back in the direction of the house. Tony paused, looking across toward the south side. "What's over there?"

"Another patio, with another bar. This side is nicer."

"What are those tall things? Sails?"

"Wind-breaks. The new roof took care of the rain problem, but it can still get pretty breezy."

He nodded thoughtfully, then looked at me with a quirked brow. "And people pay a lot of money for this?"

"Yes. Putting on a season of world-class opera is ridiculously expensive."

He looked over at the stage and shook his head slightly. I could practically hear his thoughts; he'd rather be home drinking beer and watching football. Or whatever they played in the summer—baseball.

"Would you like to go up to the mezzanine?" I said.

"No, Manny and Thomas just came in. Let's go sit down."

We made our way back to our seats. As I'd expected, Manny and Mr. Ingraham were the most formally dressed men in the house. Most of the audience were dressed casually, though a few men wore suits, and a few ladies wore long dresses. It amazed me that people dressed with so little care to attend an event for which seats cost over a hundred dollars.

But then, Superbowl tickets were also ridiculously expensive, and look how people dressed for that.

Stifling a sigh, I opened my program and flipped past the slick ads for galleries, jewelers, and real estate to find the page for *Tosca*. Tony followed my lead and was soon perusing the synopsis, for which I was almost sorry.

It wasn't a pretty story. Jealousy, torture, blackmail, murder. High drama, and the music was powerful, but definitely not a light evening's entertainment. *The Magic Flute* would have been a better first-time opera.

"The lead baritone is a wonderful singer," I said. "Victor Solano. I've heard him here before."

"Is he the one that was at Vi's tea?" Claudia asked. "I thought he looked familiar."

"Yes. He's taken her under his wing, she told me."

"That's excellent. She's off to a good start."

"She's singing tonight?" Tony asked.

"In the chorus, yes. We'll have to see if we can spot her."

"She's hard to miss."

Manny chuckled. I took my opera-glasses out of my bag and used them to inspect the Italianate columns on the stage.

"Are those the ones Edmund gave you?" asked Nat.

"Yes," I said, handing them across to her.

One of many gifts my father gave me. They were French, and antique, and entirely frivolous, ornamented with mother of pearl. I adored them.

A pang of grief caught me off guard. This was the first time I'd been to the opera since my father had died. So many times we'd gone as a family. I felt the sudden pressure of tears behind my eyelids.

"I'm going to visit the Ladies' before it begins," I said, standing.

I left my coat and my program on the seat and hurried

toward the south courtyard, needing a moment away from the others to compose myself. A couple of tears escaped, but I managed to avoid smearing my makeup, and succeeded in distracting myself.

Later, after I got home, I'd indulge in a good cry. I was about due for one.

I emerged from the washroom to hear the orchestra tuning up in earnest. The house lights blinked a warning. I returned to my seat just as the conductor took his podium, to a smattering of applause.

Nat passed my glasses back to me. Tony put them in my hand and turned his head, giving me a searching look. I smiled to reassure him as the lights went down and the overture began.

A gentle opening, almost pastoral, but with hints of brooding darkness. I let the music take over my awareness, and soon it swept me up in Puccini's lush, dramatic passion.

Tony leaned forward to fiddle with the captioning screen on the back of the seat in front of him. I left mine turned off; I usually find it distracting, and in this opera I wasn't so sure I wanted to know what the characters were saying.

The opening strains of the first act were strong and dark, setting the tone for what was to come. I kept wondering what Tony was thinking and losing my focus on the performers. When Tosca came onstage and began her love scene with Cavaradossi, Tony slid his hand onto mine.

I didn't follow the rest of the scene very well. Tony's hand was so warm, and I felt a little breathless.

I watched the lovers onstage go from adoring to bickering to playfulness, all the while wondering what would happen between me and Tony later that night. He had left his bike at my house, and we'd be back late, close to midnight. Should I invite him in?

My thoughts continued scattered until Victor Solano came onstage. A smattering of applause greeted him. His voice commanded attention, and I caught the thread of the story once more.

I liked the performer, but his character, Scarpia, was thoroughly despicable. I knew that he would deceive Tosca into thinking her lover was seeing another woman, but the language bothered me more than I expected. I understood a little Italian, and I couldn't help glancing at Tony's captions now and then.

Go, Tosca!

Now Scarpia digs a nest within your heart!

Coupled with the oppressive music, I found the words disturbing. When the act ended, I felt relieved.

We all got up, but we weren't fast enough to beat the lines that formed outside the restrooms on the terrace. Mr. Ingraham suggested the ones behind the gift shop as being less likely to be crowded, so we headed out to the front courtyard. Tony offered me his arm and led the way.

The courtyard was much less crowded, but as we passed through a narrow spot a couple suddenly stopped short right in front of us. Apparently they were having a disagreement; the woman looked unhappy. I glanced at Tony, expecting him to move past them or excuse himself, but instead he was watching from beneath a slight frown.

Cop mode. Triggered by the disagreement. I wondered if he'd had to answer a lot of domestic calls.

The woman noticed his gaze, shot a glance at her companion, and strode away toward the gift shop. The man stepped aside, grimacing, and we walked on.

Not needing to visit the restroom again so soon, I waited outside by the fountain and thought wistfully of the big petunia beds that were now gone. My gaze followed the line of the hedge where the beds had been, and I again saw the man who'd been arguing with the woman. He was standing with his back to the hedge, talking with another man who looked vaguely familiar.

As I watched, the arguing man—who had dark, curly hair combed artistically but not quite concealing a receding hairline —took two cigars from his breast pocket and offered one to the other man, who was taller and had salt-and-pepper hair. That man shook his head, and the arguing man put one cigar back in his coat.

Mr. Ingraham joined me. "Do you know who that is?" I asked him, watching the arguing man use a small, brass knife to cut the end off of his cigar.

"The tall one? I believe that's the General Director."

"No, the other one. The smoker," I added, moving away as said individual lit up his stogie.

I don't object to a little pipe smoke, but cigarette smoke makes me sneeze, and I find cigar smoke particularly vile.

Mr. Ingraham followed me, glancing over his shoulder. "I'm not sure. He does look familiar."

The others joined us, much refreshed by all appearances, and we all strolled toward the south patio. A small crowd was clustered around the bar there, where two young women were bustling away filling orders as fast as they could. One of them sliced limes with frightening efficiency, her knife flashing in the light.

"Would anyone like a drink?" Tony asked. "My treat." He turned to Mr. Ingraham and made just the perfect slight bow. I was delighted, though I worried about the impact on his wallet. The drinks wouldn't be cheap.

"That sounds lovely, Tony," said Nat. "I don't know about the others, but I'll gladly accept."

Tony took orders. I didn't dare insult him by declining.

"Just coffee for me," I said, when he got around to me. "The port's still with me."

His eyes narrowed for a second. "Cream and sugar?"

"Yes, please."

A breeze, cold and damp, swept across us, making me wonder if we were in for some rain after all. Suddenly I missed my coat.

Tony got in line at the bar while the others stood chatting near the wind-breaks: tall structures of canvas mounted on poles that were at least twenty feet high and looked a little like giant Roman blinds. I tagged along with Tony, thinking he might need help carrying the drinks.

"This is nice of you," I said as we waited.

"Least I could do."

"You didn't have to do anything."

"Yes, I did."

I let it drop.

We carried the drinks back to the others. I wrapped my chilled fingers around my coffee and took cautious sips, enjoying the heat. This was only the first intermission; by the time we got to the end of Act Three it would probably be downright cold. I wished I'd brought a blanket for Tony, then decided that sharing mine with him might have its advantages.

"Any chance we'll see Vi tonight?" Nat asked.

"Yes, she's going to meet us by the stage door after the performance," I said, gesturing with my cup toward a door in the wall south of the proscenium.

"Did you see her in the choir scene?" asked Mr. Ingraham.

"I think she was the one in the dark blue hat," I said.

"Yes, I thought so, too!" said Nat.

By the time we'd finished our drinks, the lights were blinking again. We returned to our seats and swathed ourselves in coats and blankets.

Act II: Scarpia having Cavaradossi tortured within Tosca's hearing, while urging her to reveal the hiding place of the revolutionary Cavaradossi was protecting. When she finally caved in and told him, Scarpia had Cavaradossi brought in so that he could gloat. I found that scene particularly disturbing; Scarpia caressing Cavaradossi, practically embracing him as he sang "The hangman's noose awaits you."

There was electricity in the air, the kind that comes from the best of performances. It held me frozen, though in this case I was frozen in dismay.

Then the blackmail. Scarpia promised Tosca he would let Cavaradossi live if she yielded herself to his—Scarpia's—lust. She finally agreed, and coaxed a letter of safe-conduct from him, so that she and Cavaradossi could get out of the country after his "fake" execution.

When Scarpia approached to claim her, Tosca produced a knife and stabbed him, so swiftly and fiercely that the audience gasped, me included.

This is Tosca's kiss!

I'm not a violent person, but I wanted to shout, "You go, girl!"

The lights came up, and we all heaved a sigh of relief. Mr. Ingraham leaned forward.

"Anyone need to get up, or should we all stay here and huddle?"

Tony looked at me. "You mean that's not the end?"

"No, there's one more act."

Exasperation flicked across his face, though he hid it quickly. I threw back the blanket and stood, fastening my coat's buttons.

"Actually, I think I'd like a walk. Will you join me?" I asked Tony.

"Sure."

We went up to the Stravinsky Terrace, and Tony bought us both some coffee. The breeze was now quite chilly, and we sheltered in the lee of a wall while we sipped the scalding heat.

Above, I heard voices from the members-only bar. Mr. Ingraham probably had access to it, I realized. He could have bought a round of drinks with no waiting. How kind of him not to say so.

"Sorry it's such a heavy piece," I said to Tony. "There are light-hearted operas, this just isn't one of them."

"I guess you didn't choose it."

"No. But I did want to hear Mr. Solano sing. He's got such a marvelous voice."

"That's the bad guy?"

"Scarpia, yes."

Tony nodded, gazing reflectively toward the stage. "See, I have to deal with guys like that all the time."

"Oh! I'm sorry. This really isn't the best opera for you."

He shrugged. "I'm enjoying the company, at least."

"If you want to, we could go."

He looked at me, dark eyes catching mine and making me tingle. Finally he shook his head.

"That's tempting, but I don't want to take you away from your friends."

"Nice of you."

He smiled. "I'm a nice guy, if you can believe it."

"Oh, I believe it."

" — practically snogging him right on stage. Neil wasn't happy," said a man's voice above us in a distinct accent.

Tony glanced up, then looked at me and whispered, "Snogging?"

"British slang. It means making out."

"Yeah, I know. I saw *Harry Potter*. But what's a Brit doing here?"

"It's an international company. He could be here with one of the artists, or *as* an artist. Or he could just be visiting Santa Fe."

Tony tilted his head, looking up, but there was no one in view. I swallowed the last of my coffee.

"Please excuse me. I'll be right back."

I hurried to the ladies' room, where there was fortunately no waiting. Many of the audience had elected to remain in their seats...and probably a few were asleep. Though how anyone could sleep through Puccini, I didn't know.

When I rejoined Tony, he hastily removed his hands from his pockets.

"You're cold. Shall we go back in?"

"Yeah. Really glad you brought that blanket."

"I always do. Even if the weather's ideal, it can get cold toward the end of the evening."

At the gateway in the low adobe wall surrounding the audience, we nearly collided with the arguing woman I'd seen earlier, now swathed in a dark fur coat. She was alone, and looked no less argumentative: more so, if anything. We yielded to her and I watched her stride across the house and out into the southern patio.

Tony and I hurried back to our seats and the comfort of my

blanket. We tucked the edges around ourselves. Manny and Nat were sharing a blanket, too. Mr. Ingraham and Claudia each had their own, and Claudia had donned a close-fitting, vaguely Russian-looking fur hat. I peered at it, trying to decide if it was real fur.

"No," she said, as if she'd read my mind. "But it's a good imitation."

"As long as it's warm."

My thoughts drifted back to the arguing woman as we waited for the intermission to end. I suspected that her fur coat was real, and that the color of her pale blonde hair was not. She had large eyes and a small chin, and was probably pretty when she wasn't angry.

The lights finally dimmed and Act III commenced. I tensed for a moment, until I remembered that Scarpia was dead. A horn played a melody, not quite a fanfare, with lilting tones that calmed my anxiety and foretold the dawn.

A single figure came onstage: the shepherd-boy. I gasped, realizing that it was Vi.

Nat turned to look at me, eyes big. I nodded, then looked back at the stage.

Vi was dressed in shepherd's clothes, with a cap over her auburn curls. She sang briefly; two verses, sweet and simple. I glanced at the captions.

> *I give you sighs,*
>
> *There are as many*
>
> *As there are leaves*
>
> *Driven by the wind*

Nothing to do with the story, really. Just scene-setting, to get the audience back into the opera. I watched Vi's face, serene, perhaps a little sad.

It was over too soon. Vi left the stage, and a man with a lantern crossed it. Behind him, the scenery shifted to become the jail where Cavaradossi was being held.

The music intensified as Tosca came in and the two lovers

began planning their doomed escape. Tony's hand found mine beneath the blanket. I lost track of the drama onstage.

Could this work? I must have already asked myself a hundred times. There was no way to be certain. On an emotional level, Tony and I connected just fine. Socially: that was the question.

I would probably be as uncomfortable at a gathering of his friends as he was, here tonight. He'd been so patient, though. So generous, when I knew going in that this wasn't his kind of fun. At the very least, I owed him reciprocation.

On stage, Tosca sang of the future she pictured for herself and Cavaradossi, a glorious future filled with happiness, which she would never see. Her lover knew it would not happen, but she clung to that bright hope.

Was I equally naïve?

The jailer took Cavaradossi away, to stand before a firing squad for his supposedly fake execution. From beyond the grave, Scarpia reached out to flip the lovers a final bird: the bullets are real, and Cavaradossi is dead. Tosca, thinking he's pretending, begs him not to move until the soldiers have all gone.

A shout, and a hubbub of voices offstage. Tosca froze briefly, glanced toward stage left, then again told her lover not to move. As last she felt safe and told him to get up—and discovered his death was real.

The rest happened quickly. Voices and clamor offstage again, this time from the right. Scarpia's officers returned, accusing Tosca of killing him. Tosca ran up to the top of a balcony at the rear of the stage, and with a wordless cry, leapt over it to her death. Even though I'd been expecting it, I gasped.

End of opera. I was glad. A marvelous performance all around, but I felt drained and a bit depressed.

I let go of Tony's hand to applaud. The chorus took their bow, then the bit parts—we shouted "Brava!" for Vi—then the soloists. When everyone but Scarpia, Cavaradossi, and Tosca had taken their bows, an lengthy pause followed. Some of the audience rose to their feet, anticipating Mr. Solano's entrance.

But he didn't enter. Tosca and Cavaradossi came on, holding hands, and bowed. They were smiling, but Tosca looked a bit wild-eyed.

The audience shouted "Victor, Victor!"

Still no Scarpia.

Tony jumped in surprise and reached for his pocket. Phone on buzz-mode; he took it out, grimaced, and leaned over to mutter an apology in my ear.

"Sorry, gotta go."

He got up and hurried out to the south patio, phone to his ear. I watched, expecting him to leave the grounds, but instead he headed for the stage door.

It was cracked open; someone was there. Tony paused, pulled out his wallet and flashed his badge, and disappeared inside.

3

"Oh, no!" I said. Nat, next to me, gave me a questioning look. The audience was still cheering, still calling for Victor Solano.

"Something's happened," I told Nat.

The cast took another bow, led by Tosca and Cavaradossi, then left the stage. The audience cried out in protest. The applause began to falter, and voices filled the house, questioning, speculating.

I stood, grabbed my blanket and my other belongings, and hurried after Tony. The stage door was closed. I pounded on it, to no avail.

Mr. Ingraham appeared beside me. "Where's Tony?"

"In there. He got a page. Something's terribly wrong." I tried the handle, but it was locked. I kept pounding.

"Ellen, that won't do any good."

"I have to see Tony."

"Why?"

I stopped. Why, indeed? I'd been going on pure instinct, the knowledge that there was trouble and that I wanted to help.

Tony was doing his job, though. I'd just be in the way.

The stage door opened a crack, and a man in black clothes, wearing a headset and a stressed frown, looked out.

"I need to speak to Detective Aragón," I told him.

"I-I'm sorry—"

"Please, just ask him to call Ellen. Can you do that?"

The man nodded and closed the door. I wondered if he would actually deliver my message.

A feminine wail sounded from somewhere behind the door, then ended abruptly.

The restless voices of the audience were getting louder. Everyone knew something was wrong.

The man we had seen earlier—tall, with salt-and-pepper hair

—brushed past us, knocked on the stage door, and called, "Roger, it's me." The door opened to swallow him, then clapped shut again.

Nat, Manny, and Claudia joined us. "Ellen?" Nat said.

"Tony's in there. Something awful must have happened!"

"Maybe you should come away, dear."

"I'm his ride home."

"Ladies and gentlemen," said a man's voice over a loudspeaker. "We apologize for the inconvenience. It appears that a serious crime has been committed on the premises, and we must ask that you each leave your name and contact information with security as you leave the theatre. Thank you for your cooperation and your understanding."

My heart sank. What kind of serious crime would merit such a step? Or require Detective Aragón's assistance?

Why hadn't Victor Solano taken his bow?

The noise from the audience reached an angry crescendo. The stage door opened once again, and Vi stepped out, still in her shepherd's costume. Her eyes were red, as though she'd been crying, though her makeup was still perfect.

"Vi! What happened?"

"Ellen, I need to talk to you. Come over here."

She led me away from the door and the crowd that was beginning to gather there, into the south patio. The rest of Mr. Ingraham's party followed.

Vi turned to me and drew a ragged breath. "Detective Aragón asked me to tell you that he's investigating a crime. He'll be here for a while—he said you should go h-home."

She was shaking. I laid a hand on her arm. "Vi, what's happened? Is Mr. Solano ill?"

Her face crumpled and she shook her head, fresh tears filling her eyes.

"He's dead."

I heard Nat gasp behind me. I gathered Vi into my arms, even though she was taller than I.

"Vi, I'm so sorry. Oh, my dear!"

She gave one sob, then collected herself and withdrew. "I'd better go back. Detective Aragón said none of us should leave."

"Can you tell me what happened?"

"All I know is someone found him in his dressing room during the curtain call. Detective Aragón is standing guard until someone comes to help him. He won't let anyone go in the room."

"Oh, my God."

"Thank you, Vi," said Mr. Ingraham. "We'll let you get back."

"I'll call you tomorrow," I said.

She nodded, then hurried back to the stage door. The crowd gathered there let her through, and the door opened for her.

"We'd better go, Ellen," Mr. Ingraham said gently.

I nodded, overwhelmed by sadness. Victor Solano was a brilliant singer, in the prime of his career. And we had all, unknowingly, heard his final performance. I would rather not have been able to make that claim.

We joined the milling throng of audience members filing out of the theatre with awful slowness. Security guards at the front gate were frantically recording everyone's name and phone number. We all gave ours, and were finally allowed to go up to the parking lot.

"Ellen, would you like me to drive you home?" Manny offered when we reached the row where we all were parked.

I shook my head. "Thank you, but I'll be all right." I turned to Mr. Ingraham. "Your part of the evening was wonderful. The opera was wonderful. I wish..."

"Yes," he said, enfolding me in a brief hug. "Be careful going home, Ellen."

I nodded, then hugged Nat, Manny, and Claudia. We all needed hugs, right then.

I said good night to them all, then dumped my gear in the back seat of my car, got in, and sat just breathing deeply for a minute. When I was steady, I started the car and drove home.

The garden smelled of roses and lilies. I let myself in the back door and just stood in the hall, glad to be home, sorrowing over how the evening had ended.

I'd forgotten the tray that I'd brought the cakes on.

I shook my head. It didn't matter. I'd call Mr. Ingraham later.

I went upstairs and put away my opera gear. I had caught up Tony's program as well as my own. I put them both in the sitting area of my suite, thinking I'd return Tony's to him, though perhaps he wouldn't want a souvenir of this evening.

I changed out of my finery and into a set of satin pajamas, made myself a cup of hot milk with nutmeg, and curled up in my favorite armchair.

Poor Tony. What a mess. He'd probably be there all night.

I tried to imagine what he was dealing with. It sounded very much like Mr. Solano had been murdered. There must be a hundred potential suspects—the whole cast, the crew, orchestra, staff—anyone who had access to backstage. Not to mention the audience. Anyone could have slipped back to the dressing room if they knew where they were going, and the murderer apparently did.

How could someone commit murder in the middle of a performance and get away with it?

I had taken the Opera's backstage tour a few times, and knew that there were no private dressing rooms. There was one large room each for the men's and women's chorus, and one shared dressing room each for the principal men and principal women. "There are no divas here," the tour guide had said.

So the murderer had needed to find a time when Mr. Solano was alone in the principal men's dressing room. I suspected that was nearly impossible.

I picked up a program and turned to the cast list for *Tosca*. The male soloists were Scarpia, Cavaradossi, Angelotti (the man Cavaradossi was protecting, who only appeared in Act I), the Sacristan (also only in Act I), Spoletta (the torturer), and Sciarrone (another of Scarpia's men).

Scarpia died at the end of Act II, so the murder could have happened any time during Act III. Vi had said he was found during the curtain call. When were the other principal men most likely to be away from the dressing room?

Cavaradossi was onstage for most of Act III, all except the beginning. Spoletta was around for a good part of it; he was probably backstage when he wasn't actually onstage. Sciarrone had come on at the end of the act, I recalled.

But the two men who were only in Act I would probably have been in the dressing room for all of Act III. It was their place to relax, and the most likely place they would be between their time onstage and the curtain call.

Unless they had filled in with the chorus, who were onstage as other prisoners in the jail during Act III. I didn't think that was very likely, but it was possible. I'd have to ask Vi.

Poor Vi. The murder alone was upsetting enough, but she had also lost her mentor. What a terrible blow.

The *Tosca* curse. Whether or not the legend was real, this event would only add to it.

I'd finished my milk, but I wasn't sleepy. My brain was still busy trying to puzzle out the murder. It was futile; I didn't have enough information, but I couldn't stop thinking about it.

I got up and rinsed my mug, then walked out into the hall and to the window overlooking the front yard. Tony's bike was parked where he'd left it, down on the street in front of the house. I wondered what he was dealing with now.

Other police must have arrived and taken over guarding the crime scene. Probably evidence technicians were going over it, maybe the coroner. Tony would be asking questions, trying to establish who had been in or near the room, who had last seen Victor Solano alive.

A wave of cold realization went through me. Maybe the two principal men who were only in Act I were the ones who had killed him.

They were the most likely to have had opportunity. Motive? Other than professional jealousy, I didn't know. It could be anything.

Not enough information. I really should stop this.

I took a hot shower and went to bed. Saturday was always a

busy day, and I would need to be fresh and cheerful, as opposed to tired and sad.

I lay waiting for sleep, thinking about Tony and the chaos he was dealing with. As I began to drift off, I heard a melody: gentle, mournful, and lovely—familiar, but I couldn't place it. I wondered who was playing it, just as I fell asleep.

The next day was unusually busy, even for a Saturday. By the time I finished a quick breakfast of tea and a croissant, eight messages were stacked on the reservation line, all but two of them wanting to come in that day. I was trying to fit them into the schedule when Kris came in, wearing a dress of black and white vertical stripes that looked like a throwback to the seventies.

"Did you hear about the murder at the opera?" she asked, stepping into my office.

So it was officially murder. News must have traveled fast. I wondered if Tony had a suspect.

"I was there," I said.

"Oh, was last night your party? Awesome! Did you see anything?"

Did I?

I shook my head. "It happened backstage. Kris, we have six people wanting reservations today. Can you help me fit them in?"

"Let me handle it."

I handed her the notes I had jotted down. "I didn't erase the messages."

"Good. Is there tea?"

"I was about to make some."

"Great. Thanks."

She went into her own office, and I sat staring at the chimney that anchored the wall between us.

Had I seen anything? Onstage, or perhaps in the audience?

The only thing that came to mind was the arguing woman in the fur coat. Anger had radiated from her. I wondered who she was.

Maybe I'd ask Tony. I got up and went out into the hall, stepping to the front window. His bike was gone. I felt an odd stab of disappointment.

Not wanting to go downstairs, I went across to my suite to make a pot of tea for myself and Kris. I put together a tray and carried it back across the hall, setting it on the credenza in my office.

"Here you are," I said as I brought a cup to Kris.

"Thanks. All set on the reservations, but two more have come in. Do you want to stay open late?"

I gave a small sigh. On busy days, we sometimes stayed open an extra half-hour or more to fit in a few late reservations. I didn't really feel like it that day, but it was good business.

"How late?"

"Six-thirty, maybe seven."

"All right. No later than seven, though."

"Got it." She held out two slips of lavender message paper. "These are for you."

I carried the messages back to my desk, but didn't look at them until I'd fixed myself a cup of tea, *with* sugar. It was that kind of morning.

One of the messages was from Mr. Ingraham, asking me to call when it was convenient. The other, same message but with a bit more urgency, was from Willow Lane.

I leaned my head in my hands. I could just guess what she wanted.

Another ghost to add to her tour.

I finished my tea and went downstairs, to find Julio dancing in the kitchen, intent on a tray of watercress sandwiches. He looked up and took off his headphones.

"Full house today," he said. "Can you put in some scones for me? It's time to start the first batch, and I have to finish these."

"Sure thing," I said, going to the sink to wash my hands.

"There's a tray in the fridge, but not set up for baking. We'll have to go to frozen in the afternoon unless I get time to make some more."

I put on gloves, took out a baking tray and lined it with parchment. "Has Kris sent down the updated list? We're staying open late."

Julio nodded. "That's why I'm scrambling, here."

"Interested in some overtime?"

He gave me a pained look. "I've got a date. I could do an extra half hour."

"Maybe you won't have to."

I helped Julio until it was almost ten-thirty, then went up front to make sure everything was ready in the gift shop. Rosa was there to open, and Iz was setting up trays in the butler's pantry. A glance out the front windows told me that all the tables on the *portal* were already set. There were people waiting outside the front door.

"We're booked up outside, too?"

Rosa nodded. "Booked solid, and we're still getting calls."

This was beyond a busy day. What was going on?

I helped Rosa open up and seat the waiting customers, then hurried upstairs to Kris's office. She was on the phone. I waited while she recorded a reservation.

"Tuesday's booking up," she said as she hung up. "And Wednesday's half-full. Do you want to extend hours for the week?"

"I'll have to check with Julio. Any idea why the rush?"

Kris shook her head. "A lot of first-timers, though."

My phone rang. I stepped over to my desk to see who it was, intending to let the call go to voicemail.

It was Tony.

I caught up the phone on the third ring. "Tony?"

"Hi. I need to talk to you." He sounded exhausted.

"It's crazy here today. Would tonight be all right?"

"What time?"

"Seven thirty?"

"OK."

He hung up. I swallowed annoyance; it was just his habit, and he must be under a lot of stress just now. I put the phone down and went downstairs.

Between helping Julio in the kitchen and making sure everything was going all right in the parlors and outside on the *portal*, I was on my feet all day. I made a point of talking to any guests I didn't recognize, asking them where they'd heard about the tearoom. This paid off halfway through the afternoon, when a couple a few years older than I, seated by the window in Jonquil, told me they'd heard that Victor Solano had been here and liked it.

"Oh?" I said, feeling a little uneasy.

"Yes," said the woman, a trim brunette in an elegant linen dress. She glanced at her partner. "We were at the opera last night...have you heard...?"

"I was there, too," I said. "Such a tragedy."

She nodded. "While we were waiting to leave, someone in line told us Mr. Solano loved the Wisteria Tearoom. So we thought..."

"I see. Well, I'm sorry for the way you found us, but thank you for giving us a try."

"We'll be back," said the man, smiling. "Everything's delightful."

"Thank you."

I made sure they had everything they wanted, then escaped to the kitchen. Julio greeted me with an empty tray.

"We've gone through the Aria Cakes. I can make more of those, or more scones, but not both."

"We have frozen scones?"

"Yes."

"Make the cakes. What am I making?" I hefted the tray.

"Cucumber sandwiches."

I grabbed an apron and went to work. My brain was at work elsewhere.

How many of our new guests were from the opera? How far had this idea spread? Mr. Solano might have mentioned his visit to the tearoom, but I doubted he had urged people to try us.

Maybe just a mild positive recommendation from him, backed by the weight of his stature, had started an avalanche.

I had highly conflicting feelings about that. I was glad that I was too busy to think about it much.

Tray of cucumber sandwiches, then a tray of frozen scones into the oven. Julio set me to making almond buttercream icing for the cakes, then toasting sliced almonds. He made the tea syrup while the cakes were baking. I went out for another round of the parlors, then returned to help assemble the cakes. Julio insisted on garnishing them himself.

"We're almost out of violets," he said.

"Already? I'll order more. Use the broken pieces."

He nodded, already picking through the diminished supply. I dashed upstairs to call the supplier and place a rush order for more candied violets, hoping they'd arrive by Tuesday.

I had a bed of violets out back. Maybe there'd be some blooming, still. I'd check in the morning.

I passed Kris on her way home in the doorway as I headed back downstairs. On a normal Saturday she would have been gone by two, but she had stayed to help with the reservation line, which was still going crazy.

"How is it?" I asked.

"Booked solid through Thursday. Friday will be gone by Tuesday morning. Probably Saturday, too."

I let out a deep breath. "Thank you for staying."

She nodded. "See you Tuesday."

I'd be paying a lot of overtime for this week. I hoped the extra business would cover it.

I went back down to the kitchen and found Julio putting the garnish on a tray of thirty Aria Cakes. He looked tired.

"These should get you through the rest of today. I can come in Monday afternoon to get a head start on the week."

"Thanks, Julio. Is your roommate still looking for work?"

He shook his head. "He found a job at Santacafé."

"Any chance he'd like to come in for a few hours?"

"He's full-time, and it's high tourist season. There's no way."

"OK. I'll see what I can do. Enjoy your evening."

"Thanks."

I turned back to the kitchen. Mick was hard at work at the washing station. I put the Aria cakes in the fridge, checked on the scones in the oven, and carried the timer with me as I went up front.

In the gift shop, Dee stood at the register ringing up purchases while a short line of guests waited patiently. A lot of the new visitors were browsing there, which gave me hope for my bottom line.

I checked on the parlors. The *portal* was now sunny and rather warm, but the tables were shaded by the wisteria vines, and were all full. Rosa circulated with a fresh pot of tea.

My timer went off, and I hurried back to the kitchen to take out the scones. I set them on the work table to cool, then went into the butler's pantry where I found Iz setting sandwiches on trays.

"You were supposed to go home at three!"

She cast me a wary look. "Julio asked if I could stay. It's all right, isn't it?"

"Yes, yes—thank you! Only I don't want to ruin your plans."

"I don't have anything planned tonight."

"Well, you're a life-saver. Thank you, Iz. I'll bring you the scones."

I helped her with the trays, then helped Rosa clear up front, then we were suddenly done. The last guests had been served. I sent Iz home, grabbed a teapot, and made a final round of the parlors and the *portal*.

Two more parties told me they were here because of Victor Solano. One had been at last night's performance, and the other had heard from friends who were there. I thanked them for coming.

Dee and Rosa had things under control. Mick was catching up on the china. I went upstairs to check messages, balked at the number on the tearoom voicemail, and looked through the small pile of lavender slips on my desk.

Call from Claudia Pearson. A second call from Willow. A call from a reporter at *The New Mexican*—yikes. Kris would want me to answer that one, and my friend Gina would yell at me if I didn't. I was too tired, though. I set it aside for later.

I checked my phone, where I had a message from Nat and one from Gina; apparently *The New Mexican* had already run a story on the murder. I started to call Gina back, then remembered that Tony was coming over.

Later. I would deal with it all later.

I took the morning's tea tray back to my suite and made a fresh pot of Darjeeling for myself. In case any of the staff needed to find me, I carried it back to my office, and sat sipping at my desk as I pulled up the online edition of *The New Mexican*.

OPERA STAR MURDERED AT SFO

Great. It was officially murder.

I skimmed the story. A little knot of pain beneath my breastbone kept me from reading it too closely. I knew that pain well. It was the onset of grief.

A knock made me look up. Dee was standing in the doorway.

"We're going," she said, "unless you need us for something."

"No, no." I stood. "Thank you, Dee. Are we closed?"

She nodded. "Mick is finishing up. Rosa's gone home."

"I might need you to put in some overtime this week, if you can."

"Sure."

"We'll talk about it Tuesday. Have a great weekend."

She grinned. "*You* get some rest, ma'am. I think you're gonna need it."

I followed her downstairs, said goodbye to her and Mick, and surveyed the kitchen. Mick had tidied up, but I knew that Julio would not approve of the state in which I'd left the work area. I did my best to restore it to perfection, then surveyed the contents of the fridge.

Four Aria cakes left. Half a dozen finger sandwiches. One

deviled egg and two scones.

Dinner.

Actually, ridiculously late lunch. I'd been on my feet all day, and hadn't realized until I opened the fridge that I was starving.

I put the scones, sandwiches, and egg on a plate and carried them back to my office. Normally I didn't raid the tearoom's kitchen for meals, but I was too tired to think about cooking.

I poured myself another cup of tea and nibbled a scone. Called Mr. Ingraham's number and got voicemail. I couldn't bring myself to call Willow, but I called Nat and told her about the madness at the tearoom. She wanted to know if I'd seen the story in the paper, and if I'd like to come over for dinner.

"Can I take a rain check? I'm beat."

"Come tomorrow, then, sweetheart. Promise?"

"Promise. What can I bring?"

"Nothing, sweetie. Just a good appetite. Manny's grilling."

"In that case, I'll skip lunch."

"You could bring Tony if you like," she added.

"I'll ask. He's pretty swamped too, though."

We talked a little longer, then I said goodbye and started to call Gina. My private doorbell, which only friends knew how to find, rang. I put the phone down and hurried downstairs to the back door.

Tony stood outside, back in his motorcycle duds, slouched against a pillar of the *portal* and frowning. I opened the door and he straightened.

"Hi," I said.

"Hi." His shoulders drooped, and his eyes were heavy.

"You look exhausted. Would you like some tea?"

He cocked his head. "Got any bourbon?"

"Ah...no. Port? Or gin?"

"Gin? You drink gin?"

"Gin and tonic. Grown up limeade. Great for hot summer evenings."

He sighed. "Actually, I should stay sober. I'm working."

"I thought you might be. Come on in."

I led him upstairs to my office, poured him a cup of tea, and invited him to share my dinner. He picked up a sandwich, examined it from all angles, and took a bite.

"That's watercress and lemon butter. Like it?"

"Green," he mumbled through a mouthful.

"Very." I took one myself. "I was just on the phone with Nat. She asked me over for dinner tomorrow, and said to invite you."

"Doubt I'll have time. Does she need a definite answer, or is it a 'drop by' kind of thing?"

"Drop by is fine, I think. Six-ish. Manny's grilling. You have Nat's address?"

"Somewhere."

"Let me give it to you again."

He punched it into his cell phone, then reached for another sandwich. "These are good."

"How's the investigation going?"

He swallowed a bite. "I need to ask you some questions."

I nodded. He'd probably been through the interview drill a couple of dozen times already. This was a formality; he knew exactly where I'd been all Friday evening.

I took a sip of tea and waited. He got up and started pacing, staying toward the chimney wall where he wouldn't have to crouch beneath the sloping roof. The frown had deepened.

He stopped abruptly and turned to me. "I'd like to bounce a theory off you."

I swallowed my surprise. "All right."

"First I want to know what you think might have happened."

"Tony, I..."

"You saw the same things I saw. If you *noticed* the same things, I want to know."

"OK." I poured myself more tea and took a sip. "Last night I got home and started thinking. I know I don't have complete information, but Mr. Solano had to have died during Act Three. I'm guessing near the end of the act, since he wasn't found until the curtain call."

Tony stayed where he was, staring at me from beneath dark

eyebrows. Not so much as a nod.

"Well, the most likely suspects are the cast, because the crew and everyone else are supposed to stay away from the dressing rooms, especially the principals' dressing rooms."

"That doesn't rule the others out," Tony said.

"I know, but that's where I'm starting. I looked at the program to see how many male principles were in the cast. I've seen the dressing rooms backstage. Mr. Solano would have been sharing with the other principal men—five of them. Of those, two were not onstage at all during Act Three. So either they were away from the dressing room for some reason, or they were involved in the crime."

He continued to gaze at me for a moment, then unfolded his arms. "Not bad. Those two are each other's alibi. Matthew Carter and Geoffrey Harrison. No one else can confirm it."

"Oh?" I was pretty sure I remembered those names: the Sacristan and Angelotti.

Tony grimaced. "They claim they were having a quickie in the rehearsal hall."

My jaw dropped. "During a *performance*?"

He shrugged. "That's what they say."

I was embarrassed. I knew that opera, like any of the arts, attracted people who enjoyed alternative lifestyles. Would Tony now think it was a hotbed of gay love?

I took a bite of sandwich, thinking as I chewed. "But why would they want to kill Mr. Solano? That's where I don't know enough."

"Neither do I. They're pretty convincingly upset about his death. Other cast members describe their reaction after the curtain call as being shocked."

"You don't think it was them."

"It's too early to think anything."

"Was that what you wanted to bounce off me?"

"No."

"You want this egg?"

"No."

I ate the egg and watched him pace a little more, less agitated this time. He ran a hand through his hair, then returned to the visitor's chair at my desk.

"Not a word of this to anyone else," he said. "Not your aunt, not even your best friend."

"OK."

He leaned forward, elbows on his knees. "What do you know about the director?"

"The director of *Tosca*?"

"Yes."

"Nothing. I could look up his name—"

"Nothing at all? You've never met him, or seen him?"

"No."

"What about his wife?"

I shook my head. "I don't know anything about him, really."

"They had an argument during the performance."

Argument. A faint bell rang in my head.

"Was she the arguing woman?"

Tony's brows twitched together. "The what?"

"Remember when we went up to the gift shop, and there was a couple in front of us who stopped walking? I thought they'd been arguing."

Tony raised his chin. "Go on."

"Well, I was out in the courtyard with Mr. Ingraham a little later, and I saw the man from that couple talking with another man, and lighting a cigar. I asked Mr. Ingraham who he was, and he thought he might have been the director of *Tosca*. He said the other man was the General Director."

"OK."

"Then later I saw the arguing woman again. Remember? In the second intermission, we almost ran into her. She was wearing a fur coat, and heading for the south side of the theatre."

"Did you see where she went?"

"No..."

"Damn."

"I saw her go out the south gate and assumed she was

heading for the bar," I added. "I guess she could have gone through the stage door, but that would have attracted a lot of attention, wouldn't it? It's not the sort of thing you do—going backstage during a performance—even if you're the director's wife."

"She didn't go through the stage door."

I took a sip of tea. "She could have gone around, outside," I said, thinking back to the last time I took the backstage tour. "That wouldn't have been as conspicuous. I think there's a breezeway to the south that leads to the back of the stage. It's a long walk, though. She would have had to pass the costume shop and the props room to get to the dressing rooms. A lot of people would have seen her."

A slow smile crept on to Tony's face. "You're good."

"*Did* she go backstage?"

"She did. She was overhead giving Sandra Usher a piece of her mind right before Act Three."

Sandra Usher was the soprano who had played Tosca. I didn't need the program for that one.

"So she wasn't mad at Mr. Solano?" I asked.

"Apparently not."

"So that's a dead end. Do you have a suspect?"

Tony got up and started pacing again.

"You don't have to answer that," I said.

"If I'm going to use you as a sounding-board..." He slowed to a stop and turned to look at me. "Hell, I've already told you more than I should."

"I won't say anything. Scout's honor."

He laughed. "Were you a girl scout?"

"Yes, until high school. Then I got more into band and let scouts drop. Were you a scout?"

His smile vanished. "No."

Because his family couldn't afford the cost? Fees, uniforms...things I had taken for granted....

Tony came back to his chair, but didn't sit. He leaned his hands on the back and stared at me, his hair almost brushing the ceiling.

"Other than Carter and Harrison, we don't have a suspect. Mrs. Passaggio is on the maybe list, just because she had opportunity and was...agitated."

I thought back to the cigar-man. I supposed he might look Italian. His wife didn't.

"Why was she angry with Sandra Usher?" I asked.

"According to the person who overheard her, she was accusing her of sleeping with Mr. Passaggio."

"Oh, good lord! Right before she had to go onstage?!"

Tony shrugged. "People lose control. That's when bad things happen."

"She wasn't the only one who lost control!"

"No."

Our gazes held. I felt as if Tony wanted something from me; wanted me to guess something that would solve the case. Unfortunately, I was pretty brain-fried.

"What a mess," I said. "I'm so sorry you have to deal with this, Tony."

His eyes softened. "It isn't your fault."

"But if you hadn't been there with me, someone else might have gotten the call. I guess the police department knew where you were?"

"I had told a couple of people, yes. That's how they knew I was at the scene."

"So..."

He sat down, pulling the chair closer to my desk so he could lean his elbows on it. "It's *good* that I was there. I was able to secure the crime scene pretty fast, and get the house security people to take contact information."

"And now you just have to interview a few hundred people."

He grinned. "That's what beat cops are for."

I picked up my teacup, but it was empty. I put it back down. "I just feel bad. Like I caused you a bunch of extra work."

"Don't." He picked up a cucumber sandwich, inspecting it. "I would probably have been assigned to the case even if I hadn't been there. As it is...I think it's helped that I was there to see the opera."

"Helped?"

He nodded and swallowed a bite of sandwich. "Nobody else in the department knows much about opera. Because I was there with you, I'm kind of the local expert now."

"Oh!"

"And that's why I came to talk to you tonight. You know way more about this stuff than I do. You might make a connection that I can't. If you don't mind my bouncing ideas off you..."

"Not at all. I'm glad to help if I can."

"So I'm considering you an unofficial consultant, all right? But I'm serious about not saying anything to anyone. Not even your priest."

I smiled. He knew perfectly well I wasn't Catholic.

"I promise I won't."

"Good."

I picked up the last sandwich. "Want this?"

He shook his head, then frowned at my plate. "This isn't your dinner, is it?"

"Lunch, actually."

"Jeez! Let me buy you a steak, for Chrissake!"

"I'm not hungry enough now. Unless you haven't eaten?"

"I had a burger."

"Another time, then." I ate the sandwich and poured out the last of the tea into my cup. "Have you talked to the British man yet?"

"British?"

"The one who was talking about snogging? He was up in the members' bar; he must have been in the audience."

Tony stared past me, as if trying to remember. "No, I haven't talked to him. If he was in the audience, he's on the list that the beat cops are handling."

"Maybe you could ask them to refer any Britons to you?"

He nodded slowly. "Yeah. Do you remember exactly what he said about snogging?"

I leaned back and looked up at the ceiling, thinking back. "'Practically snogging him right onstage', I think. I figured he was talking about Tosca and Cavaradossi. And he said something about someone being upset."

Tony's eyes narrowed. "Who? Do you remember?"

I closed my eyes, trying to recall the moment. I took a deep breath and let it out slowly.

"Neil."

I opened my eyes to find Tony staring at me intently. "Neil Passaggio."

"Is that his name?"

"Yes. And his wife accused Sandra Usher of sleeping with him."

"So...if he was upset by Sandra Usher kissing—whatever his name is—Cavaradossi..."

"His name is David Ebinger."

"Ebinger, OK." I paused, struggling to keep the names straight.

"If Neil Passaggio was jealous of Usher kissing her costar," Tony said, "that supports Mrs. Passaggio's accusation."

"Ugh! But that doesn't explain the murder."

"Unless Sandra Usher was also sleeping with Victor Solano."

I stared at him. "We're going to need a program just to keep track of all the backstage affairs!"

"Fun, huh?"

"You're enjoying this?"

"It's my job. And yeah, I do enjoy making progress on an investigation."

I, however, did not find it all that enjoyable. Turning over all the detritus of people's private lives, just to see what could be found. I couldn't help thinking of compost.

"Have you talked to Sandra Usher?" I asked.

"Briefly, last night. I'll be going back. I left her alone today. She was pretty upset."

"I imagine everyone was."

"Yeah, but different people show it differently. Some of them were doing the stiff upper lip thing."

"Like who?"

"Ebinger, for one."

I picked up the last scone, pulled it apart, and offered half to Tony. He took it, his fingers brushing mine and sending a tingle up my arm.

"OK, you think Passaggio was jealous of Usher and Ebinger," I said. "And maybe Usher and Mr. Solano."

"Right."

"If Usher and Ebinger *were* involved, and she was also involved with Passaggio *and* Solano...she'd be exhausted."

Tony laughed. "OK, maybe it's a bit of a stretch. I don't think she's actually involved with Ebinger."

"Because if she was, wouldn't Ebinger also have a motive to kill Mr. Solano? I mean if she really was involved with all three of them."

Tony looked around my office. "You don't have a white board, do you?"

"Sorry, no."

"Can you give me some paper, then?"

I got out a legal pad and a pen and handed them to him. He set the pad on my desk and commenced sketching a diagram of circles with names in them: Usher, Passaggio, Ebinger, Solano. Then he drew lines between the romantic connections, with question marks over some of them.

"I guess this was a crime of passion," I mused. "No one in their right mind would plan a murder during a performance."

"Stranger things have happened," Tony said, frowning at his diagram.

"It would take nerves of steel! Anyone could have walked in. Carter and Harrison *should* have been in the dressing room."

"I wonder if they made a habit of an Act Three quickie?" he said.

"Or Act Two, for that matter. They're both just in Act One."

"But the chorus isn't onstage in Act Two. There would have been a lot more people backstage."

"Good point. Although if they always took their rendezvous away from backstage, to the rehearsal hall or even out in the woods, it might not matter so much."

"Hm." Tony let out a sigh. "Gonna have to sleep on it. I'm beat."

I refrained from making a pun about beat cops. "Did you get any sleep last night?"

"Couple hours."

He tore the page with his drawing from the pad, folded it, and slid it into a pocket of his motorcycle jacket, then pushed the pad and pen back toward me. I could see the indentation of his circles and arrows in the paper.

"So is Neil Passaggio a suspect?" I asked.

"Not sure. Need to ask a few more questions, but I think he goes on the list."

"Who overheard Mrs. Passaggio telling off Sandra Usher?" I asked.

He leaned back and stared at his knees.

"If you don't mind telling me," I added.

He raised his head and met my gaze. "It was Vi."

"Oh, no!"

"She was pretty ripped up about the whole thing."

"Mr. Solano was her mentor. Of course she was upset! Oh, damn—I was going to call her today."

"It's not that late."

"She's probably onstage. They didn't cancel tonight, did they?"

"Nope. *The Magic Flute* must go on."

"Then she's definitely on—she has a role in that one." I took out a pad of sticky notes and wrote myself a reminder to call Vi the next day.

"So she was close to Solano?" Tony asked. His voice was gentle, but I could smell the cop attitude hanging on the words.

"Tony Aragón, Vi did not kill Victor Solano!"

He held up his hands in a gesture of surrender. "Didn't say she did. I have to consider all possibilities."

"She was devastated! She was on the verge of tears last night when she told me he was dead!"

"Hey. I like Vi."

His quiet tone deflated my indignation. I rubbed my forehead.

"Sorry. I'm really tired."

"Me, too. I should leave you alone, let you get some rest."

He stood and headed for the hall. I followed.

Dusk had fallen while we were talking. I turned on the hall light.

"You get some sleep, too," I said.

"Yeah. Got a couple of things to deal with first."

We went downstairs. The light in the dining parlor was on. Tony looked in, frowning. I flipped the switch, turning it off.

As I unlocked the back door, Tony turned to me. "I never got the chance to thank you for last night. Believe it or not, I enjoyed the evening."

"That's nice of you. It turned out to be rather a trial by fire," I said, and then thought of *The Magic Flute*.

"Well, at least Thomas has a *Tosca* story he can dine out on," Tony said.

I laughed, though it caught in my throat. Dark humor, masking a tragedy. How cop-like.

Tony's fingers brushed my cheek, and I looked up to find him gazing softly at me.

"Let's get that steak soon," he said.

I nodded. "I'd like that."

My chest felt tight, making my breathing shallow. For a second I thought he was going to kiss me, but he just smiled and stepped away.

"Thanks for your help."

"Any time."

I watched him get on his bike and cruise away. Weariness wrapped around me like a quilt, muffling my thoughts and making it hard to move. I locked the door and went upstairs to my suite, where a hot shower and bed were calling to me.

I slept in. Luckily I had left my phone in my office, and didn't hear it ringing. When I carried my second cup of tea in there, three texts and two messages were waiting on my personal phone. I didn't dare check the tearoom voicemail.

The texts were from Gina, Rosa (saying her brother might be available to help in the kitchen during the coming week), and an old school friend who had heard about the murder and wanted to know if I knew anything about it. The messages were from Mr. Ingraham, with whom I was now officially playing phone tag, and Vi.

I checked the time. Vi's call had come in about twenty minutes earlier, so she must be awake. I called her back.

"Hi, Ellen." Her voice was a bit wobbly.

"Hi. I'm sorry I didn't call yesterday. We were crazy busy here."

"It's OK. I was pretty worthless yesterday anyway."

"Have you had breakfast? Want to come over?"

"I had some granola."

"Well, how about some tea?"

I could hear her thinking, and wondered if maybe she wasn't up to it yet.

"Actually," she said with a sigh, "that sounds really nice."

"Come on over, then. Ring the back bell."

"OK. Thanks."

"See you in a few."

I scurried downstairs to pop some scones in the oven, then returned to change out of my nightshirt into some casual clothes. Back down to put the kettle on, and out into the garden to look for violets. I cut a double handful and put them in a tall shot glass. Later I'd candy them for the Aria Cakes, but just now they were for Vi.

I carried them to Marigold, the most private of the sitting areas in the tearoom, and one of the coziest. A window to the south overlooked the rose garden. I cracked it open for a breeze, then went to the butler's pantry to start a pot of tea and to fetch china and silver and napkins.

By that time the scones were done. I put them on a plate and dished up some lemon curd and clotted cream. Thought about adding some Aria Cakes, then decided they might be a sad reminder so I left them in the fridge. Instead I nabbed the last of the lavender shortbread cookies that Julio had made on Friday.

I put everything on a tray, added a small candle, and took it to Marigold to lay the table. I had just returned to take the infuser out of the teapot when the doorbell rang.

Vi looked small, as impossible as that seemed for someone of her stature. Her shoulders were hunched, and her eyes were a bit red. In a purple tee-shirt and jeans, with her hair pulled into a ponytail, she seemed young and rather forlorn.

I drew her into a hug, whispering condolences. She let out one shuddering sigh before we parted.

"Thanks, Ellen. It's good to see you."

"Come on in. Tea's ready."

She followed me into the pantry and gazed around at the canisters of tea leaves and shelves of china while I found a cozy for the teapot. "Wow, I miss this place."

"Well, we miss you, too. No, I'll carry it. You're a guest today."

We walked up to the front and slipped through the silent gift shop, around the corner to Marigold, tucked behind the shop on the far side of the chimney wall. Too warm for a fire, alas, but the candle added a spark of comforting light. Vi settled into one of the rust-colored velvet wing chairs with a sigh and helped herself to a scone while I poured.

"It's so nice to have some quiet," she said. "I haven't had much chance to just rest."

I watched her spread curd on half a scone and take a bite. "Well, you can stay as long as you like. I could use some rest, too."

"You said it was busy yesterday."

"Yes, we were open late. Looks like this whole week will be busy."

I didn't want to mention why; didn't want to bring up Mr. Solano or the opera until Vi was ready to talk about them. Which maybe she wouldn't be, today.

She reached for the other half of the scone. "I've missed these, too. Oh—how pretty!"

She'd seen the violets. She picked up the glass and raised them to her face, closing her eyes to inhale.

"My mother never could get these to grow at our house."

"They need a shady spot," I said. "I have them under the lilac bushes."

"I'll tell her."

"How is she? I haven't seen her in a while."

"She's fine. Keeping me fed. There's no way I could cook with my schedule."

"Mm." I nodded, then picked up a piece of shortbread.

"Ellen..."

I glanced up at the soft misery in her voice. Grief had seeped through her company face; she looked at me like a broken-hearted child.

I put down my teacup and took her hand. "Yes," I said.

Yes, I'm listening, yes, it's horrible, yes, say whatever you want. Or nothing.

"I woke up this morning thinking it was a bad dream," she whispered.

"I wish that were true."

"Everyone's out of their mind, getting angry at each other over nothing, falling to pieces."

"You didn't."

"Not right then." She laughed softly. "I was a wreck when I went home."

"You were entitled."

A tear slid down her cheek. She ignored it.

"I keep wondering...who would want to kill him? He was so kind!"

Another tear followed the first. Vi took a tissue from the box I'd set on the table between us with the candle and the violets.

"I don't know," I said, "but Tony will figure it out."

"Detective Aragón? Oh, he was so wonderful! He came in like Superman, taking charge of everything. I was so glad, because it was chaos until he showed up. I was surprised to see him, though."

"Had I not mentioned he would be in our party?"

She shook her head. "Good thing he was. He marched right up to the dressing room, chased everyone away, and closed the door. Then he stood in front of it like a bulldog."

I couldn't help smiling at the image. Pit bull is what came to mind, more precisely.

"It must have been obvious that it wasn't an accident or a heart attack," I said, thinking aloud.

"Oh, yeah. It was obvious. I thought you knew."

I waited, watching her.

"That's the worst part," she said. "So vicious. They not only wanted Victor dead, they destroyed his voice."

"Destroyed?"

"They slashed his throat."

4

A vision of Tosca and her knife rose up in my mind. The ultimate irony: slain in the same way he'd just been "killed" onstage.

"It was so horrible." Vi mopped her face and took another tissue.

"You saw?"

She nodded.

I had no words of comfort. My mind painted the scene for me: Solano seated at his dressing table, mirror surrounded with lights, reflecting the slumped figure and the blood—stage blood, mingling with real blood...

I gave myself a small shake. Time to redirect my thoughts, and Vi's, too.

"His cover will take over the role, I assume? They wouldn't cancel..."

"Oh, no." Vi gave a short, bitter laugh. "The rest of the performances are all sold out now. The last tickets went yesterday."

Sometimes people were despicable, I thought.

Aloud, I said, "You'll get through it."

"Yes. I was glad we had a performance yesterday. It was a good distraction. When I'm not doing something I start to feel so helpless..."

"When is the next one?"

"Of *Tosca*? A week from tomorrow. Lucky—it gives Matthew a whole week to rehearse. They're running him through the blocking today."

"Matthew Carter?" I asked.

"Yes, he's Victor's cover for Scarpia."

The Sacristan. A new motive for murder suddenly occurred to me. Could he have done it for the lead role?

Terrible, terrible thought. I pushed it aside; time enough to examine it later. Vi was my priority at the moment.

"When's your next performance?" I asked.

"Tuesday. *Magic Flute.*"

"And you're off until then?"

"No, in the afternoons we have final rehearsals for *Cesar Chavez.* It opens Saturday."

"That's the premiere, right? Is it good?"

"I think so. Not very pretty, perhaps, but it's powerful."

"What's your favorite part of it?"

I encouraged her to talk more about the other operas in the season, figuring it would do her good. I mentioned the apprentice showcases, then mentally kicked myself because it brought the sadness back into Vi's face.

"Victor helped me so much, and now he'll never see the result."

"Maybe he will."

She gave me a wistful smile. "Maybe."

"I'd like to hear you. Which night should I come?"

"Oh, well—the second one will probably have fewer mistakes. We'll all be nervous the first night."

"Maybe that's when I should come, then. I'll send you calming vibes from the audience."

She chuckled. "You and Mom. My fan club."

"Well, I am your fan. You sang the shepherd wonderfully, by the way. We were delighted to see you."

A shadow of grief draped her face, then she mastered it. "Thank you. I was so excited."

"Was the regular performer unwell?"

A nod. "She called in sick that afternoon. Just before call, so I didn't have time to rehearse, but I knew the part."

She looked troubled. I picked up the teapot to freshen our cups.

"Do you know her well?"

"Lydia? Not well, no. She...well, she was trying to get Victor's attention, I think."

"A lot of people were, I imagine."

"Yes." Vi sipped her tea, frowning into the dark fireplace.

I wondered if Vi had become emotionally involved with Victor Solano, beyond friendship. It seemed unlike my impression of him to meddle with someone as vulnerable as she—young, an apprentice, looking up to him—but I heard Tony's voice whisper that all possibilities had to be considered. Could Vi's grief reflect a deeper involvement with Solano than I had thought?

"He told me—oh, I'm sorry." She dug her phone out of her pocket and glanced at the screen, then put it away again. "Sorry, Ellen. I forgot to turn it off."

"It's the weekend. Work-time rules don't apply. And you're a guest, remember?"

She gave me a weary smile. "This is so nice. Thank you."

"You're very welcome."

"I've been feeling like I'm onstage all the time...like I have to pretend...but it isn't like that here. I can talk to you."

"Yes, of course."

"That helps a lot. You don't know how much."

I thought back to my initial, stunned grief over my father's death more than a year before. "I think I can guess."

She took my hand and squeezed it. We sat silently for a minute.

"I'm really lucky," she said eventually. "Lucky that I knew Victor. He was so supportive."

"He seemed like a wonderful person, the time I met him."

"Yes. Oh, I wish you'd had the chance to know him better. He was so *good*."

Was he? Then why would anyone want to kill him?

"You know my first day with the company, he came up to me and said, 'A Carmen in the making!'"

"Did he?"

"Before he'd even heard me sing! I said, 'How do you know I'm not a coloratura?' and he said, 'I can spot a mezzo-soprano a mile away.'"

"Sounds like he was flirting."

"Oh, he flirts with everybody. But he was just trying to help me relax, you know?"

I smiled, but this didn't reassure me. Maybe I should talk to Vi's mother. She'd probably have a better idea of what Vi's relationship with Mr. Solano had been.

Or maybe I should just leave it alone.

But the puzzle itched at me. Why had Victor Solano died? Who had hated him enough to destroy his voice—if only as a symbolic gesture—while taking his life?

The sheers stirred at the window, making me look out at the garden. Sunshine wakened the fragrance of the roses, and a breeze carried it in to us. Clouds had begun to bloom, gathering in white puffs, teasing with the possibility of afternoon rain.

"He treated me like an equal," Vi mused. "Not all of them are like that. He made me talk to the principals—made sure I met them all and that they acknowledged me. Like I was one of them, not just chorus."

"Well, you are more than chorus. The apprentice program is a big deal."

She nodded. "I know. But Victor said I should pretend I had already finished it, and was moving on to a career. He said if I acted like an equal, they would treat me like one."

"And is that true?"

"Mostly. Sandra—Miss Usher—has been nice. She even invited me to come to tea here this week. She's bringing a bunch of people."

"Is she? I haven't had time to look at the reservations."

"Yes, on Tuesday. I can't come; I have a rehearsal. But it was nice of her to invite me."

"Were she and Mr. Solano close?"

Vi met my gaze with an inquiring look.

"Apparently he spoke well of the tearoom," I said. "We're getting a lot of reservations from the opera crowd this week. I wondered who might be spreading the word."

"Oh. Well, it could be Sandra. I don't know. She was friends with Victor, but she's seeing someone else."

Hm. I wondered if it was the tenor, David Ebinger. I didn't want to press Vi for gossip.

"Do you like her?" I asked instead.

She sipped her tea. "Yes. It helps that I'm a mezzo. That sounds petty, but it really is true that people are competitive. There's so much money involved. It makes people act crazy."

"I have no idea what opera singers are paid. Is it a good living?"

"Well, it depends on a lot of things. The company's budget, whether you're a principal, past reviews, all that. I won't be making much until I have some solo roles under my belt, but the top performers are paid pretty well."

"While they're on top."

She smiled, laughter crinkling the corners of her eyes. "Yes, exactly. It's like dancers, or even sports stars. Their time at the top is limited, so they have to make the most of it."

"What do you think you'll do next?"

"Apply for my second season, if they'll have me. Apprentices are allowed to return once."

"And after that?"

She shrugged a shoulder. "See who else will hire me."

"Are there any companies you'd especially like to get into?"

"Well, the Met, of course, but they won't take me yet. I'll probably have to go to Europe for a couple of years."

"That sounds exciting."

"As long as I can afford it. I don't want to be a burden on my mom."

"Maybe we could do some fund-raising for you. Would you like to sing here again? You could have the profits after I cover my costs."

"Ellen! That's so sweet of you!"

"Well, I want to support you. I'm your second-biggest fan, right?"

She put down her teacup and reached over to hug me. She smelled freshly-scrubbed, soap with a hint of verbena.

"You're so good to me," she said.

I gave her shoulders a squeeze, then let her go. "We'll talk about it after the season."

"Yes."

It occurred to me that her return to the tearoom, if it happened at all, would be temporary. Eventually she'd fly—off to Europe or somewhere, wherever she found a company that would give her a chance. I'd be sorry to lose her, but happy to see her realize her dreams.

"When you're at the Met, I'll come to New York to see you."

She laughed. "You don't have to."

"I want to. I can stay with my brother." I picked up the pot, which felt suspiciously light. Lifting the lid, I saw that there was less than a cupful of tea left. "I can make some more."

"No, I'd better be going. But thank you so much, Ellen."

"Let's do this again. Next week? Or the week after?"

"Starting next Monday we go to the full performance schedule. I'll only have a couple of days off in August."

"Let's touch base later this week, and if you're not too exhausted we'll get together on Sunday."

"Sounds perfect."

I walked with her to the back door, waved goodbye from the *portal,* and watched her drive away. Returning to Marigold to tidy up, I thought back over what she'd told me.

It sounded like there were some tensions—social, and maybe political—going on behind the scenes at the Opera. That didn't surprise me. I'd done some amateur theatre in high school, and there was more drama backstage than onstage, or so it had seemed.

I carried my tray to the kitchen, unloaded the china into the dishwashing station, and turned the oven on low to get ready for candying the violets. I emptied the ones I had cut into a colander, then decided I might as well do them all at once, and went out to the garden with scissors and a small basket. Another fifty flowers were snipped, leaving the violet bed severely depleted.

I eyed the bowls of pansies I had on the *portal*. Not yet, I decided, but if the violets I'd ordered didn't arrive, I'd have to raid the pansies.

I carried my booty back to the kitchen, added it to the violets in the colander, gently washed them all and left them to dry while I went upstairs to attend to my various unanswered messages.

Mr. Ingraham wanted to invite me to dinner on Friday. "Just a small, at-home gathering," he said. "Bring Tony."

"I'll have to see. It's going to be a busy week, and I might be working late on Friday."

"Well, call me in a couple of days, when you have a better idea."

"I will, thanks."

I called Willow, and was guiltily grateful when it went to voicemail. Probably she was running a tour. I left a brief message, then dialed Gina. Voicemail again; she might be showing properties.

I checked for texts, sent Rosa a thank-you and yes, please ask your brother to come in, and emailed the tearoom staff warning that it would be a busy week and asking anyone who was willing to work overtime to let me know.

A sense of doom had been growing on me. I gave in and brought up our reservations calendar.

The whole week was booked solid through Saturday, including the outdoor tables, and there were half a dozen names on the waiting list. Kris had booked seatings up through 6:00 p.m. every day, which meant we'd be open until 7:00 or later.

My heart gave a small lurch of dismay, and I started making notes for Monday's grocery order. We'd need extra eggs, butter, and cream, probably more lemons, and sliced almonds, just for starters. I'd check with Julio before placing the orders.

Curiosity made me look for Sandra Usher's reservation. I didn't find her name, but a party under the name of Kowalski had booked the dining parlor for Tuesday afternoon.

The dining parlor was usually the last room to be scheduled, because it was large and not as cozy as the flower seating areas. It had a full, formal dining table rather than the comfy chairs and low tables that filled the rest of the tearoom. Larger groups, like showers and birthday parties, landed in the dining parlor, but it mostly stood empty.

It wouldn't, this week. Except when large parties had the room, Kris had two smaller parties booked to share the dining table, something we'd talked about but never had to do. I would have to put all the leaves in the table. Maybe do a big floral centerpiece, to give the two parties a little separation.

It was going to be a tough week. I was grateful for the business, but couldn't help wishing the timing had been different.

I went down to the kitchen, got out an egg, and cracked the white into a small bowl, putting away the yolk for later. I tossed the violets in the colander, emptied them onto a paper towel and spread them out to dry a little more while I washed the china from Vi's visit. Then I moved the violets to a parchment-lined cookie sheet, painted them with egg white, sprinkled sugar over them, and stuck them in the oven, turning it off.

I took perverse satisfaction in writing a note to stick on the oven door: CANDIED VIOLETS, DON'T TOUCH.

Julio was always leaving notes like that.

Deciding I needed to de-stress, I fixed myself a glass of ice water and carried it out front. Sun shone through the wisteria vines to dapple the front *portal*. The breeze was kicking up stronger.

I stepped down and strolled through the garden, enjoying the roses' fragrance and the bright eyes of anemones, zinnias, and daisies in the beds by the house. The camellia and the two peonies I had planted a year ago were starting to thrive. I pondered whether I could make dahlias happy, maybe against the south wall.

Over the mountains, the clouds were a mashed-potato heap. I wondered if Manny's grilling would get rained out, then decided he wouldn't let it happen. He'd be out there with an umbrella if necessary. I could see him hunched against the rain, with the grill moved into the most sheltered corner of Nat's patio, shielding his precious meats with his body.

My stomach grumbled. The last time I'd eaten something besides tea food was yesterday morning. I didn't want to have lunch before Manny's feast, but I needed something to tide me over, so I went up to my suite and had an apple and a slice of cheese.

With a few hours of leisure before I was expected at Nat's, I decided to try to find out a little more about Victor Solano. I walked across the hall to my office, pushed the tearoom paperwork aside, and started web-surfing.

I found a number of Victor Solanos besides the singer. No website, but he was listed on several opera company websites, mostly from past seasons, and on SFO's for the current season. I'd already read his bio, so I skimmed the company listings and looked for articles that mentioned him.

I found several reviews, including a recent one in the Albuquerque Journal about his Scarpia at SFO. Glowing. Most of the others were positive, but one New York critic apparently disliked his voice, not only in the opera he was reviewing but in a couple of previous ones he saw fit to mention.

That smacked of politics to me. How had Solano managed to offend that particular reviewer?

Out of curiosity I surfed on the reviewer's name, resulting in a long list of reviews and one rather petulant blog post from, apparently, an ex-boyfriend.

Wild scenario: gay reviewer makes a pass at opera singer, is turned down, and retaliates with slam review.

Pretty far-fetched. I went back to surfing Solano, this time keeping an eye out for any romantic associations.

I found none.

Absolute zero; not even a photo of him out on a date. Apparently he was very private about his romantic affairs.

Why would a man be so protective of his love-life? Particularly a celebrity who was often in the spotlight and who enjoyed it. I'd expect such a person to show off his romantic conquests, not hide them.

Possibly he was into some weird kink that could damage his career if it were known.

Or was illegal.

I frowned at my monitor. That just didn't fit with the man I'd met, though any stage performer was capable of convincing deception. But to me he had *felt* like a good person. I'd known a few bad ones, and just being in their presence had made me uncomfortable. I didn't react that way to Victor Solano.

I sighed, unable to unravel that particular knot. Not enough information. I'd try again later.

I surfed on Neil Passaggio and found a few articles. He was a former singer, which I hadn't known, and an up-and-coming director of opera. One article called him a "fiery tenor."

Unlike Solano, he showed off his romances. There were lots of photographs of him with young singers from three years or more ago. Then a huge barrage of announcements of his wedding, followed by a bunch of pictures of him and his wife.

The arguing woman. Arguing with him, and yelling at Sandra Usher.

She didn't look argumentative in the photos I found online. I was surprised to see that her smile made her look quite lovely.

She was not involved in opera, unlike many of the women in photos of Passaggio that predated her advent. Michelle Passaggio (née Martin) had been an interior designer before her marriage. If she had continued that career, I didn't find any mention of it. She looked to me rather like a trophy wife, except that she was classier than most.

And trophy wives were often gold-diggers, which I just didn't see in Michelle. As a director, Passaggio would certainly make good money, but he was no Donald Trump.

Well, enough of that. I was starting to feel like a stalker.

I shut down my computer and went downstairs to the dining parlor to pull the extra leaves for the table out of the closet. As I stepped up to the door, the floor creaked beneath my foot and gave a little.

"Oh, blast."

I did *not* need to have to repair the floor right now, thank you. I prodded the offending board again with my toe and it wiggled. Not good.

Getting down on my hands and knees, I pulled back the corner of the oriental rug that filled most of the room, and looked more closely at the floor boards. I didn't see any rot, for which I was thankful.

The loose board was right up against the corner of the room, an end piece about eighteen inches long. It looked slightly narrow, and I wondered if it might have shrunk. The floor was old: solid oak, possibly original to the house. In Santa Fe's dry climate, wood shrank and warped and twisted in all kinds of interesting ways.

I pushed at the loose board to see how much I could wiggle it. It slid to one side and then away from the wall. I poked at it and the end near me popped up, surprising me into making a startled noise.

The near end was sticking up about half an inch. I took hold of it and gave a gentle tug, and the whole piece came up.

"Damn it," I muttered.

I'd broken my floor.

The piece of wood itself was undamaged. Maybe it really had just shrunk.

I peered at the space beneath, thinking unhappy thoughts about spiders. The floor was sprung, and I could see one of the supports running across the gap close to me. At the other end of the space was something I took for a clump of insulation.

Except that if this was the original floor, it probably wasn't insulated.

I looked closer. Maybe it was an old sock or something; it looked whitish.

I laid the board aside and fetched a flashlight from the kitchen. Shining it into the gap, I saw that what I'd taken for insulation was actually paper.

Multiple folded papers, to be precise. Tied with a scrap of ribbon. My heart started beating faster.

After a careful inspection for spiders, I reached in and picked up the bundle. A deep layer of dust covered it. I shook it over the hiding space and tapped it a couple of times, careful to be gentle. Still, it crackled in my hand, and exuded a fragrance of old, musty paper that made me think of the many happy hours I'd spent deep in back sections of the city library.

I turned the bundle over and saw handwriting, a thin script that looked as fragile as the paper it rested on.

El Capitan Señor Samuel Dusenberry
Fort Marcy Post
Ciudad de la Santa Fé de San Francisco de Asís

5

I put down the flashlight and cupped the bundle of letters in both hands, afraid of damaging them. If they had really belonged to Captain Dusenberry—and they looked old enough —they might be important historical documents. I should hand them over to Bennett Cole at the Museum of New Mexico.

No way. Not before I read them.

A ball of excitement settled in my gut. I suspected the letter on top was from a woman; the handwriting was careful and beautiful, and the exaggerated mode of address seemed playful. But maybe I was reading too much into it.

I got up, threw back the lace tablecloth from one end of the dining table, and laid the bundle on the polished wood. Pulling up a chair, I wondered if I should untie the ribbon or try to slide it off. Now that I looked more closely at it, I saw that a desiccated rosebud was tied into the bow.

Shouldn't untie it, then. I pushed gently at the ribbon, which was loose enough to move. With aching slowness I nudged it toward one end of the bundle. About an inch from the end it stopped moving so easily, and I was so annoyed I growled.

The ribbon wasn't going to budge any farther. Frustrated, I pinched the end of a letter in the middle of the bundle and wiggled it. Luck was with me; it gave, and I was able to pull it free. I pulled out two more letters, keeping track of the order they were in, and by then the ribbon was loose enough to remove. I set it carefully aside, restored the letters to their proper order, and placed them on the table in front of me.

I glanced up at the chandelier. Nothing moving.

Hope you don't mind, Captain. I'm curious.

Taking a deep breath, I picked up the top letter. It wasn't in an envelope; the address was written on the outside of the page, and when I turned it over I saw that it had once been sealed with a dab of red sealing wax. I lifted the top edge and carefully spread the letter flat on the table. It creaked a little, but the creased edges had been softened, perhaps by many readings, and I was able to unfold it without damaging it.

Muy distinguido señor,

Oh, great. It was in Spanish. Mine was passable, but not fantastic.

I skimmed it, noticing some references to music and a "baille" which I believed to be a dance. Also the incongruous word "Exchange," immediately following "La Fonda."

La Fonda was the name of the hotel on the southeast corner of the plaza in Santa Fe. It had been there forever, certainly since Captain Dusenberry's time.

So did the letter writer want to make an exchange of some kind at La Fonda?

I had no clue.

I skipped to the signature: Maria Hidalgo. The Hidalgos were a prominent Santa Fe family. They were among the first settlers, and returned after the Pueblo Revolt. They had land and major influence back in the day.

I took a quick glance through the rest of the letters. They all appeared to be written by the same person, but after the first three or four the addresses changed from Spanish to English. I set the Spanish ones aside and happily opened the first of the English-looking ones.

Dear Capitan Dusenberry,

Many thanks for your most excellent company and escort to the concert at the Exchange. The music and the evening were of great delight, most especially the voice of the lovely soprano, Miss Lago. I thought the lyric of her aria most striking.

Speriam che in contento, finisca l'affanno
Non sempre è tiranno il fato ed amor.
I will remember these words when my heart fails me.

How lovely it would be to form a musical group, as we discussed, so that we might all together enjoy music whenever we pleased. My sister would join us, and I will speak to some of my friends who might also have an interest. You will, I hope, be willing to come and play the pianoforte for us? And perhaps to lend your voice, for though you are modest, in truth you are a fine singer.

I look forward to your visit on Thursday.

Favor de escribirme pronto,

Maria Hidalgo

Spanish *and* Italian. Yi.

Though the lyric should be surfable, if it was anything near accurate and not too obscure.

I sat gazing at the letter, feeling a tingle of excitement. So many new details about Captain Dusenberry! He and Señora—Señorita?—Hidalgo were friends. That gave him a connection to a powerful Hispanic family, something that would surely be useful to a military officer.

And he played the piano. I couldn't help smiling. I knew he was a music lover, but to see it confirmed pleased me immensely.

More puzzling, "Exchange" had showed up again, and it appeared to refer to a place. Could "La Fonda Exchange" once have been the name of the hotel? That sounded so odd.

I folded up the letter and restored it to its place in the stack, then carried all of them and the ribbon upstairs to my office. I surfed on "La Fonda Exchange" and learned that "Exchange Hotel" had been its name during the territorial years. Apparently it was a common name—I found references to Exchange Hotels in other towns, including Las Vegas, New Mexico.

I pulled up a translator and typed in the Italian lyric. Only partial success, but the gist of the first line seemed to be "hope that happiness finishes the anxiety."

Surfing on the lyric itself produced the entire text of the aria from which it came, which turned out to be Mozart, from *The Marriage of Figaro*, along with a translation. Sung by the Countess Almaviva, the aria expressed cautious optimism that her life would soon improve.

Why had Maria Hidalgo chosen to quote from that particular aria? It wasn't just because of the music or the performance she'd heard. She said they were words she would remember.

I'd seen *Figaro*, but not recently. I recalled that the Countess and her maid exchanged clothes, and that mischief ensued, which eventually was all sorted out into a happy ending. Now I was curious, so I resolved to read the whole libretto.

Not today, though. I needed to get ready to go over to Nat's for dinner.

I glanced at the time and gasped. Four-thirty! And I'd left a mess in the dining parlor!

I found a shallow box to hold the letters and the ribbon with its dried rose. It just fit into my desk drawer alongside the bank bag fat with Saturday's receipts. I locked the drawer and hurried downstairs to straighten the dining parlor.

The floorboard and flashlight lay on the floor beside the gap where I'd found the letters. With a bit of effort, I wiggled the board back into its place, and put the corner of the rug back over it.

I straightened the tablecloth, set my flashlight on the table, and opened the closet, being careful not to step on the hidden compartment. I pulled out the table leaves and leaned them against the wall; I'd put them in the table later.

Returned the flashlight to the kitchen. Dashed back upstairs and jumped into the shower. As I scrambled into some clothes, I thought I heard distant music. I stood still and listened.

It sounded like the stereo was on downstairs.

I closed my eyes and indulged in a sigh. Not again.

I finished dressing, grabbed purse and keys and a sweater in case it got cold later, and walked slowly downstairs. The stereo was definitely on, and it was playing Mozart: the Andante from

Eine kleine Nachtmusik.

OK, that was too weird to be coincidence. The only way anyone could know that the letter I'd read referred to Mozart was if they'd read it too, and I was pretty sure no one had opened that hiding place in the floor for a very long time.

Which meant that Captain Dusenberry was for real.

I didn't have time to sort it out. I paused outside the pantry, but didn't go in to turn off the stereo. Instead I looked around me, at the hallway, the stairs, the doorways to the pantry and the dining parlor, the back door with its lights throwing indirect sunlight onto the oak floor.

This was my home. I'd lived here less than a year, but it was the place where my heart rested. If I had to share it with a ghost, at least he was a gentleman.

I let myself out and got in my car. My plan was to stop by the grocery store and pick up some of Manny's favorite beer. A glance at the clock on the dash told me I had just enough time.

The checkout line was longish. While I was waiting, I thought I should call Nat and let her know I was on my way. Unfortunately, my phone wasn't in my purse, or my pocket. I'd left it in the office, I was pretty sure.

Quietly chiding myself, I smiled at the cashier and paid cash for the beer. Tried not to be too lead-footed as I drove to Nat's.

She lived on the north side of town, not terribly far from the Opera. Her views were to the east and south: the mountains, and after dark a glimpse of the lights of Santa Fe.

The sun was still an hour or so from setting. I could smell mesquite smoke as I pulled into Nat's driveway. Another car was there; a silver BMW that I was pretty sure belonged to Claudia Pearson. I smiled; I liked Claudia.

Nat had been friends with Sylvia Carruthers, who was Claudia's boss until she died. Claudia had inherited Sylvia's job of directing the Santa Fe Preservation Trust, and all the headaches that went with it. She was quiet and classy where Sylvia had been pushy and loud, but they both had the same passion for history and the same kindness of heart.

I got out, collected my beer from the back seat, and followed my nose onto the deck and around the north side where Manny was on duty at the grill. He gave me a big smile and a wave.

"*¡Hola, chica!*"

"*Hola* yourself. I brought *cervesa.*"

"Bless you! The girls are making some kind of concoction, a cross between a margarita and a cosmopolitan."

"That sounds terrible."

He set down his tongs long enough to give me a hug, then shooed me inside. My stomach, awakening with proximity to the juicy smells coming from the grill, gave a long, low growl.

Nat and Claudia were in the kitchen, dressed far more casually than when I'd last seen them. Nat was in a multicolored broomstick skirt and a yellow blouse with puffy sleeves, and Claudia had on a slinky knit top in a dark shade of mauve over pipestem jeans. They greeted me with hugs and demands that I sample their handiwork.

It was pink, sort of. A kind of cotton-candy pink with a touch of salmon.

"What's in it?" I asked, despite my fear that I'd be better off not knowing.

"Vodka, triple sec, cranberry juice, lime juice and tequila," said Nat, filling a shot glass and handing it to me. "Taste."

I took a wary sip. It wasn't bad, really. Milder than a margarita, but I suspected the cotton-candyness hid a knockout punch.

"Wow," I said, slightly breathless.

"We're trying to decide what to call it. I like 'Margrapolitan' but Claudia doesn't."

"How about 'Doña Tules'?" I said.

"There's a thought," said Claudia. "A touch of history."

Nat hefted a pitcher that was half full of the concoction. "Want a whole one?"

"Thanks, but I think I'll start with a beer. Is there room in the fridge for these?"

"There should be, now that Manny's taken the meat out."

"What's he grilling? It smells fantastic."

"Elk steaks and venison sausage."

"Ah...his hunter friends are having a good season."

"They had it last year, actually. These are leftovers. I think they're clearing space for this year's haul. Let's go out on the deck, shall we?"

I tucked my sixpack in the fridge between a dish of marinated green beans and a bowl of potato salad, opened a beer, and tagged along after Nat and Claudia out to the deck. We sat in comfy chairs on the east side and gazed at the mountains. Occasionally a gust of aromatic breeze would waft over us from the north.

I yawned. "Thanks for inviting me, Nat. I needed a break."

"You said it was busy yesterday."

"Yeah, and it looks like it will be all week. Apparently Mr. Solano said he liked the tearoom, and word has been going around in opera circles. We're booked solid."

"Wow! Do you need help?"

"Maybe. Rosa's brother is going to come in."

"Can he cook?"

"I have no idea. I'll see what he's good for when he gets there. He plays the guitar beautifully, but that's not what I need this week."

"Opera circles," mused Claudia over her martini glass of cotton-candy. "I wonder if Thomas had anything to do with it."

"That hadn't occurred to me," I said. "You think he might have?"

"He does love a good story."

And he was at the tearoom for Vi's event. Well, if I owed my busy week to Mr. Ingraham, I could only be grateful to him.

"Claudia, what do you know about La Fonda?" I asked. "I've been reading some old nineteenth-century letters and it sounds like there were concerts and maybe dances there."

"I can believe that. It was the biggest building other than the church, back then. And the church, of course, wasn't nearly as big as the basilica is today."

"Bigger than the Palace of the Governors?" Nat asked.

"I think so, and it had a ballroom. The Palace didn't."

"Is there a good history of the hotel in print?" I asked.

"Not that I know of. You could check with the museum, or there might be some records in the state archives."

I took a swig of beer. Part of me wanted to tell them about my find, but another part of me wanted to keep the letters to myself, at least until I'd had a chance to read them all. I was afraid everyone would insist that I turn them over to the museum. And I would...but not just yet.

"Hey," Manny called from around the corner. "What does a guy have to do to get a beer around here?"

I jumped up. "I'll get you one. No, you stay put, Nat. I bet you've been cooking and cleaning all afternoon."

"Bring the pitcher," she called after me.

I fetched a beer and the pitcher and brought them back, by which time Manny was moving sausages onto a platter. He took a deep swig from the bottle, then gave an appreciative "Ahhh!"

"Those done?"

"Yes. Tell Nat to bring out the sides."

I conveyed this message, which caused Nat and Claudia to spring into action. I offered to set the outdoor table while they carried out the potato salad, green beans, and a basket of garlic bread that had been hiding in the oven. By the time we were done, Manny appeared with his platter heaped with meat.

"I hope you invited more people," I said to Nat, looking at all the food.

"The Lindholms, but they weren't sure they could make it."

"Tony said the same thing."

"More for us," Manny said, taking his seat and helping himself to a steak.

I tried a little of everything. The veggies were wonderful, of course. Manny always made sure that Nat had the best produce, which would have made me jealous except that he did the same for me.

"Oh, Manny—I'm probably going to need extra lemons and

cucumbers this week. And maybe some shallots."

"Just let me know by two tomorrow."

"OK."

Julio had said he would come in for the afternoon; I'd draw up an estimate of what we'd need in the morning and have him approve it before I adjusted the week's orders.

"Got some nice organic peaches in," Manny said. "First of the season."

"From Colorado?"

"Yes."

"I'll take a couple of pounds for me." I couldn't quite afford organic produce for the tearoom, though that was one of my hopes for the future.

My seat faced the north, and though there were hills in the way, I knew the Opera wasn't far away. "You know, it just occurred to me that we should have gone to *Cesar Chavez*. Are you interested in it, Manny?"

He shrugged. "That's history, as far as I'm concerned. I can take it or leave it."

Nat chuckled. "Like any opera."

"No, I like going with you to the opera. Chance to dress up."

"That's the spirit!" said Claudia. "Better keep him, Natasha."

"As a matter of fact..." Manny said, glancing at Nat.

Her gaze rested on him fondly. "Oh, well—now you're letting the cat out of the bag," she said, teasing. She looked at me and broke out in a beaming smile. "I've accepted Manny's proposal. We're getting married in the fall."

"Nat!" I jumped up and hugged her, then ran around the table to hug Manny. "Uncle Manny!"

"Ahem. My nieces and nephews say '*Tio*'."

"*Tio Manuel*. That's fabulous!"

"Here's to the happy couple," said Claudia, raising her glass.

I grabbed my beer. We drank several more toasts so that everyone was sure to have consumed enough liquor. The pink stuff in the pitcher underwent serious depletion.

"Doña Tules is almost gone," Nat said, looking at the pitcher.

"We're going to need to make more."

"Not on my account," said Claudia. "I have to get myself home in one piece."

"Well, there's dessert."

"I'll have one," I said, feeling reckless and wanting to please my aunt.

Nat stood, divided the last of the pink between her glass and Claudia's, and headed for the kitchen. I tagged along.

"Bring me another beer while you're in there," Manny called after us.

The kitchen faced north, but the living room to the west was bathed in orange light from the setting sun. I leaned against the counter and watched Nat concocting more Doña Tules.

"Have you made any plans about the wedding?" I asked while I watched her squeeze limes.

"Nothing elaborate," she said. "Just family and a few friends. I was wondering if you'd be willing to have it in your garden?"

"I'd love to! Should I ask Julio about the cake?"

"Oh, Manny would love that! He's crazy about that cake you did for the opera."

"Julio did it. Maybe he can make a larger version for a groom's cake."

"That," she said, handing me a martini glass brimming with pink, "would make Manny's day."

"No, getting married to *you* will make his day," I said, raising the glass to her.

"Then the cake will be the...icing on the cake."

She gave a chuckle, got another beer from the fridge, picked up the pitcher, and headed back to the deck. I took a swig of pink and noted its effect on me as I walked. I would definitely need some dessert to help me get over it.

Manny and Claudia were chatting about the upcoming Spanish Market and Indian Market, two of the big tourist events of the year in Santa Fe. Like most locals, I tended to avoid them —because, traffic nightmare—but this year I might walk over since the Plaza was so close to the tearoom.

I mused about whether to try some kind of advertising connected to the events...but that was bound to be expensive. And I didn't need it so much this time of year; certainly not at the moment. It was the slower seasons when I'd need some help getting people into the tearoom.

The pink was making me drowsy. The mountains were pink, too: pink with sunset. I gazed at them, feeling content, listening to Manny and Nat discuss where to go for their honeymoon.

A memory of Uncle Stephen, Nat's first husband, came to me. A party at my parents' house, gathered around the fireplace in the great room, Stephen playing the guitar while we sang some silly folk song. He'd been gone for almost a decade, now—cancer—and it had taken Nat a long time to recover.

I hoped she and Manny would be happy together. They were certainly happy now, and marriage should only increase their bond.

By the time the pink had faded from the mountains, it was starting to get just a little chilly. We carried the leftovers and dishes inside, and Nat fed us strawberry shortcake and coffee.

"No coffee for me, thanks," I said. "I have to get a good night's sleep. Tomorrow's going to be a busy day, gearing up for this week."

"You sure you don't want me to come in?" Nat said.

"I'm not sure at all. How would you feel about manning the gift shop?"

"I'd be glad to. Starting Tuesday?"

"Yes. Let me check the schedule. I think we'll be all right in the mornings but I could use you for sure in the afternoons. We'll be open late all week."

Nat traded a look with Manny.

"Good thing I made extra steaks," he said.

I finished my dessert, firmly declined seconds, and hugged and kissed everybody, Claudia included.

"I'll walk out with you," she said. "Nat, thank you for a lovely evening."

"And Manny, thanks for the excellent viands," I added.

"Viands." He chuckled. "Call me tomorrow with your order."

"Will do."

As I walked out with Claudia, I paused to look up at the Milky Way. The sky was a deep, velvety indigo. Santa Fe twinkled, but it was the cloudy ribbon across the heavens that drew my gaze.

"Magnificent," Claudia said. "Not many cities in the country where you can see a sky like that."

"Yes. We're blessed."

We hugged again, promising to meet soon, and went our separate ways. I drove home carefully, suspicious of the possible lingering effects of Doña Tules. When I pulled up, I saw that the hall light was on.

Interesting. Usually Captain Dusenberry messed with the lights in the dining parlor.

I approached the door cautiously, listening, looking for signs of trouble. Other than the light being on, there was nothing unusual. I unlocked the back door and went in, locked it behind me, and stood still for a minute, just listening to the house.

The stereo was not on. I noted this, pondering its meaning. Had Captain Dusenberry run out of music he liked? Or had he played it for me, not for himself?

Or was he a figment of my over-active imagination?

Smiling, I started toward the stairs. I froze as the music began.

Not the stereo. It was coming from the main parlor. My piano.

6

I stepped out of my loafers. It was my habit, and it just seemed proper, to make a silent approach to any ghostly activity in the house.

I wished for my cell phone, and resolved to make a dash for the gift shop to dial 911 if it happened to be a fleshly musician, then tiptoed toward the parlor. The music was hesitant, a melody picked out note by note. It began with the "Three Blind Mice" opening but went on from there into a different phrase. Slow and mournful.

I reached the doorway to the parlor and stood listening, observing. I heard no breathing, no movement. Only the notes from the piano: a second phrase, balancing the first, with an accidental that sounded very familiar.

Mozart.

I peeped around the doorway. There were no lights on in the parlor, but the light from the hallway lit the edges of the furniture.

No one was seated at the piano. The keyboard was closed.

This was my cue to run screaming, and if I'd been twelve, I would have. I was more than twice that age, though—and I wasn't afraid, exactly. But I did want to know what was going on.

The music didn't continue. After that accidental and one more note to resolve it, silence filled the room.

I closed my eyes and ran the phrases through my head again. I recognized them. Definitely Mozart, but which piece? He wrote hundreds.

All right, never mind. I'd figure out the source later. Meanwhile, I would establish that there was nothing wired to my piano to make it play remotely.

I flipped the light switch and the parlor lit up. Blinking at the brightness, I approached the piano and lifted the keyboard lid.

Nothing additional, nothing out of place. I moved several ornaments and a fringed shawl off the top of the instrument and opened the lid to the case. Peering down into it, I saw no strange wires or foreign mechanisms.

I closed the lid and restored the decorations to their places, then sat on the bench with my back to the instrument and just gazed around the room. The phrases ran through my head, repeating over and over. I feared I would fall asleep to them that night.

"What are you trying to tell me?"

Silence.

I could put all my Mozart disks in the stereo. Maybe Captain Dusenberry would find the right piece and play it.

Shaking my head, I drew a deep breath and stood up. I had letters to read.

I left the room, turning out the light. Stepped into my shoes and went upstairs to my office.

My phone was on the desk, right where I'd left it. I checked for messages and found three—two texts and a voicemail—all from Tony. I checked the texts first.

SORRY I BAILED 2NITE – HOPE U HAD FUN

and

CALL ME PLS

The voicemail was equally brief: "Ellen, give me a call. Need to talk to you."

I glanced at the clock. Not quite nine. Tony would probably be up.

I felt strangely reluctant to call, though.

Setting the phone aside, I unlocked my desk drawer and took out Captain Dusenberry's letters. I read through them all, starting with the one that came after the first one I'd read, and going back to pick my way through the Spanish ones after I'd finished the English ones.

They were all pretty similar. Lots of talk about music,

sometimes a mention of a *baille* or concert they had both attended. The musical group was formed and met a couple of times, much to Maria's delight, "not only for the music, but for the company of my dear friends."

The story between the lines was bittersweet. I was certain that Maria Hidalgo was in love with Samuel Dusenberry, and I gathered that he was equally fond of her.

The Hidalgos disapproved.

The last two letters had an edge of desperation. Maria repeatedly entreated the captain not to confront Reynaldo—whoever that was—and warned that his temper was "like fire." What the topic of confrontation might be I had to guess, but the captain's friendship with Maria was probably a good bet.

I reread the last paragraph of the final letter:

> *Patience is not easy, but it is the only weapon we have. Just as time will dull the sharpest blade, so too will our patience dull the harshness of my family. We will have our day. I pray for it each morning, that today will be the day that God softens their hearts.*

I laid the letter down, saddened by the sense of doom it conveyed, even after more than a century. Like Romeo and Juliet, they seemed to be losing their options, hemmed in by opposition.

Or maybe I was reading too much into it. I sort of knew the ending, after all.

But I didn't know what had happened to Maria Hidalgo. I wondered if I could find out. I really did need to talk to Bennett Cole at the Museum of New Mexico.

My phone rang, making me jump. I picked it up, glancing at the caller ID. Tony again.

I took a deep breath. "Hello?"

"Good, you're there. I was starting to worry."

"Sorry, I forgot my phone when I went to Nat's."

"Listen, I talked to Vi today."

"Yes?"

"She seemed pretty upset."

"That's natural, don't you think?"

"I just think there might be something she didn't tell me. I was wondering if you could talk to her."

"As a matter of fact, I saw her today, too."

"Yeah? What did she say?"

A complete answer to that would take a while, assuming I could remember everything we'd talked about. I gave him the highlights of our conversation, and added my suspicion that Matthew Carter might have killed Victor Solano so that he could take over the role of Scarpia.

"Murder, for a part in an opera? That's sick!"

"Murder is generally a sick act. And it's not just a part. This is the kind of role that can make a career. Vi was telling me the competition is very fierce."

Tony's silence told me he was giving it serious consideration. I was gratified.

"OK, I'll look at that. Thanks."

"Sure."

"What are you doing now?"

My heart gave a little thump. Why did he ask? Did he want to come over?

My fingers went to the ancient rosebud tied in its fragile ribbon. "Reading some very old letters that belonged to Captain Dusenberry. I found them under the floor in the dining parlor."

"Wow. I'm surprised they didn't crumble to dust."

"Well, they've been undisturbed, I think."

"Anything interesting?"

"Yes. I think they may help me figure out who killed Captain Dusenberry, and why."

Silence again.

"You want to solve a hundred-and-fifty year-old murder? Good luck with that."

I bit back a defensive reply, and took a steadying breath before answering. "From what I've gathered, there wasn't much attempt made to solve it at the time."

"Yeah, probably not. The Wild West and all."

This was a side of Tony I didn't much like. I abandoned the thought of inviting him over for coffee. I couldn't deal with cynicism. Not now.

"Listen, I've got to turn in," I said. "This whole week is going to be busy."

"Too busy to get that steak?"

"Ah...maybe. We'll be open 'til at least seven every night."

"Except tomorrow."

"Yeah. I'll still be working, though."

"Well, how about I call you in the afternoon and see how things are going?"

I let out a long breath. "All right."

"OK. Sleep well."

"You too."

"Thanks."

Dead line.

I put the phone down and rubbed my forehead. Mixed feelings about seeing Tony. I did have a lot to do the next day: deposit Saturday's receipts, look over the reservations and write up our grocery orders, give Julio whatever help he needed when he came in, reorganize the work schedule with the additions of Nat and Rosa's brother Ramon.

Identify the Mozart that was running through my head.

I wondered if I'd have time to drop by the State Archives after I made the bank deposit. I decided to try, at least to ask a few questions. Maybe I'd learn something about Maria Hidalgo.

Despite good intentions, I slept late. It was almost eight by the time I got up, brewed some tea, and got dressed. I still wasn't very hungry after Manny's grill-fest. I washed a handful of fresh blueberries, put them in a bowl with a spoonful of yogurt, and called it breakfast.

With the rest of my first pot of tea in a tall, thermal mug, I went downstairs for my Monday morning prowl. Armed with scissors, a small watering can, and a big bowl, I strolled through all the sitting areas and freshened each flower arrangement, culling faded blooms and trimming stems. I'd do new arrangements on Thursday, so that they'd be fresh for the weekend, and nurse the current ones along until then.

Except that maybe I should do a new centerpiece for the dining parlor. Vi had said that Sandra Usher, the soprano who sang Tosca, was coming.

Well, if I turned out to have time I'd do it. Meanwhile I carried the flower trimmings out to the compost bin, washed the bowl and my scissors, and went up to my office to attack the grocery orders. I made up one list of things I was sure we'd need in addition to our usual orders, and a second list of things to ask Julio about. By then it was almost nine, and I collected the bank bag and headed out to run errands.

The Archives were in a fairly new and rather imposing building on the south side of town. I waited a few minutes while the receptionist, an older Hispanic woman, helped the two people in front of me. When my turn came, I asked if there was a quick way to find out whether there were any records pertaining to Captain Dusenberry.

"Let me take a look at the catalog," she said.

A few keystrokes, and she nodded. "Yes, he was an officer at Fort Marcy Post."

"What sort of records are there?"

"Mostly correspondence. Military, and for the land office he ran. Some newspaper articles about his death."

"Any letters? Diaries?"

"I don't see any. They could be indexed under another subject."

"OK. How about Maria Hidalgo."

"Do you have her middle name? There are probably a lot of Maria Hidalgos."

"I don't. Can you check?"

She typed, long brown fingers flying over the keyboard.

"Well, you've got 230 results. Jose Maria Hidalgo, Maria

Peron y Hidalgo, Maria Sanchez Hidalgo—"

"OK, never mind on that. I'll see if I can find her middle name."

"Or what time frame?"

"Oh...1865."

"Maria Imelda Fuentes y Hidalgo?"

"Maybe."

"She lived in Santa Fe between 1841 and 1889."

"That's probably her."

The receptionist typed a little more, then reached for a piece of paper that came out of a printer behind her. "Here's a list of resources in our collection. Some of them might just mention her in passing."

I looked at the page full of text. "This is a start. Thank you."

She smiled. "Glad to help. Do you want me to show you how to request a folder?"

"I don't have time today, but I'll come back." I folded the page and stuck it in my purse. "Thank you very much."

I hurried out, aware that I'd spent more time than I had intended on this. I snaked through neighborhoods in order to bypass the heaviest traffic, but it was well past noon by the time I got back to the tearoom.

I heard music from the house as I got out of my car: salsa music. Julio was in the kitchen. I poked my head in to greet him, and got a wave back. He was mixing something, feet dancing to the boom box. He had on a black muscle shirt and black baggy pants with red, green, and yellow chiles on them, with a matching cap.

"Be right back," I said over the blaring music, and escaped upstairs. I put the deposit receipt on Kris's desk and left my purse in my suite, then made myself a quick sandwich so that I wouldn't be tempted to nibble tea food.

Refreshed, I collected my notes on the grocery orders and went downstairs again. I stopped in the butler's pantry to put the kettle on. Julio had thoughtfully turned down the volume on his boom box.

"Hey, boss," he said, nodding as I came in.

"Hi. Will you be at a stopping point soon?"

"Pretty soon, yeah. About five minutes."

"Good. I have some questions about what to order, and I'll need to start making calls pretty soon."

"Right. Just let me get this in the oven."

I went back to the pantry to pick out a teapot and decide what tea to brew. I liked lighter teas in the afternoon, and went with an orange-blossom green. I brewed it and poured myself a cup, then went back to the kitchen.

Julio was just shutting the door of the oven. "I took the violets out. They looked like they were dry." He gestured to the lunch table, where my tray of violets sat under a loose sheet of plastic wrap.

"Probably, yes," I said.

"Where did you get them?"

"From the garden."

"Bueno. They should last a couple of days. They're better than the ones from La Fleur."

"Thanks. I only wish I had more of them."

We sat at the table together and went over the grocery orders. I made corrections to my estimates based on Julio's judgment of what we'd need.

"Get extra butter and cream, and a bag of oranges. I'm going to make some orange scones, and orange curd to go with them."

"OK. Why now?"

He shrugged. "Just to mix things up a little."

"Keep some lemon curd on hand, too, though."

"Absolutely."

I dismissed the thought that this week might not be the best time to experiment with the menu. Julio was an artist, and I had learned not to question his instincts. If nothing else, changing things up would be a stress-reliever for him.

"Can you work extra hours this week?" I asked.

"Already planning on it."

"Thank you. Rosa's brother is coming in, but I don't know

how much kitchen experience he has."

"Ramon? He's done his time bussing tables at El Vaquero. He'll be able to handle simple stuff at least."

I'd forgotten that Ramon and Rosa were Julio's cousins. It made me doubly glad that I'd taken Ramon on as a temporary hire. He'd probably fare better than a stranger would in Julio's kitchen.

"He's sure a great musician," I said. "I'm thinking about hiring him to play, later in the year."

Julio nodded absently, perusing my list. "Extra raw milk, too, I'm going to have to double the clotted cream."

I made a note, and picked up my teacup. It was empty.

"Go ahead, get some more," Julio said. "I'll look over this list one more time."

I went to the pantry and brought the teapot back with me. Julio frowned at the list while I filled my cup.

"We've never been booked solid before."

"I know," I said.

"Why this week? Any idea?"

"Apparently Victor Solano told some people he liked the tearoom."

"Solano? The opera singer? The one who was killed?"

"Yes."

His frown deepened as he stared past my list to something I couldn't see.

"You disliked him, didn't you?" I said.

Julio glanced at me, then back at the list. He made a change with his pencil.

"Does it matter?"

"Not really. I just wondered why. Vi was so fond of him..."

"Yeah, well, maybe he didn't come on to her."

It took an effort not to gape. "You mean he came on to *you?* When?"

"At Vi's event. It wasn't a huge thing, but...."

"Are you sure he wasn't just being friendly?"

"I'm sure." He glanced at me again, eyes dark beneath his

frowning brows. "I get it a lot. It gets old."

Now I was seriously confused. Was Julio gay? Or did he just mean gay guys were drawn to him? He didn't seem like the type you'd expect to attract that kind of attention. Julio was not effeminate in any way. He was completely masculine, as far as I was concerned. Yes, he wore colorful chef's pants and matching hats, but he never *swished*.

It's true that I had wondered, from time to time, whether he and his roommate might be romantically involved, but other than the fact that they shared an apartment, I had nothing on which to base that notion. They were close, but they'd never acted like more than friends when I'd seen them together.

None of it was my business.

I picked up the list. "Well, if this is done, I'll go up and call in the orders."

Julio nodded, pushed back his chair, and got up. I watched him check the oven and then get out a clean mixing bowl.

I swallowed the rest of my tea, filled the cup again, and carried it upstairs. The sun was coming around to the west, now, and the upper floor was starting to bake. I cracked the windows at either end of the hall and closed the drapes over the west window, then spent half an hour on the phone placing orders.

When I called Manny, I could hear him grinning through the ionosphere. "How's your head, chica?"

"Fine. How about yours?"

"Eh, all I had was beer. Still want those peaches?"

"Yes. Got any raspberries?"

"Not yet. Give it a couple of weeks."

"How about oranges?"

"Always. How many?"

I gave him the whole list, and he promised to deliver it the next morning. We chatted a little more, then I pleaded work and said goodbye.

I headed down to the kitchen and got out an apron. "What can I help with?"

Julio looked up from measuring flour. "Stir that pot on the

stove."

I washed my hands and went over to stir. The pot held a syrupy liquid that had a familiar, deep, rich smell. "Assam?"

"Yes, that's the syrup for the cakes."

The afternoon flew by while I learned how to make Aria Cakes. We finished two batches and the cake layers for a third. Julio moved on to his orange scones, delegating the curd to me. I was rather proud that he trusted me with it.

The kitchen filled with the fragrance of oranges and the sharp tang of zested rind. Julio rolled out and cut two dozen scones and stowed them in the freezer, then stuck two scones in the oven and started a batch of our regular currant scones.

At that point, a knock on the back door made me look up from stirring curd. Through the window I saw Ramon Garcia outside, standing by the kitchen door, his black hair loose over the shoulders of a red tee-shirt with silhouettes of flamenco dancers on the front. I hurried to let him in.

"Ramon, thank you for coming. You know Julio."

They traded nods and greetings in Spanish. I stepped to the stove and gave the curd a last stir, then moved it aside, covered the pot, and turned off the burner.

"Come on upstairs and sign a W-4 for me."

He followed me up to my office, where I offered him the guest chair.

"Sorry about the heat," I said, going around behind the desk.

"Better than the kitchen at Vaquero."

As I sat, I noticed that my phone had messages. I glanced at it, saw that the most recent call was from Tony, and set it aside.

"You've worked at El Vaquero?"

"Summers, yeah. Washing dishes and bussing."

"Well, I appreciate your willingness to help us out on short notice."

"I was surprised when Rosa said you wanted me."

"Oh? Why?"

He looked down and his cheeks colored slightly. "Because of the trespassing."

I watched him, recalling the occasions early in the summer when he and some Goth-wannabee friends (I couldn't think of them as real Goths, not with Kris working for me) had come poking around in my back yard looking for signs of Captain Dusenberry. Ramon seemed contrite.

"Well, it hasn't happened since we talked," I said. "I'm satisfied."

I printed out a W-4 for him and pushed it across the desk, along with a pen. He stared at them briefly, then met my gaze. "Thanks."

I smiled. "You're welcome. Later in the summer, when this rush is over, I'd like to talk to you about coming to play here now and then."

His eyes widened and he straightened in the chair. "That would be great!"

"It might not be until fall—we'll have to see how the rest of summer goes."

"That's fine, but if it's fall it'll have to be weekends. I'll be back at UNM." He grabbed the pen and started filling out the form. "Rosa's always talking about how great this place is. She really loves working here."

"I'm glad. We love having her."

I asked him a couple more questions and offered him the same rate that I paid Mick. He agreed to it, and to coming in at ten in the morning to get a head start on the dishes. Mick didn't usually arrive until one.

"In the morning it will mostly be food-prep stuff, but about midday you'll start to get china. You'll want to do that separately from the cooking things."

He nodded. "Rosa said you have fancy dishes."

"The teapots are the trickiest. Let's go back down and I'll show you the machine."

The commercial dishwashing station was full of clean china, Mick's last load from Saturday night. I showed Ramon where the teapots, cups, and saucers were stored in the butler's pantry. He helped me unload the machine, and I watched how he handled the china. He was careful enough to allay any fears I had.

"Shall I do these?" he asked, waving toward Julio's and my accumulation of baking miscellany.

"Sure. Let's get you a timecard, though."

Duly checked in, he set to work on the bowls, measuring cups, and baking sheets with an air of confidence that could only have come from experience. I silently thanked my lucky stars. It looked like Ramon was a find.

I walked over to Julio. "Need anything more from me?"

"Just your opinion." He handed me a small plate on which rested an orange scone, still warm from the oven. I broke it open and took a bite.

"Mmm. Oh, that's lovely."

"I'm thinking about sprinkling some coarse sugar over the top. Give it a little extra texture."

"That sounds perfect." I got out a spoon and scooped up some of the orange curd, which I spread on the other half of the scone. As I bit into it, the double-dose of orange made me close my eyes. "Fabulous. Great idea, Julio!"

"Thanks."

I looked at him, and saw the small smile of satisfaction that I knew meant he was pleased with himself. Julio had a high opinion of his skill—justified, I thought—but he tended to keep it to himself.

"All right. I'll be upstairs if you need me."

The orange scone was gone by the time I made it to my office. In the privacy of that sanctum, I licked the curd from the plate, then set it aside and looked through my messages.

Willow Lane, then two from Tony. I called him back, and he answered at once.

"Hey, there. Steak tonight?"

I glanced at the clock: almost five. "Depends on when."

"Seven-thirty?"

"Sold. Casual dress?"

"Yeah. I don't have time to go change. See you then."

I called Willow and got her voicemail. I really needed to look up her tour schedule and find a likely time to call her. I surfed to her website and scanned the list of current tours. One was the tour that stopped at the tearoom, and I saw that it was scheduled to come on Tuesday afternoon. I called Willow back and left a second message, explaining that the parlor wouldn't be available for her tour to visit that afternoon, or any time during the week.

I felt a little bad about that, but we'd had a couple of booked-solid days earlier in July, and Willow had agreed to keep her tour on the *portal* then. I hoped she wouldn't mind doing that again. Made a mental note to ask Julio to bake some extra cookies for the tour guests.

I leaned back in my chair and closed my eyes. I was tired, and we hadn't even been open that day. This was going to be a long week.

Mozart flitted through my head—the same elusive phrase. I opened my eyes and realized that I was still wearing an apron.

With a small groan, I got up and carried my scone plate back downstairs. Ramon saw me come in and came forward to take it from me. He didn't put it in the machine, but set it aside with the teapot I'd used that morning.

"I'll do those when this load is done."

I untied my apron. "No, it's after five. Just leave this running and go on home. And thanks for staying to work."

A sudden smile lit his face. "No problem."

I glanced toward Julio, who was putting a tray of currant scones into the freezer. He closed it and looked at me.

"That's it. Should give us a head start. See you in the morning."

I nodded, hanging up my apron. "Thank you, Julio."

"De nada." He turned to Ramon. "You too, primo. Mañana."

"Mañana."

They bumped fists, then Ramon went to the regular sink and started washing the teapot by hand. I watched Julio go out, then walked over to Ramon.

"I forgot to mention that Julio might need your help with some of the food prep. Would you mind doing that when you're not washing dishes?"

"That's cool. I used to make tortilla chips at Vaquero."

"Great. Thanks. He'll tell you what he needs."

I tidied the pantry while Ramon finished the teapot and my plate, then I saw him out and locked the door behind him. Gathered up the aprons and towels from the day's cooking and stuffed them in the washer. Headed back upstairs for a quick shower and change.

I'd lost count of how many times I'd gone up and down the stairs that day. At least my calves would be in good shape.

In the shower, I indulged in a double handful of my favorite jasmine-scented body wash, scrubbed myself all over, then stood with the hot water pounding my shoulders for a long time. When I emerged I was relaxed, if not entirely energized.

I pulled out a lightweight sweater of soft green cashmere and my favorite pair of jeans. Not knowing whether Tony would let me drive or insist on my riding with him on his bike, I put on sneakers and grabbed a tweed coat that had been my father's. It was a little big on me, but comfy and had lots of pockets. I slid my wallet into one, cell phone and lip gloss into another, and declared myself ready.

The back doorbell rang as I was coming down the stairs. I hurried the last few steps and saw Tony peering in through the lights around the back door. I opened it and invited him in.

"If you're ready, let's just go," he said. "That steak is calling me."

I stepped out and locked the door. "Shall I drive?"

"Sure."

He glanced at me as he buckled his seat belt. "Ever been to The Farm House?"

"No. Is it as rustic as it sounds?"

"It's not fancy, but the food is good."

"Sold."

He directed me to drive to the south side of town. The Farm House turned out to be not far from the police station, in a building that had housed some other restaurant and been redecorated to look barn-like. I was skeptical, but when we went in, the savory aromas of grilled meat and fried potatoes reassured me.

We were seated by a window and given chips and salsa. To keep myself from spoiling my appetite, I broke a tortilla chip into tiny pieces to nibble. Micro-chips, I thought, grinning to myself.

"Margarita?" Tony asked when the waiter requested our drink order.

I looked up from perusing a list of local micro-brews. "Yeah. That sounds good."

"Frozen?" the waiter asked.

"Rocks. With salt."

He went away, and I ate a micro-chip. "How's the investigation going?"

Tony sighed. "Tedious. Spent all day yesterday going through the props room, looking for the murder weapon. You know they have like ten thousand props?"

"I knew it was a lot. Five productions."

"And they're all numbered and cataloged. Our evidence room should be so organized."

"Did you find the weapon?"

He shook his head and shoveled salsa into his mouth with a chip. I ate another micro-chip.

"I assumed it was Tosca's knife," I said, "but I guess that doesn't make sense."

"No. All the prop knives are dulled. And Tosca's knife is too big, anyway."

"Too big?"

"The M.E. said the weapon was a small knife. Very sharp."

"Like a pocket knife?"

"Maybe."

"Jeez. That could be anywhere."

"Yeah. When we didn't find it on the grounds, we were hoping the murderer ditched it with the props, but no luck. I spent an hour looking at switchblades."

"Switchblades?"

"Yeah. They're using them in *Cesar Chavez*. Whoever had the idea of writing an opera about him?"

"SFO commissions new works fairly frequently. Every year they do either a commissioned work or a U.S. premiere of something from another country."

"Hm."

Our drinks arrived. I sipped my margarita, which was killer strong, and mused about pocket knives. Who would be likely to carry one?

Members of the cast wouldn't have knives on them, but it would be easy enough to retrieve one from a purse or a gym bag. Really, anyone might have a small knife.

"So what did you do today?" I asked, picking up another micro-chip.

Tony grimaced. "Spent the morning going through the dumpsters. Afternoon at the forensics lab."

"Anything interesting?"

"Not really. Just eliminated a couple of things."

"Have you talked to the Brit yet?"

"Not yet. The interviewers haven't seen him. I told them to let me know."

We paused to assure the waiter that we both wanted large chunks of moo. Actually, I ordered a filet mignon, which was plenty big enough for me when accompanied by a baked potato and a small salad. Tony asked for a rib-eye, rare, with fries.

"How'd your day go?" he asked me when the waiter had sailed off toward the grill.

"Busy. Hired a new employee."

"Yeah?"

"Temporary, to help in the kitchen." Though I suspected we'd want to keep Ramon. "And Julio came in and baked all afternoon."

"On his day off? That's nice of him."

"He's a nice guy."

Tony took a pull at his margarita. "OK, let's talk through this.

Say you've just murdered Victor Solano. What do you do?"

"Oh, thanks a lot!"

"C'mon, I just want to hear your thoughts."

I crunched a micro-chip, thinking. "Well, I get out of there as fast as I can, as unobtrusively as I can."

"Which way do you go?"

I frowned. "I've got a knife in my hands, and probably some blood on them. I grab a towel or something to wipe it off, and then I stuff the knife and the towel in my pocket or my purse...no, I don't think I would have brought a purse. So it must be a pocket."

"Maybe not. Maybe you're in a slinky dress." The corner of Tony's mouth curved upward.

"Well, A: it's cold, so if I'm in a slinky dress I have a coat on over it. And B: if I have a knife, I must have a pocket. I wouldn't just carry a knife around the theatre in my hand."

"Unless you were planning to kill someone."

I glowered at him and sipped my drink. "If I were *planning* a murder I'd pick a much better time and place."

"Good point. So you just happened to have a knife in your pocket, and you went into the dressing room during Act Three and got in a fight with Solano."

"You know, that probably means the killer was a man."

"Maybe. Back to my question. What do you do?"

"OK. I stuff the knife and towel into my pocket, and go out. I can't use the stage door into the theater during the performance, so I go out the back way, by the deck."

"And from there?"

"Get to my car, assuming I have one. Drive someplace I can ditch the knife, clean my hands, and go back in time for the curtain call."

"Why drive away? Why not ditch it on the grounds?"

"Too easy for it to be found."

"Then why bother to go back once you're off the property?"

"Well, if I was in the audience then other people would have seen me, and my absence would be noticed once the murder was discovered. And if I was in the cast or on the crew, it would be even more noticeable."

"What if you were none of the above? A hired assassin?"

"Then I wouldn't go back, but people probably would have seen me. And how would I get backstage if no one knew me?"

"Same way you just snuck out. The back way."

I shook my head. "There would be people all over. It's very close quarters backstage. And anyway—if there's time to hire an assassin, then there's time to plan the murder for a safer time and place."

"Yeah, OK. It was unpremeditated. We reached the same conclusion."

"Thank you." I picked up my last micro-chip, dipped it in the salsa, which was kind of a pathetic gesture given its size, and ate it.

"But the murderer didn't leave the grounds. We checked with the parking lot crew, and no one left during the third act. By the time people started leaving, we were already having them give their names to Security." He scooped up some salsa with a chip and crunched it. "The murderer is already in our pool of suspects, it's just that it's a big pool. He—or she—is someone who could go into the dressing room without the people backstage thinking it strange. Someone known to Victor Solano, and to the cast and crew."

I nodded. That was still a lot of people. Anyone who was a part of the company, and a lot of people who were peripherally associated. Like Thomas Ingraham. He had a nodding acquaintance with Solano. I'd watched him open a bottle of red wine with a Swiss army knife, which could easily have been in his pocket.

So the question was motive. As far as I knew, Mr. Ingraham had none. Plus, I could personally attest that he'd been in the audience during the third act. But there had probably been a lot of men with pocket knives at the performance.

"Have you found anyone who heard Solano arguing with someone?"

Tony shook his head, licked salt from the rim of his glass, and pulled at the margarita. "Went over it a couple of times with everyone who was backstage. No one saw anyone go into the dressing room who didn't belong there. No one heard the fight."

"Damn."

The waiter brought our dinners, and we gave them our immediate attention. The beef was good, really tender, and perfectly prepared, raising The Farm House several notches in my estimation. I chewed a bite of meat slowly, savoring it, while I watched Tony devour two large bites of his steak and carve a third.

"You really were starving," I said.

"Missed lunch."

"That's my trick."

He flashed a grin at me and kept eating. For a few minutes we both focused on the food, though I was still thinking about the murder.

If it was a man (which I thought was more likely, because of the pocket knife), then the most obvious suspect was Matthew Carter. He had opportunity and motive. His alibi was his lover, Geoffrey Harrison, who might lie to protect him.

So how to prove he was the murderer? Either catch him and Harrison in a lie, or find someone who saw one or both of them somewhere other than where they claimed to be.

"Have you talked to Geoffrey Harrison?"

"Constantly. He and Carter are sticking to their story. And one of the chorus saw them leave the dressing room together early in Act Three, which tends to confirm it."

"Hm."

Something niggled at the back of my brain. I remembered Vi telling me about how she'd ended up singing the shepherd-boy, a role for which she was the cover.

"Have you talked to Lydia...I don't know her last name. The woman who was supposed to sing the shepherd boy?" I asked.

Tony blinked at me. "I've talked to a lot of people in the last few days."

"She called in sick just before the performance. She was supposed to sing the shepherd-boy in Act Three. That's how Vi ended up singing it."

Tony ate a fry. "OK."

"Well, what if she did that so she'd have an opportunity to get into the principal men's dressing room?"

He tilted his head at me. "Thought we'd agreed that this wasn't premeditated."

"Yes...but this is an anomaly. If I were leading the investigation, I'd check it out."

He took out his pocket notebook. "What's the name again?"

"Lydia something. I still have your program if you need it."

"No, the opera gave us a few."

We talked through the murder some more until we started talking in circles, by which time I was getting sleepy. The waiter came to see if we wanted dessert, and we both passed. When he brought the check I got out my wallet.

"No, no," Tony said, grabbing the folder. "I invited you."

"Well, thanks. Next time I'll treat."

"You're the lady. You don't pay."

"That's not really fair."

"Who said anything about fair? I thought you were old fashioned."

I bit my lip. "Customs are changing." I didn't want to say what I was also thinking, which was that I knew his salary wasn't huge.

"Well, the custom in my family is that the man pays."

"All right. If you won't let me treat you, maybe you'll let me make you dinner next time."

He gave me a sly look. "In your tiny kitchen upstairs, or in the big fancy kitchen?"

I laughed. "It's not *that* tiny. I can't do a five-course meal up there, but I can handle a regular dinner."

"Good. I like the upstairs better anyway."

Because my bed was right there? I drank the last of my margarita to hide the sudden heat in my cheeks.

"You also need to decide on a movie," Tony said, pulling out his wallet.

I sighed. "Not this week."

"Yeah, not for me either. Gonna be working long hours on this for a few more days at least."

"There's a point where the likelihood of solving the crime diminishes, right?" I said.

He stuffed several bills into the check folder, then gave me a sharp look. "We're not there yet."

"I hope you find the weapon."

"Me too."

I drove back to the tearoom, running through the list of suspects in my head again. My list was not anywhere near complete, and I had reasons against just about everyone on it being the killer. I needed the whiteboard Tony had talked about. I wondered if he actually had one for working on the case, and if so, whether it was covered with multicolored scribbles.

I pulled into my parking space and turned off the engine. "Thanks for dinner. You were right, the food's great there."

"Thanks for letting me use you for a sounding board."

"Glad to help."

I couldn't read his expression in the shadowed darkness. Behind him, a light from up the street shone through the leaves of my lilac bushes. He leaned toward me and kissed me on the cheek.

I caught my breath, but he was already getting out of the car. I got out, too, and locked it.

Tony headed for his bike. "Call me if you think of anything else."

"OK. Good night."

He waved a hand, then backed the bike away, turned it, and cruised out toward the street. I watched, impressed at how quiet he was being when I knew how loud that bike's engine could get.

Feeling disappointed, I headed for the house. The light on the back *portal* was on, as were the lights in the hall and the dining parlor. I didn't remember whether I'd turned the outside light on, but I was sure I'd left the inside ones off.

"Well, hello to you, too, Captain."

Not really in the mood for ghost antics, I unlocked the back door and stepped in slowly, listening. As usual, I heard nothing to indicate that there was anyone else in the house.

I walked down to the main parlor. The light there was off. I flipped the switch, just to confirm that it was undisturbed.

But it wasn't. Vi sat curled in one of the blue wing chairs in Iris, weeping.

7

"V i!" I hurried to her, kneeling by her chair and taking her hand. "What's the matter? What brought you here?"

She sniffed and rubbed at her eyes. "I'm sorry. I shouldn't have come in, but I still had my key, and I didn't want to go home, because Mom doesn't like to see me cry..."

"Of course you can come here if you need to, but what is it? Can you tell me?"

"I just miss Victor so much. Things haven't been going very well."

"That's not surprising."

"I didn't realize how much of a difference he made just by being there. Everyone's really tense now, and there's a lot of fighting. A couple of people have said some things to me that they just wouldn't have said before."

"Oh, honey, I'm so sorry. Would you like some tea? Gingermint?"

She sniffed again. "That sounds nice."

"I'll go put the kettle on. Be right back."

I hurried to the pantry and filled a kettle. Fetched the teapot I'd used that afternoon from where Ramon had left it to dry. I was measuring tea into the infuser when I heard the piano.

Mozart, again. The same phrase I'd heard before.

How did Vi know that phrase?

I ran back to the parlor, intending to ask her, and found her clutching the arms of her chair, staring wide-eyed at the piano.

The keyboard cover was still closed.

The music ended just as it had the previous time I'd heard it. I knew that the song, whatever it was, went on from there, but I couldn't remember how.

"Ellen!" Vi whispered in an awed tone, staring at the

121

instrument.

"Yes. It's happened before."

"I thought the ghost was just a story."

I shook my head. "I'm really beginning to think it isn't."

The kettle began whistling.

"Will you be all right here for a minute?"

"Um."

"Or you can come with me."

She shook her head, and seemed to pull herself together. She straightened in her chair and rearranged her purple broomstick skirt, still staring at the piano. "I'll be all right."

"OK. Just scream if you need me."

I hurried to the pantry, poured hot water over the tea leaves, grabbed some cups and saucers and put them on the tray with the pot and the timer, and carried it all back to the parlor. Vi hadn't moved.

I set the tray down and sat in the other blue chair, watching my guest. At least she wasn't crying any more.

I waited, watching the timer count down. I didn't want to push Vi to talk, and I didn't want to discourage Captain Dusenberry from making more music. But both of them were silent. When the timer went off, I caught it on the first beep and shut it down.

The sound seemed to shake Vi from her reverie. She watched me remove the infuser from the teapot and set it on a spare saucer. I poured for us both and handed a cup to her.

"Thanks." She took a sip, then sighed. "These past few days have been so strange. I feel like I'm drifting around on an alien planet sometimes."

"What brought you here tonight?"

"Oh—I guess it was really nothing. It just bothered me at the time."

"Then it wasn't nothing."

"I'm over-sensitive, I think. I got upset when I shouldn't have."

"Over...?"

"We had the first dress rehearsal for Cesar Chavez today, and the director was sitting out in the house with a bunch of bigwigs, and he kept stopping us, so we were running late. So the chorus came on in Act Two and he stopped the show and yelled at me for missing a cue."

"Yelled at you?"

"Yeah. It was my fault. I got distracted by something out behind the stage. A beer can or something catching the sunlight. I was upstage, at the top of a platform, and I wanted to sneak a look at the mountains. So I wasn't paying attention and missed my cue."

"Well, that's no reason to yell at you."

"He was in a bad mood anyway, because the rehearsal wasn't going well, and Neil and Charles and everyone were watching. I think he just needed to yell at someone, and I gave him the perfect excuse."

She drank some more tea, then set her cup down, glancing toward the piano. It was silent. The captain had apparently made his point, whatever it was.

"Pretty skirt," I said.

"Oh, thanks." She smiled ruefully. "I'm so predictable."

"Not at all. You look stunning in purple. You have every right to take advantage of it."

"But it's my name. How tacky, right? Any self-respecting kid would have rebelled and chosen orange for a favorite color. But I can't help it—I've always loved violet."

"Me, too. You observe how unselfish I am, by being willing to share it with you."

That got her to laugh a little. I refreshed our tea.

"How's your mom?"

"Oh, she's fretting over me. I can't explain why, but that just makes it worse."

I nodded. I knew the feeling.

"I'm thinking...."

I waited, watching her. She seemed to slump a little.

"Maybe I wasn't cut out for opera after all."

I bit back the urge to protest, sure that her mother would have done so. Instead I sipped tea and answered as calmly as I could.

"Why is that?"

"I guess I didn't realize how much Victor protected me. It's so awful now. Everyone's on edge."

"That's temporary, don't you think?"

"Some of it might not be. Sandra and David never did like each other, and yesterday at rehearsal they had a terrible fight."

"Really?" I thought back to the as-yet-unidentified Brit's comment that Tony and I had overheard: *practically snogging him onstage.* If he hadn't been talking about Usher and Ebinger, whom had he meant?

My mind flashed back to the performance, to the opening where Cavaradossi and the Sacristan opened the opera together. I remember thinking it had gone on a long time. Then the Sacristan went off and Angelotti, sung by Geoffrey Harrison, came on. Could there have been an exchange then that I had missed?

"It was awful," Vi said. "Neil yelled at them both, and then called off the rehearsal."

"Wow!"

"It was running late anyway, and they had to change the sets for the evening's performance. It takes a while to move those big pieces up from downstairs."

I remembered the Italianate pillars and trellises, the gigantic church set, and the prison, all from *Tosca.* "They store them on the bottom level, right? There's so little room backstage."

"Yes, it all goes up and down on the B-lift."

"The what?"

"That's what they call the stage elevator. It's so quiet they can move things even during a scene."

I thought back to my backstage tours, but only had a vague recollection of the elevator. I decided I needed to take the tour again and refresh my memory.

As soon as I had a free morning.

A click of china drew my attention. Vi had set down her empty cup and saucer. I reached for the teapot, but she shook her head.

"I'd better go. Mom'll be starting to worry. Thanks for listening, and for not minding my barging in."

"Not at all. Mi casa es su casa."

We both got up, and she enfolded me in a goddess-like hug. "Don't be surprised if I come crawling back, asking for my old job."

"You are welcome to your old job whenever you want it, but I expect you to report to it on your feet, not your hands and knees."

She grinned at me. "Because Miss Manners disapproves of crawling."

"In the parlor, certainly, if one is over the age of five."

Vi laughed. "You always cheer me up."

"I'm glad. I hope things get better at the opera."

She looked sad, then squared her shoulders and found a smile. "Me too. Thanks, Ellen."

I saw her out, then went back to collect the tea tray from the main parlor. Pausing at the doorway, I looked back before turning out the light.

All quiet. All still, except for one crystal on the main chandelier in the center of the room, swinging gently back and forth.

I slept lightly, disturbed by questions about the murder. When I woke, I couldn't even remember the questions, much less any answers.

I sent Tony a text suggesting he look into the argument between Usher and Ebinger, dealt with a few personal messages, then headed downstairs to see if Julio needed my help. It wasn't yet nine, but to my surprise, Ramon was already there, wearing an apron and spreading butter on slices of bread. He looked up at me with a grin.

"Morning, boss!"

"Ellen, please."

"Rosa said you'd say that."

I glanced at the dishwashing station, but it was empty. He had already put everything away. I went to the pantry and started a pot of tea, then came back and asked Julio what I could do to help.

"Nothing," he said. "You're going to have enough to do today. Ramon's all the help I need."

"OK. Well, if that changes, let me know. I'll be upstairs."

I took my pot of tea up with me. Kris came in the back door as I was starting up the stairs. She went straight to work peeling messages off the reservation line. I poured each of us some tea, then left her to it while I made a to-do list for myself.

At the top of the list was keeping an eye on Ramon. I didn't mind that he'd come in earlier than I'd requested—for all I knew, Julio had asked him to—but while that kind of initiative was fine for this week, I couldn't let it keep happening when our business dropped to a more normal level.

Number two on the list was to sit down with Kris and discuss Ramon's hire (about which I hadn't yet told her) and overtime in general.

After that it got more eclectic. Call Willow. Spend some time at the state archives researching Maria Hidalgo. Figure out the Mozart.

To the bottom of the list, I added "take SFO backstage tour." That one was niggling at me, though I couldn't say exactly why. I did want to see the B-lift again, but I wasn't sure what use that would be.

I went back to the top of the list. Ramon's schedule I'd deal with later; talking with Kris about him was top priority. I topped up my teacup and carried it into Kris's office along with the W-4 I'd had Ramon fill out.

Kris was on the phone, apologizing to a client for the fact that we were booked up at the time she wanted. I waited while she talked the client into a date the following week, then placed the form in front of her.

"Surprise."

"Oh, good! The way things are going we're going to need a couple more."

"Still getting a lot of calls?"

"Thirty-seven when I got here. I've gone through about ten, but two more have come in. We're booked through next Wednesday now."

"Holy..."

"Yeah. The Solano Effect is going strong."

We discussed advertising for another assistant chef and two servers. I decided to first ask the existing staff if they had friends who were looking for work. If we could get another Ramon or two, we wouldn't need to spend money on ads.

My hope of finding time for the archives and the backstage tour receded. I went to my desk and dialed Willow's number, expecting more phone tag, but she answered after two rings.

"Willow! Did you get my message?"

"Yes, thank you. Sorry I couldn't take the call yesterday."

"I hope you don't mind that we can't accommodate your tour today. I called as soon as I realized."

"It's fine. That's not why I've been trying to reach you."

"Why, then?"

She paused. "I need you to be open-minded. I have a message for you."

Oh, boy. "OK."

"Water."

"Beg pardon?"

"Water. It's very important."

I picked up my pen and tapped it on my to-do list. "Who is this message from?"

"It came through my spirit-guide. It's from a concerned entity. I'm not sure who."

"All right. I don't know what it means, though."

"Just let it rest in your awareness. You'll see the connection when the time is right."

Oooookay.

"Um, thanks. Listen, you're bringing your tour today, right?"

"Yes, and on Wednesday, and I'll be doing an extra one on Friday. The first two are booked to the max."

Her maximum was twenty. Had the Solano Effect spilled over to the spirit tours?

"Just this tour?" I asked. "I mean, not the history one, or—"

"The Spirit Homes tour is the only one that sold out, yes. It is peak tourist season, though. All the numbers are up."

"Well, let us know when you get here. We'll have some iced tea for your customers on the *portal*."

"That's very nice of you, Ellen. Thank you."

"See you this afternoon."

I hung up, and pulled my list toward me. I crossed out Willow's name and wrote "Water" at the bottom of the list, then gazed at it and shook my head. This was turning out to be a weird day, and it wasn't even eleven o'clock yet.

Kris brought me a message from one of our suppliers—they were out of the sliced almonds we needed. I scrambled to find another source that wouldn't cost an arm and a leg. By the time I was done with that, Nat had arrived, peeking into my office from the doorway.

I scribbled "Nat's wedding" at the bottom of my list, then got up to greet her.

"Tea?" I lifted the pot on my credenza. "Oh, we're out."

"I'm fine. I just wanted to let you know I was here. There are some people just browsing in the shop, and Iz asked if I could cover for her so she can help serve."

I went downstairs with her, bringing the empty teapot with the idea that I'd brew more, but the tearoom was open and all the seatings were already full, with most of the outdoor tables full as well. I ended up helping Iz and Rosa serve while Nat manned the register in the gift shop. I did poke my head into the kitchen a couple of times, to warn Julio that the almonds wouldn't come in until Wednesday, and that we'd need iced tea for twenty tour guests in the afternoon.

"Gonna need more paper cups, then," he said. "And we need more lemons for tomorrow."

"I'll call Manny."

I kept an eye on the clock and made sure to be downstairs at two, which was when the Kowalski party was scheduled to arrive for the dining parlor. I hovered in the gift shop, and my suspicions were confirmed when Sandra Usher came in, leading a half-dozen men and women who had the lean and focused look of performing artists. I was sure I recognized a couple of them from the cast of *Tosca*, though I didn't know their names.

"Welcome to the Wisteria Tearoom," I said, smiling. "Let me show you to the dining parlor."

Ms. Kowalski-kum-Usher, in a scarlet dress and huge sunglasses, luxurious dark hair spilling over her shoulders, smiled and followed me out into the hall. I escorted her party to their room, where the table was already set with china and water goblets and teapots under velvet cozies. I pulled the door closed, and while the guests were arranging themselves around the table I spoke to Ms. Usher.

"I was at your performance on Friday. It was magnificent."

She removed her sunglasses and gave me a guarded look. "Thank you."

"Please accept my condolences on the passing of your colleague. I hope the company is recovering."

"We'll manage," she said in a softer voice. "Thank you."

Rosa came in with the first of two three-tiered food trays, and I went to fetch the second while she poured tea. As I placed the tray on the table Ms. Usher addressed me.

"You're the owner?"

"Yes, I'm Ellen Rosings."

"Tell us about your ghost! This *is* the haunted room, isn't it?"

"This is the room where Captain Dusenberry was killed, and where the majority of manifestations have been reported."

I continued with the story of Captain Dusenberry's unfortunate fate, feeling like I was channeling Willow Lane. I'd heard her spiel often enough to do so. I'd also answered the same questions from my own customers so frequently that I knew what the guests wanted to hear about. I was careful to make no claim that the "reported manifestations" proved the ghost's existence, and kept my personal opinions to myself.

I kept Maria Hidalgo to myself, too. I needed to learn more before I'd share her with anyone.

Ms. Usher's party seemed satisfied with my descriptions of lights turning on and off and crystals dancing. The latter made them all look up at the chandelier, which of course was stock-still.

"We've also had the stereo come on unexpectedly on several occasions," I said.

"So Captain Dusenberry is fond of music," said one of the men I recognized, a lean-faced brunet with sparkling dark eyes and a wry lilt to his voice, which was deeper than his spare frame had led me to expect. "Does he like opera?"

"Actually..." I hesitated, not sure if I was ready to mention the piano. I looked at Ms. Usher and decided to compromise.

"There's a musical phrase that's come up more than once. I'm sure it's Mozart, but I can't place it. If you'll forgive me..." I sang the little fragment, la-la-ing it, extremely conscious of the inadequacy of my voice in the company of these professionals.

Ms. Usher picked up the next line without a blink. She sang softly, but the power of her voice still raised a thrill in me. The words were Italian; the tune hauntingly sad despite the major key. We all held still until she concluded the brief passage.

"*Nozze di Figaro*," said the brunet.

"Yes, 'Contessa, perdono,'" Usher said, glancing at me. "My favorite moment in the opera."

"Thank you! It's been bothering me for days!"

"Look!" said one of the women, pointing toward the chandelier.

Everyone raised their eyes and exclaimed. A single crystal was swinging back and forth.

I left them to enjoy their tea and their speculations. In the pantry I checked on Rosa and Iz, who assured me they had everything under control. I poked my head into the kitchen to verify that the iced tea was ready, then dashed upstairs.

I didn't have time for a web search, so I wrote "Contessa, perdono" on my to-do list. The only thing that immediately came to mind about *Le Nozze de Figaro* was that Vi had sung an aria from it at her tea.

I checked with Kris, then went down to the gift shop to lend Nat a hand. Many of the customers were shopping, and we were kept busy until Willow's tour group arrived. They stood clustered at the south end of the *portal*, overlooking the rose garden. I helped Iz serve them iced tea, and went back inside just in time to see Ms. Usher's party leaving. She came up to me and offered a hand.

"Thank you so much. We all had a marvelous time. Poor Victor was right; your tearoom is an absolute delight."

"Thank you. That was so kind of him."

She gave me a sad smile and turned to the lean-faced brunet, who had come up beside her. "Matthew has his work cut out to fill Victor's shoes, but he's rising to the challenge."

A little tingle went down my arms as I met his gaze. Could this elegant man have committed murder? Hard to believe, in his presence.

"Then you're Mr. Carter," I said. "I wish you success in your new role."

He gave a gracious nod. "Thank you."

Another man came up beside him—shorter, blond, broader in the shoulders—and I recognized him as "Angelotti," Geoffrey Harrison. The warm look they exchanged left me in no doubt of their relationship. They also, both of them, seemed entirely calm.

They were professional actors, I reminded myself. If anyone could look calm when they felt otherwise, they could. It occurred to me that none of them seemed especially distraught about their colleague's death. But then, someone who felt distraught would no doubt have declined an invitation to a tea party.

All of Ms. Usher's guests were friendly together, I observed as they spread out in the gift shop, pointing out pretty things to one another. I realized as I watched them that David Ebinger wasn't in the party. That seemed to confirm that he and Ms. Usher were not, in fact, an item. If they had been, she would surely have wanted him to join her on this outing.

I saw the party out, and on my way back to the pantry I was waylaid by Ramon. "You didn't get lunch. It's waiting for you upstairs."

"Thank you! I'll go up as soon as—"

"Julio said to send you up now, or the soup will get cold."

The firmness in his face tempted me to laugh. I settled for a smile. "Yes, sir!"

I went upstairs and followed the savory aroma of cream and onions to my sitting area by the front window. Sunlight spilled in through the gauze curtains, dappled by shadows of the highest branches of the wisterias, shifting gently in the breeze.

A tray awaited me with half a turkey sandwich, a bowl of potato-leek soup adorned with watercress leaves, and an egg-cup of baked custard. Ramon came up after me with a tall glass of ice water.

I couldn't help a sigh of relief as I settled into an armchair. "This is lovely. Thank you so much. Tell Julio he's a genius."

"He said you're not allowed to go back to work for at least half an hour."

"He's becoming a tyrant! Tell him thanks."

Ramon smiled as he set the water on the tray, then left me to myself. I resisted the urge to fetch my phone, or even my to-do list, from my office. Julio was right. I needed a break if I was going to get through this week without running myself into the ground.

The soup was delicious. When Julio had found time to make it, I couldn't imagine. I ate the meal slowly, savoring every bite and each complementary flavor.

If Julio continued the way he'd begun, I would have to resign myself to losing him in a year or two. Right now he was still having fun, but our menu was too limited for a young man of his talent. He needed a full-fledged restaurant, where he could exercise the entire scope of his abilities. So I would have to find a permanent assistant chef for him—Ramon had said he'd be going back to UNM in another month—who could be trained to take his place.

My thoughts turned to Ms. Usher and her party. Apparently they had been drawn, not only by Victor Solano's recommendation, but like so many of my other guests by the story of Captain Dusenberry. Even Mr. Solano's recent demise had not damped their interest in my Victorian ghost.

I foresaw that I would eventually yield to the hints and nudges of Kris and of Willow Lane, and start using Captain Dusenberry to advertise the tearoom. With a shudder, I rejected the thought. The Wisteria Tearoom was first and foremost a haven from the stresses of modern life, a place where one could enjoy an hour or two of good food and good company. That a colorful ghost story was attached to it was incidental.

Two colorful ghost stories, sort-of. There was Mrs. Carruthers, who had also died in the dining parlor. I regularly fielded questions about her, too, and though I never hesitated to assert that there had been no sign of her presence, I couldn't deny that she added to visitors' interest in the room.

A dreadful thought assailed me. Could the piano music be her doing?

"Sylvia, no!" I murmured.

Even as I thought it, I rejected the idea. Sylvia was not musical as far as I knew, and had not been a fan of opera. Whereas Captain Dusenberry had been; witness his pleasure in the concerts at La Fonda, and the musical group he had formed with Maria Hidalgo.

The niggling at the back of my brain took a sudden leap in volume. The phrase that Ms. Usher had identified for me was from *Figaro*. Had the Captain and Maria Hidalgo seen a performance of it?

I frowned, recalling Maria's letters. There had not been a full opera performance; indeed, a town the size of Santa Fe in the 1860s, basically a frontier town, would not have justified the expense of a full opera production. But they had nonetheless heard selections of opera music performed in concert by traveling musicians, such as Miss Lago, who had sung that aria that Maria had quoted...

I gave a little gasp, and set down the custard cup.

That aria was from *Figaro*.

I jumped up, cast a guilty look toward the stairs, and slipped into my office. The clock on my computer showed that my half-hour wasn't quite up, but this wasn't work—exactly—and I couldn't wait.

I looked toward Kris's office through the entryway it shared with mine. I couldn't see her at her desk from that angle.

I took out the letters and found the one with the reference to the aria Miss Lago had sung. The letter didn't give the character's name, but a quick web search on the lyric provided it. The aria in question was sung by the Countess Almaviva.

Contessa, perdono.

I searched on those two words, found the song, a translation, and a video clip of the scene. I put on my headphones to listen. The character asking the countess's pardon was her husband, the count. That was the Three Blind Mice part.

In the next two lines, the ones Sandra Usher had sung for me, the countess forgave her husband for his infidelity. The climax of the opera, and a beautiful piece of music.

Why had Captain Dusenberry fixed on that passage of music? Was he asking Maria Hidalgo's pardon? Except that he hadn't been unfaithful to her. As near as I could tell, he'd been just the opposite. If he'd lived, I felt sure he'd have married her.

If he'd lived.

Dear heaven. Had he been murdered because of his love for Maria, and hers for him?

I wished I had some of his letters, instead of only hers. I *had* to get to the archives and spend a few hours hunting down whatever they had about him. Maybe he'd left a diary or something that had been forgotten over the years.

I heard footsteps coming up the stairs. Hastily, I locked the letters back in the drawer and returned to my abandoned lunch. I was just picking up my half-eaten custard when Nat joined me.

"Well!" She sank into the other armchair with a sigh. "How do you do this every day?"

"It's not usually this busy." I offered her a bite of the custard, but she waved it away.

"I had some earlier. That boy Julio's a genius!"

"I know. Has it settled down in the gift shop?"

"No, but Dee came in and sent me off to take a break. I've been wanting to talk to you ever since Sandra Usher was here. That *was* her, wasn't it?"

"Yes. They were all from the Opera."

"She didn't look terribly upset about her co-star's death. Did she say anything?"

"Not about that. She and her guests wanted to know about Captain Dusenberry."

"Oh, for Pete's sake."

I scraped the last of my custard from my cup and held it on my tongue, enjoying the creamy sweetness for as long as I could make it last.

"You'll need me all week?" Nat asked.

"If you don't mind. I'm going to look into hiring another server or two, so with luck you won't have to do this for long."

"I don't mind, Ellen. I'm delighted to see you having such success."

I gave her a weary smile. "Thanks."

The success was complicated, and it was eating what spare time I had, but I was grateful. I had to be grateful. My bank account insisted on it.

We chatted a little about her wedding plans, then went back downstairs. It was nearly five, so I sent Nat home, insisting that I didn't want to invoke Manny's wrath.

Julio and Ramon were both gone, and Rosa was just leaving. Dee and Mick, my end-of-day team, were putting away clean china. The last of the customers were enjoying their tea. Everything was caught up, so I went back to my office, where I found a small pile of message slips, a note from Kris, and another from Julio with a few more items to be ordered. I made a couple of calls, then looked at my to-do list. A conjunction caught my eye:

- Take SFO backstage tour
- Water

An image came into my mind: the pool of water between the orchestra pit and the audience. A tingle ran down my arms.

Why was it important, though? It was just a giant trough of water. A pretty architectural detail.

A place where a knife might be hidden.

I sucked a deep breath. Maybe it was a dumb idea, but I felt compelled to check it out. I wrote a note to Kris, letting her know I'd be out of the office in the morning, then I pulled up SFO's website to look up the time of the backstage tour that ran every weekday during the season.

I didn't want to tell Tony my idea. If it came to nothing, it would be a waste of his time. I'd slip down to look at the pool during the tour, and if I spotted anything in the water I'd call him immediately.

I wished I could go at once, but the same reason that made it impossible would also keep anyone else away from the water: the opera would be gearing up for the evening's performance. People would be in the house constantly; no opportunity to slip in and fish anything out of the pool. I worried that it could happen overnight, but if so it might have happened already. I didn't think I'd feel this compulsion to look if there was nothing to be found.

And anyway, I had other reasons for wanting to take the tour. If I was to help Tony, it would be good to refresh my memory of the backstage area. Something else might jog my memory or spark an idea. I had to go.

So I had to work late, because the tour would eat my whole morning. I took a deep breath and tackled the rest of my messages.

I rose early, threw on a sun dress, and hurried down to the kitchen to talk to Julio. He was making scones and had Ramon peeling cucumbers. Music played on his boombox: flamenco, not salsa. I glanced at Ramon, wondering if it was his music, or at least his choice.

"You're up early," Julio said, dumping out his batter onto a floured section of his work table.

"I have to go out for a couple of hours this morning," I said. "Is there anything you need me to bring you, or anything I can help with before eight-thirty?"

"Don't think so."

"I'll check with you before I go, in case you think of something. Oh, and we're probably going to hire a couple more servers, at least temporarily. So if either of you knows someone who might be interested, ask them to call."

Julio nodded, intent on his work. Ramon glanced up with a smile.

I made a quick tour of the parlors and gift shop. Everything there was ready for opening. Iz and Rosa would set up the outdoor tables when they arrived.

Back to the office, where I took out the previous day's receipts and did the bank deposit, hoping to relieve Kris of that burden at least. I would drop off the deposit on my way to the opera. I wrote her a second note explaining this, and warning her that applicants for temporary server positions might be calling.

At 8:20 I fetched my sun hat from my suite, fixed myself a travel mug of tea, and headed downstairs with the bank bag tucked under my arm. I poked my nose in the kitchen, was shooed away by Julio, and went out to my car.

The morning was brisk, with bright clouds over the mountains promising a chance of afternoon rain. Cheered by this, I dropped the deposit in the night drop at the bank and then headed north out of town.

The opera's parking lot was nearly empty. I found a space in the shade of a tree at the end of a row, and since I was a little early I sat finishing my tea and trying to calm down.

Being there again brought back all the awful memories of the night Victor Solano had died. I let them flow past, hoping my emotions would settle. Vi's face, shocked and horrified as she told us what had happened, stuck in my memory. And Tony, clicking into professional mode, heading backstage, looking more cop than opera-goer despite his suit.

Dragging my thoughts away from Friday night, I got out of the car and headed for the box office, where I was to pick up my ticket for the tour. As I walked toward the theater with its complicated support structure, I realized that the last time I'd done the tour was before the second theater had been demolished. Maybe I'd learn something new.

A dozen or so people were already gathered outside the box office, waiting for the arrival of the tour guide. I paid for my ticket and joined them, imagining how best to slip away from the group and inspect the pool.

I'd need a flashlight. I took out my keychain and checked the small flash I had on it, which was working. It wasn't very powerful, but I hoped it would be enough. A knife blade should catch it.

Unless the knife was folded. I pressed my lips together, wondering if I should dash back to my car for the flashlight I kept in the glove box, but that one was larger and might be too conspicuous. Also, I thought as the tour guide came up and introduced himself, I didn't have time.

The guide was an older gentleman, a volunteer, who had been coming to the opera for decades. I listened impatiently while he talked about the history of the company and passed around some photos of John Crosby, the founder, and the first theatre. I kept thinking of Tony and what he'd be doing if he were there.

He'd be watching everyone but the tour guide, probably. I looked at my fellow tourists, all seemingly innocent. A couple were opera fanatics, and several were obviously not locals. Two tall women who were together wore grins of absolute delight. Reminded that I was supposed to be enjoying myself, I summoned a smile.

At last we moved, walking down to the gate and into the courtyard. As always, I glanced toward where the petunia beds had been. The fountain wasn't running.

I had to wait through a couple of stops before we got into the house itself. I used the time to practice my Holmesian skills of observation: I looked at the guide and the tourists, trying to notice something about each, then I looked at my surroundings. The grounds were immaculately clean; no trash anywhere, not even any dead leaves. Someone was in the bar on the Stravinsky Terrace, cleaning.

When we finally entered the house, I listened to the first part of the guide's speech, then ambled down toward the orchestra pit. The stage was set with terraced steps and a few fanciful adornments at the sides, vaguely Egyptian in style, mostly golden. *Magic Flute*, I guessed. Probably the previous night's performance, unless they were already set up for tonight's.

But no; Vi had mentioned they were doing final rehearsals during the day for *Cesar Chavez*, which was to open on Saturday. So they must not have changed the set yet. I doubted they'd rehearse on the set for a different production.

I reached the pool and noted that the water in it was still. On Friday night, it had been rippling just slightly; there must be a pump somewhere that circulated the water, and was presently turned off.

I strolled along the pool as if casually admiring it, and surreptitiously aimed my flashlight into the water, which was much shallower than I'd expected, only a few inches deep. I swept the beam along the bottom, looking for any anomalies. There were none. I walked the whole length of it and even leaned over it a little to make sure I'd seen the front edge. Nothing.

I turned back, intending to double-check, but the tour guide had brought the others down to join me, so I smiled and asked him a question about the pool. He responded with the history that I already knew. The other tourists showed interest. I continued to peer into the water, though I didn't dare use the flashlight.

Frustrated, I followed the group to the south patio. As we were leaving the house, a guy in jeans and a tee-shirt—a crew member, I surmised—came onto the stage and prepared to move one of the set pieces.

The guide led us through the stage door into the backstage area. The walls and floor were painted black, making the space seem even smaller than it was. The guide pointed out the stage manager's console, which included a video monitor and lots of technical-looking control panels. I half-listened to his talk while I continued to look around.

More crew members had joined the first guy. They started disassembling the terraced platforms and stacking the pieces at the back of the stage. Getting ready to load it all onto the B-lift and take it down to storage.

The tour moved into a short hallway. A rack of costumes stood there, making it even more crowded and tempting us to touch the beautiful fabrics, which the guide quickly warned us not to do. He talked about the dressing rooms but didn't allow us to go in. He stood with his back to the women's chorus dressing room, which made us face away from the principal men's dressing room. Behind him, just inside the doorway, a floor-to-ceiling set of cubby shelves filled with shoes drew the eye. Each space was labeled with a character's name.

I was sure the guide's choice of where to stand was deliberate; he wanted to minimize our curiosity about the fact that we were right beside the scene of Friday's murder. The lights in the principals' dressing rooms were off, whereas the women's chorus room was brilliantly lit.

I stood at the back of the group, placing myself where I could look into the principal men's dressing room. I didn't expect to see much of anything, and I didn't, but I felt I had to acknowledge the place where Victor Solano's life had ended so violently.

The dark walls backstage only accentuated the air of drama and mystery. By contrast, the inside walls of the dressing rooms were light, and the mirrors and lights made a striking scene against the gloomy backstage area.

Theatres all have their histories, colorful and often (if the theatre had been around long at all) including ghost stories. If SFO didn't already have ghost stories, it soon would. I'd have to ask Mr. Ingraham. He'd probably know.

The guide ushered us back toward the stage, then down some steps. At a half-landing we entered the props running room and stood just inside the entrance while the guide talked about the creation and storage of the hundreds of props needed for each season. Beside me was a wall rack holding dozens of parasols. I could imagine Tony's despair upon realizing he had to search everything in the place.

We went back out to the stairs and on down them. The guide gathered us at the foot of the steps, waiting until we were all down.

"We'll look at costume crafts next, and then the back deck," he said.

A gentle mechanical whir began, drawing our attention toward the stage at our right. The guide glanced toward it.

"That's the B-lift. They're bringing it up so they can load set pieces on it and take them down to storage. We'll look at—"

One of the tall women screamed. The floor of the B-lift had passed us, rising upward on a single, giant piston and revealing the space below.

A body lay in it—what was left of one. All I saw was a muddied glimpse of purple and black.

8

This way, everyone!" The guide began shooing us past. "Straight back, onto the deck. Quickly, please!"

A wave of a dreadful odor reached me and I cringed, a primal reaction to a smell that said "get away, not safe." An older woman in the group collapsed. Before I could go to her, two others were there. I took a step backward, my hands shaking as I took out my phone and called Tony.

Purple and black. I squeezed my eyes shut.

"This way, everyone! All the way back, please!"

"Aragón."

"Tony," I said, profoundly grateful to hear his voice.

"Yeah? Ellen?"

"You n-need to come to the opera."

"I'm kind of tied—"

"Right now. There's another...ah..." I was having trouble breathing. People were shouting but I didn't understand them.

"Ellen?"

"Hurry, Tony, please." I gulped. "Another body."

"Shit," he said, then the phone went dead.

I still had my eyes shut. I couldn't make myself open them. They started leaking tears.

"Ma'am? You need to come this way, please."

The tour guide. Shaking, I blinked a few times until I could see past the tears.

"This way," he said again, reaching hesitantly toward my arm.

I moved forward, looking straight ahead, feeling numb horror.

Purple and black. That's what Vi had been wearing when I last saw her. She wore those colors a lot.

143

Any self-respecting kid would have rebelled and chosen orange for a favorite color. I can't help it—I've always loved violet.

Oh, God. Vi.

I stumbled and the tour guide caught my arm.

"I'm all right," I said. "I'm all right."

I kept repeating it silently, a throwback to when my father had died. A mantra against despair.

I was not, in fact, all right, but the words kept me going until I was outside, on the broad deck behind the stage, joining the rest of the tour who were huddled together. The woman who had fainted was being supported by a man about her age; husband, probably. The others looked shocked or numb, stared toward the B-lift, whispered speculations.

I shivered and rubbed my arms, despite the warm weather. My teeth were chattering. Shock.

Raised voices came from the backstage area. There were wide sets of steps on either side of the B-lift. I'd forgotten that, though I'd seen them before and remembered them being used for grand entrances of the chorus in past operas. Now the stage crew were scrambling up and down them, calling to each other, shouting questions and instructions. The B-lift had stopped partway up between the steps. It looked odd there.

I turned away, looking westward. The Jemez Mountains lay serene and blue in the distance. Closer by, the dusty hillside was dotted with piñon trees and sage. Two big water towers rose up from the hill, a little to the left. Storage of the runoff from the opera's many rooftops, I remembered from a previous tour. They saved it all for watering the landscaping.

"This way, please, everyone," said the tour guide. "We'll go inside now to where you can sit down. The police will want to talk to you."

He led us down some stairs and south to a building I didn't remember. It was large, and a sign announced it as the Stieren Orchestra Hall. This was the back of the building, and the doorway we went through led to a lower level; like the theatre, most of the building was above us. We passed through a hallway to a conference room, where the guide invited us to sit down. He was on the phone, figuring out what to do with us, no doubt.

Phone. What had I done with mine? I didn't remember.

I looked in my purse and found it in its usual pocket. I must have put it away without realizing.

I sank into a chair, grateful to be off my feet.

We were in that room forever, it seemed. People would talk for a while, speculating on what had happened—was it an accident? Or suicide?—and then lapse into silence.

If it was Vi, and I was terribly afraid that it was, then it couldn't have been suicide. She'd been upset when I saw her, but not enough to take her life. She had a brilliant career ahead of her.

Oh, Vi.

I closed my eyes, trying to block out the voices of the others, trying to keep myself together. I just had to make it until Tony got there. Then everything would be all right.

My phone rang, startling me. I took it out, expecting to see Tony's number, but it was Rhonda Benning.

Oh, God.

I wanted to chicken out and let it go to voicemail, but I couldn't do that to poor Rhonda. I stood and went out into the hall to answer the call.

"Hello?"

"Ellen, it's Rhonda. I'm sorry to bother you, but I was wondering if you'd seen Vi. She didn't come home last night."

I bit my lip. "The last time I saw her was night before last. She dropped by after her performance."

"But not last night?"

"No. I'm sorry."

I couldn't tell her about the body. What if it wasn't Vi? Much as I wanted to ease Rhonda's mind, if I told her anything it might just make everything worse.

"Could...she have stayed with a friend?" I asked.

"I've checked with everyone I could think of," Rhonda said. "No one's seen her, and she's not answering her cell."

"Oh. I really wish I could help...."

"Thanks, Ellen. If you hear from her—"

I swallowed. "I'll tell her to call you."

"Thanks."

We said goodbye, and I returned to the conference room. My stomach was in knots.

The tour guide came in— I hadn't realized he was gone—and passed around a clipboard, asking us all to write down our names, addresses, and phone numbers. I complied, then sat staring out the doorway.

Vi wouldn't kill herself, and I doubted she'd be careless around the stage. So someone had pushed her, or knocked her unconscious and dropped her into the elevator pit, and then lowered the platform.

I squeezed my eyes shut. If you fell in the pit, could you get out? There must be a way—too much of a risk without some way to escape. My mind told me that I had glimpsed a ladder mounted to one wall, black on black.

Which meant that Vi hadn't been able to climb out. She'd been unconscious. Or...already dead?

I shuddered.

Maybe it wasn't Vi. Stop thinking it's Vi, I told myself.

"Can't we go home?" a plaintive voice behind me said.

I turned my head to see the woman who had collapsed. Her husband was murmuring to her. Others were checking their watches.

Oh, God. The tearoom!

I took my phone out again. Almost eleven. I was debating whether to call Kris when a uniformed police officer walked in, accompanied by a woman who looked like a security guard, carrying the clipboard we'd all signed.

"Thank you for your patience, everyone," the guard said. "The police would like to interview each of you briefly, then you'll be free to go home." She glanced at the clipboard. "Ellen Rosings?"

I stood.

"And Melvin Steinberg."

A gruff-looking older man joined me. We went into the hall and it was all I could do to keep from squeaking when I saw Tony. I hurried to him and he caught me in a quick hug, then put me at a distance. All business.

"Come out here." He nodded down the hallway. The uniformed cop was leading Mr. Steinberg in the other direction.

Tony led me outside the way we'd come in, to a parking lot behind Stieren Hall. I blinked at the bright sunlight, and though we stood in the shade of the building, I could feel the heat reflected from the pavement.

"Tell me what you saw," Tony said, taking out his notebook.

I told him. "Tony, I'm afraid it m-might be Vi. She liked to wear purple and black."

"That doesn't mean anything. Don't jump to conclusions."

"But her mother just called me. She didn't come home last night after her performance."

His brows folded into a frown. "We can't make a positive I.D. yet. Have to wait for the M.E."

I nodded and swallowed, blinking back the threat of more tears.

"You OK?"

I drew a shaky breath. "Not really."

"Come here."

He led me south, away from the theatre. I followed, sniffed once, tried to pull myself together. We walked around the corner of the building and I saw that the paved area we were on connected with the patio to the south of the theatre.

Tony stopped walking and put his arm around my shoulders. "What are you doing here, anyway? I thought you were going to be busy all week."

"We are, but I had an idea. I didn't want to bother you with it, and I figured if I took the tour I could check myself."

"What idea?"

"Don't laugh."

"OK."

"I thought the murder weapon might be in the pool by the orchestra pit. If the murderer needed to hide it quickly...."

He looked surprised. "What made you think that?"

I couldn't tell him about Willow's suggestion—not if I didn't want to get laughed at. "Just a hunch," I said. "But I didn't see anything, so never mind."

"It's not a bad idea. We didn't look there, since it was in full view of the audience. But we'll check it out, since we're here."

"You don't have to do it just to make me feel good."

"Hey."

He turned me to face him, both hands on my shoulders. His gaze steadied me.

"I value your opinions, OK? You've already helped us a lot on this. So don't ever hesitate to tell me your ideas, even if you think I'll laugh. OK?"

I nodded and sniffed again, trying to smile. "OK."

"Where's your handkerchief? Don't you always carry one?"

"Um, yeah." I dug in my purse.

"You've had a shock." Tony's voice was gentle. I looked up and saw his eyes—soft, not the hard cop gaze—looking at me with concern. "Are you all right to drive home?"

I nodded. "Yeah."

"I want you to go there now, and take an hour to lie down or just sit quietly. No jumping into work. If you think of anything more—if you remember anything else—call me."

"OK."

"And please don't talk to anyone about what you saw. Not even Vi's mom."

"Right. I didn't tell her anything."

"Good."

He hugged me and I clung to him, fighting back sobs. He bore it patiently, and I managed to keep from breaking down completely.

"Go home and cry, babe. I'll call you when I have any news."

"OK." I let him go and mopped at my face with my handkerchief. "Thanks, Tony."

"Thank you for calling me right away. You did the right thing."

I managed a smile.

"Want me to walk you to your car?"

Yes.

"No, I'm all right. You have a lot to do."

"OK. Take care. I'll call you."

He brushed his thumb across my cheek, then walked away. I watched until he disappeared around the building, heading back for the theatre. The crime scene.

I took a deep breath, then turned and headed for the parking lot.

The tearoom was bustling. It took some effort, and a bit of prevarication, to avoid getting sucked into the activity. I finally claimed a headache and told the staff that I wanted to be left alone for an hour.

As I was heading upstairs to my suite, I heard a firm tread behind me. At the top of the staircase I turned to find Nat frowning at me.

"Are you sick?" she asked.

"N-not exactly. I just need some quiet."

"What happened?"

"I can't talk about it, Nat. I'll tell you later, OK?"

"Ellen!" Her face and her voice showed dismay. I had to fight back a sudden onslaught of tears.

"Just give me an hour or so," I said. "Please."

"Oh, sweetie! Of course." She caught me in a swift hug and then stepped back. "Can I bring you anything?"

I shook my head, and tried to smile as I unlocked my suite.

"Tell Kris, OK?"

Nat nodded, still frowning in concern as I gently closed the door between us.

Sunlight blew in on a warm breeze through the window I'd left cracked, setting the gauze curtains swaying. The suite was otherwise dark.

I walked to the kitchenette, leaving the lights off, and filled a kettle for tea. The routine calmed me: warming the pot, choosing which tea, measuring the leaves. When the kettle boiled I poured the water slowly, inhaling steam with the first hint of tea aroma. I set a timer and retreated to my favorite chair to wait.

Now that I was alone and free to indulge in hysteria, the tears wouldn't come. There was a hard knot in my chest and I knew the feeling. Defense.

I knew how to do this. I'd done it before. It wasn't easy but it was manageable.

But I had to wait. No point in grieving until I was certain.

The timer went off and I got up. I filled my favorite mug with tea and indulged in honey and milk, turning it into a sweet.

Oh, yeah. I hadn't had lunch.

My stomach clenched at the idea of food. I abandoned the thought, and paced aimlessly, both hands wrapped around my mug, sipping now and then.

Part of me wished I hadn't gone to the opera that morning. But if I hadn't been there, Tony wouldn't have heard about the—new body—until much later. So it was good that I was there. Just upsetting.

Who would want to murder Vi?

Someone who wanted her roles? But she was an apprentice. Bottom of the totem pole. Nothing to gain from her death. There was someone covering the solo parts she had, but it would be another apprentice, most likely. No, the gain, if there was any, wasn't enough to offset the risk.

So who else?

The murderer. If Vi knew something about Victor Solano's death, his killer might feel threatened by her and decide to get her out of the way.

My throat tightened. What a nightmare.

I couldn't follow that train of thought any more. I let it slide away, and emptied my mind, just pacing from my sitting room to my bedroom and back. When I ran out of tea, I took my mug back to the kitchenette and left it there.

Numb, I returned to my bedroom. Darkness enfolded me; the window there was closed and covered. I kicked off my shoes, crawled under the comforter on my bed, and lay still.

Images came to me, though I tried to think of nothing. A glimpse of purple and black. The pool in front of the orchestra pit. A pocket knife, folded shut. Then one with a corkscrew deployed. Mr. Ingraham's tailgate party.

I clung to that one, because it was a good memory. I had enjoyed that party. Good food, good company, Tony relaxing with my friends. It had been such a nice evening, until the end of the opera.

Murder. I turned over and buried my face in my pillow.

Why was murder a part of my life? It wasn't because of Tony. It was the other way around; murder had brought Tony into my life. I was glad to know him, but I could do without the emotional trauma.

Three, possibly four murders since the tearoom had opened. Not all here, thank God, but all in my face, more or less. I felt inclined to complain.

Whine, whine, whine. I let the thoughts flow through me. If there was any place where I was entitled to indulge in self-pity, it was in my own bed.

Music drifted into my awareness. Not through my ears, but in my mind. Piano music. No, vocal—a capella, then with an orchestra. I frowned, knowing I recognized it, but not placing it.

Oh. "Contessa, perdono."

Make that five murders, if you counted Captain Dusenberry. That one had happened over a century ago, but here in my house. That definitely counted as in my face.

Nothing I could do about it. Throw in the towel and close the tearoom? Hell, no. I was building something, maybe the most important thing I'd ever done. I was not going to let a few paltry murders interfere.

Can't let the bad guys win. I could hear Tony saying that.

Somehow, I drifted to sleep. I woke up to a persistent knocking on my door. Glanced at the bedside clock: 3:08.

"S'minute," I called.

I slid out of bed, found my shoes, and pushed my hair back from my face. I probably still looked like hell but I didn't much care.

I opened the door a crack and looked out. Nat was outside with a tray.

"It's been over two hours. Julio sent up some lunch for you."

I didn't have much appetite, but I didn't want to be rude. I reached for the tray.

"Let me set it down for you. Were you sleeping? I'm sorry to bother you, but they're getting anxious downstairs."

I opened the door for her and stepped back, then closed it behind her. Nat set the tray on the low table in my sitting area. It held a plate of sandwiches and a bowl of fresh fruit.

"Thanks, Nat."

"Is your head better?"

I hesitated. "A little."

"Mick was listening to the radio and he heard a breaking news announcement. A body was found at the Santa Fe Opera."

I sighed and sat in my chair, tucking my feet up under me, leaving my shoes on the floor. Nat sat in the other chair.

"Is that what's bothering you? Did you find the body?"

"Not exactly. The whole tour group saw it."

"Oh, dear heaven. No wonder you're upset."

"Tony asked me not to talk about it."

"I see."

Silence stretched out between us. Nat knew better than to badger me with questions or small talk. Like my father, her brother, she had infinite patience.

I gazed out the window, heard voices drifting up from the *portal* below. I sat up.

"Oh! The spirit tour!"

"Dee's handling it," Nat said.

"Oh. Thanks." I relaxed again. Amazing how weary I felt, considering I hadn't done much and had just had a two-hour nap.

"Mind if I pass along a couple of things people asked me to tell you?" Nat said.

"Go ahead."

"Kris has a couple of applications for temporary servers that she'd like you to look at."

"That was quick!"

"They're friends of staff, apparently. She passed the word around."

"OK."

"And Sandra Usher wants to book the entire tearoom for a private party next week."

"Wait...the whole tearoom?"

"Yes. Kris gave her an outrageous quote and she didn't even blink."

"But we're booking up next week already..."

"Kris says she can swing it. Just needs to rearrange a few reservations, but she wants your approval before she starts on that."

"Man, I go away for a couple of hours..." I pressed my hands to my temples. "What day?"

"Next Wednesday, from one to five."

A week away. "OK."

I felt bombarded, but what was I going to do? Turn down a lucrative private party?

"Kris has the details, and would like to go over them with you. Ms. Usher wants a special menu."

I turned my head to look at Nat. "Not if Julio says no."

"Julio likes the idea. He's looking forward to it."

I took a deep breath. "OK."

In that moment, I realized I was no longer in control. The tearoom had a life of its own. Sure, I could have said no...but that would have been an act of insanity. My staff thought they could handle this—they wanted to do it—and I'd be nuts to forbid it.

Never mind that I needed a day or two, which I didn't have, just to sort out my own stuff.

Nat's hand slid onto my forearm, warm and comforting. I

sighed and moved to clasp it.

"Thank you, Auntie Nat."

"Good Lord, you haven't called me Auntie in years!"

I gave her a feeble smile, and finally the tears came.

She sat with me, quiet comfort, while I mopped my face and sniveled. Nothing left to explain; she knew it all. Well, mostly all.

I had too much going on, as usual. I needed to set some of it aside.

When I was cried out, Nat got up and fetched me a glass of water. "Drink this, and eat one sandwich, and then if you're ready go talk to Kris. I'll go downstairs and make sure everything's all right."

I held the glass with both hands, like a child afraid of dropping it. "Thanks."

"You're welcome, honey." She kissed my cheek. "I'll be back before I leave."

She slipped out, quietly closing the door. A moment later I heard her and Kris talking briefly, then Nat went downstairs.

I followed her instructions, though the sandwich didn't taste like anything. I put the rest of the food away in my fridge, and went to the bathroom to wash my face. Caught a glimpse of my hair when I looked in the mirror.

"Yikes!"

I brushed it and pulled it back into a ponytail, then blew my nose once more and put on my shoes. Ready to face the world, or at least my job, I went across the hall.

Kris had on a skin-tight black silk dress with long sleeves and a deep neckline which was decorously obscured by a lavender lace scarf. She welcomed me without comment and we had a very businesslike conversation, with no mention of dead bodies. She suggested scheduling interviews with the two potential new servers on Monday.

"It shouldn't take long, and you could go ahead and show them the ropes if you decide you like them."

"Do you know either of them?" I asked.

"Yes, one is a friend of mine, Dale Whittier. Very reliable."

"And the other?"

"A friend of Ramon's. Thea Swift."

She placed their applications before me on her desk. I gazed at them without registering any details. There went half a day of my free time.

"All right, but not until the afternoon. I need the morning to myself."

"Fine. I'll schedule them for...say, one and three?"

I nodded. Kris put aside the applications and launched into the plan for Sandra Usher's party. I paid attention as well as I could, but my mind did wander a bit. Ordinarily I'd be interested in all the details of planning such a party, but I just couldn't find the enthusiasm. I was sliding into numbness again. A symptom of overload.

I gave Kris the go-ahead to book the party and do whatever rearranging of the schedule it required. In response to my query whether reservations were slowing down at all, she shook her head.

"You might want to think about raising prices."

I blinked. "We've only been open three months!"

She shrugged. "Just saying. If you want to slow the reservations down a bit, that might do it."

"I'll think about it."

"The house across the street is for sale, by the way."

I looked up sharply, but she was making a note on her computer. I knew the house she meant: an historic home with distinctive faux-brick plastering, formerly owned by Vince Margolan, which he'd been turning into a gallery and in which he tried to throttle me.

"Let's pay this one off, first," I said.

I would never buy that house, but there was no need to be rude about the suggestion. Possibly the Hutchinses, who lived on the corner, would be interested in expanding their B&B.

"Well, that's all I have right now. I'd better get on the phone to these two," Kris said. "I left some messages on your desk, but there's nothing urgent."

"All right. Thanks for staying on top of things, Kris."

She flashed me a rare smile and turned her attention back to her computer. I went into my office, sat at my desk, and stared at the pile of message slips.

A rumble of thunder surprised me into looking up. There was still sunlight outside, but when I went to look out the window I saw dark clouds gathered over the Sangre de Cristos. The morning's promise had come through, at least for the mountains.

I looked at my watch. Four o'clock: tea time. Right on time for the summer rains.

I opened the window, hoping to catch the smell of rain. Too far away, but I left the window open and stood enjoying the breeze that set the sheers dancing. With luck, the rain would reach us eventually.

I was still standing there, thinking about the rain dances my brother and I had done as children, when I heard Nat go into Kris's office and talk with her briefly about Ms. Usher's party. She looked through the adjoining doorway and smiled.

"There you are. You look better."

"I could hardly look worse. Why didn't you tell me my hair was a rat's nest?"

"Was it? I didn't notice."

"Faithful Auntie Nat."

She collected me into a hug. I needed that, and I held on to her greedily for a minute. When we finally parted she grasped my shoulders and looked me over with a critical eye.

"Did you eat?"

"Yes, ma'am."

"All right. Do you want to come home with me for dinner?"

"Thanks, but no. I'd just be a lump."

"It's all right to be a lump with your family."

"Not tonight, Nat. Thank you."

"Are you going to Thomas's on Friday?"

"Oh! Crap! I forgot to call him back." I stepped to my desk, but my phone wasn't there. Still in my purse, which was still in my suite.

I stopped, recognizing the tension between my shoulders. Stress, caused by trying to please too many other people. I couldn't afford that right now.

"You know what? I think I'm going to wimp out on that."

"Company might do you good," Nat said.

I pictured dining with Mr. Ingraham and friends, and knew that the conversation would be dominated by the new murder. "No," I said. "Not this time. I'll call him with my regrets."

"Let me make a suggestion for something else. No, an offer: I'll call and book you a massage at Ten Thousand Waves."

"Oh, Nat—"

"You need some time away from the tearoom. If you're not up to socializing, then I prescribe some TLC. My treat, for your birthday."

"You already gave me a birthday present."

"Well, you're my only niece so I get to spoil you all I want."

I smiled. "Thank you, Auntie."

"Stop that." She kissed my cheek, and I caught a whiff of her perfume, sweet and floral. "Feel better, sweetie. Don't come downstairs, everything's under control. I'll stay until closing."

"But Manny—"

"Manny's experimenting with the grill again. He found a TV show on PBS where they cook absolutely everything on a grill. I think he's making grilled quiche."

"Ack!"

"Yes, well. We'll see. Now you relax on this beautiful chaise longue that you never use, and read a novel or something. Can I bring you some tea?"

"No, I'm fine."

"All right. See you tomorrow."

I followed her to the doorway. She turned around and frowned at me.

"Just getting my phone," I said, gesturing to my suite. "And a book."

Nat stood at the head of the stairs and watched me go across to my door. I had to laugh, which I supposed was her intention.

She actually waited until I went back to my office, book and phone in hand, then waved as she went down the stairs.

I glanced through the messages on my phone, but there was none from Tony. Ignoring the rest, I left the phone on my desk and went over to the chaise.

Nat had helped me find it, and bullied me into buying it even though I'd balked at the price. It was antique maple, with beautiful carved scrollwork along the back and green velvet upholstery. I turned on the stained-glass lamp over it and took a moment to admire the glowing colors.

This was a corner I had created for myself, and Nat was right: I didn't use it enough. Tucked beneath the sloping roof, with a view of the window, the chaise was a perfect spot for cozy alone-time. I stretched out on it, sighed, and opened my long-neglected book: *Cotillion* by Georgette Heyer. It was a very silly book, and I'd read it many times. I still loved it.

Before I knew it, Kris was in the doorway saying good night.

"Don't get up. I made an appointment for Monday with Dale, and left a message for Thea. And I got the reservations all switched, so Ms. Usher's party is good to go."

"Did you tell her?" I asked, wondering if Ms. Usher had heard about the new tragedy at SFO.

"I left a message."

"OK. Good night, Kris. Thanks."

With her departure, I had the upper floor to myself. Some of the tension in my back dissolved. I hadn't realized it was there.

There were a million things I should do. I ignored them all, and dove back into *Cotillion*. Now and then I heard a door close downstairs, but I was able to ignore that, too. Not until my private doorbell rang did I look up.

To my surprise, it was dark outside. I smelled rain. Going to the window, I found the sill was wet. I closed the window, then left my book on my desk and hurried down to the back door.

Tony was standing outside, raindrops glinting on the shoulders of his leather jacket, helmet in one hand and a white carry-out bag in the other. I invited him in with a gesture. He stepped over the threshold, looking at me with serious eyes.

"It's Vi," I said.

He nodded.

9

D amn it," I said, tears sliding down my cheeks. Tony put his helmet and bag on the floor and gathered me into his arms.

"I'm sorry, Ellen," he said in my ear, his voice rough.

I didn't bother trying to stop crying. He held me and occasionally murmured comforting nothings. When I finally wound down, he picked up his paper bag, and I saw the blue and red logo of Blake's Lotaburger.

"Green chile cheeseburgers," Tony said. "You might not be hungry, but you should eat anyway."

"Actually, that sounds good," I said. "This is your dinner?"

"Yeah. Gotta go back, but I didn't want to break it to you on the phone."

I sniffed. "Thanks. Come on in here."

I led him into the kitchen, and we sat at the staff's break table. There were two chocolate malts and a bag of tired fries along with the burgers.

"Want some coffee? I could make some," I said.

He shook his head as he shrugged out of his jacket. "Don't bother. Coffee's easy to find."

I took a bite of my cheeseburger, and was instantly transported back to high school. I closed my eyes, savoring the distraction.

"Did you work today?" Tony asked.

"Not much. I mostly sat around being numb. Took a nap for a couple of hours."

"Good."

"How's the investigation going?"

"Well, kind of chaotic at the moment."

Questions came to mind, but I wasn't sure I wanted to know the answers. I ate a couple of fries and sucked at my malt.

"I'm going to want to talk with you about this," Tony said.

"Not tonight, but in a day or so."

"OK."

"Did you remember anything else?"

"No. All I can think of is that Victor Solano's murderer must have thought she was a threat."

"Yeah, that's our working hypothesis. Can't find that she had any enemies."

I shook my head. Vi was the sweetest person in the world. Why would anyone...

I couldn't think about that. I returned my attention to my meal, trying to spark my flagging appetite.

"Really nice of you to bring me dinner," I said, managing a smile. "That's two meals I owe you."

"Who's counting?"

"When we're back to normal, I'm going to make you a five-course dinner."

"Boy howdy."

I feigned offense. "Well, if you don't appreciate it—"

"I've been living on mostly junk food for five days. At this point, I'd appreciate spaghetti and meatballs and a bottle of wine."

"I can do that."

He grinned. "You can do better, I'm sure."

I took another pull on the malt. "I'm going to hire two more servers."

"Wow. Still booming, eh?"

"Louder and louder."

I was getting full, so I put the rest of my burger down and watched Tony finish his. For a man who ate mostly junk food, he was in pretty fine shape. He looked tired, though.

"How's your family?" I asked.

"Hell if I know. Been a week since I talked to any of them."

"I'd still like to have you bring your mother and grandmother to tea. When things have settled down, I mean."

He smiled. "They'd like that. Thanks."

"I have an ulterior motive. I'm curious to meet them."

"They want to meet you, too."

They do?

Now I was *really* curious: what had Tony told his family about me? I was surprised he'd told them anything, until I remembered that he'd borrowed his mother's car once to take me to dinner.

Had he told them I was Anglo? The thought brought back some of our less comfortable discussions. We were still feeling our way toward a balance, coming from rather different cultural and social backgrounds.

Tony polished off his burger and stuffed a few fries in his mouth. I took one more fry and nibbled at it, though I wasn't really hungry anymore.

He pulled at his straw until his malt rattled its last gasp, then stuffed the cup and the wrappers into the Blake's bag. "I'd better get back. You done with that?"

I nodded. "Full. Thanks, Tony."

"You need to get a dog. Shame to let that go to waste."

"Take it with you if you like. I'm sure you could find a dog without any trouble."

"Ha, ha."

He stuffed my abandoned sandwich and the rest of the fries into the bag. I relieved him of it and put it in the trash compactor. He put on his jacket and grabbed his helmet, and I walked with him to the back door.

The air was cold and damp and delicious, and the night was quiet, as if waiting for whatever came next. Not even a cricket singing.

"Looks like it's stopped raining," I said.

"Yeah. Well, good night. Get some rest."

"You, too. You're not made of steel, you know."

"Says who?" He grinned, putting on his helmet. "I'll call you."

"Good night."

I watched him walk out to his bike. He coasted it down the gravel driveway to the street before starting the engine. Considerate of him.

He did that a lot; surprised me by an act of courtesy or an elegant turn of phrase just when I figured he was in total cop mode. I wondered if that was his nature, or if he was making extra effort for my sake.

I went back to the kitchen, put the rest of my malt in the freezer, tidied up the table, and turned out the light. I was on my way to the stairs when the piano began.

"Contessa, perdono." I recognized it now.

An expression of condolence? Or an actual apology?

I couldn't think why Captain Dusenberry would need to apologize to me. I walked down the hall to the main parlor and turned on the light.

The piano was closed. The music continued to the end of the phrase.

"How are you doing that?" I said aloud. "Are you plucking the strings?"

It was just the melody line, though it sounded more confident now than it had previously. Maybe he'd been practicing.

I moved the ornaments off the lid and opened the sound box again. Turning my ear toward the strings, I could just sense a latent vibration.

It was real. I had not imagined the music. I wasn't the only one who had heard it. Vi—

Oh, Vi.

I sat in the nearest chair and gave one gusty sob. I didn't want to cry any more; I was tired. I took a few deep breaths.

"Damn it."

The piano played a single, low note—a C, I thought. I got up and looked in the sound box, and saw one hammer settling back into place.

So that was how he did it. He was hitting the hammers, one by one. Like hunt and peck typing. How, I had no clue. Maybe Willow Lane could explain it.

What did low C mean? It was the ultimate tonic.

Tonic. As in restorative?

I was too sad to smile, but I wondered if Captain Dusenberry was a punster. Or maybe a C, the tonic, the foundation of the most basic scale, was meant to indicate agreement. Either way, I did find it strangely comforting.

I confess, I resorted to a sleeping pill. Actually an eighth of an over-the-counter pill; anything more would have me dragging all the next morning. I didn't like drugging myself to sleep, but my thoughts would have haunted me if I hadn't shut them up. I had learned that the hard way when my father died.

I woke feeling sad but reasonably refreshed. A faint smell of coffee reached me; it was coming through the window in my sitting area, which I'd forgotten was cracked open. I pulled on my robe against the morning chill and hurried to investigate how much rain had come in, and whether I needed to do emergency cleanup.

The wind must have been from the north, because there wasn't a mess of water under the window. The sill was slightly damp, but that would soon dry. Already the sun was shining on an ironically cheerful morning.

I put on a plain gray dress and went downstairs, said hello to Julio and Ramon, and stepped out into my garden with my clippers, gloves, and an empty vase. It was really an excuse to walk among the flowers: "the sweetness of the wet garden." I cut a few roses and lilies, and paused to smell each bush, though the rain had carried away a good deal of scent. The most fragrant roses were up and running, though.

I lingered for half an hour, making a mental list of little garden chores that needed attention. The violets were putting out more blossoms.

I paused, closing my eyes. Vi had been more than an employee. She was a friend. I'd known her less than a year, but it still hurt like hell to think she was gone. It was just so wrong.

And by damn, if there was anything I could do to help catch her killer, I'd do it.

I bent down and clipped a few violets, then went inside and found a tiny vase for them. The larger vase I left on my credenza while I brought the violets to my desk.

I fired up my computer and checked the website of my preferred local news station. As I'd feared, they had found the story. ANOTHER DEATH AT SANTA FE OPERA blared at the top of the screen. There was even a sidebar story: "Curse of *Tosca?*" Mr. Ingraham would have kittens.

I skimmed the lead story. They mentioned no names, but they did say the victim was one of the apprentices.

I'd have to talk to my staff.

I texted Tony:

OK TO TELL MY STAFF ABOUT VI? STORY IS ON THE NEWS.

Even if I didn't tell them they'd probably guess. I just wanted to give them some closure.

I poked through my message slips until my phone buzzed with Tony's answering text:

YES.

I went down to the kitchen and wrote on the whiteboard beside the time clock: STAFF MEETING MAIN PARLOR 10:30 a.m. Julio and Ramon were the only ones in at the moment, so I told them about the meeting, then went up front to the gift shop to collect the previous day's receipts, which I'd forgotten to take upstairs overnight. Fortunately, Nat had locked the cash drawer, and when I opened it I saw that she had already set it up for the new day, with the checks, charge slips, and extra cash in the bank bag.

Heaping silent blessings on my aunt's head, I took the bag upstairs and wrote up the deposit. It was, I knew, a way of avoiding my messages, which I didn't feel like answering. I'd have been happy to spend the day in hermit mode, but I'd been mostly useless the day before and I needed to reassure my staff that I was still functional. Sort of.

When the deposit was done I locked it in Kris's desk, then I made a pot of tea (yes, more procrastination), and finally sat down at my desk. I sorted the messages into "answer now," "later," and "delegate" piles, then glanced at the clock—8:52—before starting in on "answer now."

Top priority was Mr. Ingraham. I braced myself for a conversation about Vi, but either he hadn't heard or he was being particularly considerate. He said everything that was kind and polite, wished me well with my busy week and hoped that he'd be able to welcome me to his home on another occasion. Truly the gentleman.

I got through two more messages before Kris came in. By the expression on her face, it was clear that she'd heard the news, and reached her own conclusions.

"I hope Usher doesn't cancel," she said.

"We can't be surprised if she does."

"I'd better put everything on hold." Kris helped herself to tea, then went into her office.

I returned to my messages, calling people I didn't really want to talk to and listening politely to their ideas and concerns. Only one of them mentioned the opera story, and let it drop when I responded noncommittally.

By the time I got through all the "answer nows," it was quarter to ten. I replenished my tea and made a few notes to help me through the staff meeting. It wouldn't be fun, but at least I wouldn't stand there stupidly. At quarter after, I went across to my suite for two clean handkerchiefs, then headed downstairs.

Everyone was in the tearoom except for Dee and Mick, who wouldn't arrive until the afternoon. I went into the main parlor and Nat joined me there. I noticed the shawl on the piano was askew and stepped up to adjust it.

"Have you been playing the piano?"

"N-no. Why?"

Nat shrugged. "I know you used to play it a lot when you were troubled."

"Yeah, I did. Haven't had much time lately."

I'd have to take some time to play, after hours. It would probably feel good.

The staff began to gather. Iz looked at me intently as she

entered, then sat in one of the farthest chairs. Rosa came in with Ramon, who whispered to her as they took seats. Kris came in last, phone in hand, while Julio hung in the doorway.

That was everyone. Time to bite the bullet. I stepped forward.

"Thank you, all. Some of you may have heard that another death occurred at the Santa Fe Opera yesterday. I'm very sorry to tell you that it appears to be Vi Benning."

A small sound drew my attention to where Iz sat. I glanced that way, but she was staring at the floor, hands clasped tightly in her lap.

"The police are investigating her death. Not much is known so far." I cleared my throat, which was threatening to close. "Vi was more than a friend. She was part of the tearoom. I'm sure you all feel this loss, as do I. We'll always remember her."

The words were inadequate. There would never be adequate words. Blinking, I swallowed.

"If anyone needs some time off, or would like to arrange for some counseling, please come see me in my office. Thank you."

They dispersed. Nat gave my shoulder a squeeze, then went off to tag new merchandise in the gift shop.

"Can I talk to you when you come up?" Kris said.

"Sure. Be there in a minute."

She went out, leaving me alone with Iz, who still huddled in a wing chair. I went over to her and sat in the matching chair beside her.

"Iz?"

"It's not fair," she said in a low, angry voice.

"No, it isn't."

"She helped me...."

Iz had always been quiet, almost too shy. Vi had been her opposite, vivacious and outgoing, but she had taken pains to include in the tearoom's early days Iz and had won her affection. She had made it easier for Iz to adjust to her job, and made her feel important and valued.

Rosa and Ramon hadn't yet been hired then. Dee and Mick had. I'd have to deal with their reactions later.

I laid my hand over Iz's. She gulped out an angry sob. I considered giving her a hug, but Iz was quite a private person and I didn't want to overstep her comfort zone. Instead, I gave her one of my handkerchiefs.

"Do you want to go home? We can probably manage..."

"No. I'll do my job." She wiped defiantly at her nose.

"All right. If you change your mind, just let me know."

I stood and turned to go. Iz caught my hand, stopping me.

"Thank you, Ellen," she said.

"Thank you for being willing to stay." I squeezed her hand, and she let me go. I left her to collect herself in private.

Rosa was in the pantry setting up trays for the first arrivals. The smell of scones baking pervaded the atmosphere. I offered to help but she shook her head.

"It's fine. Thanks, but I'll be OK."

"Look after Iz, all right? She and Vi were close."

"I will," Rosa said.

I went into the kitchen. Julio was beating something in a large bowl, scowling. Ramon was at the prep table laying out sandwiches for trimming. I watched them both for a minute.

Julio and Vi had been especially close, and I was a little worried about him. He tended to bury stuff that bothered him instead of letting it out.

I resolved to talk to Kris about getting a counselor in for the next day. One day wouldn't solve long-term grief, but it could get us started in the right direction.

I went upstairs, to be greeted by Kris. She invited me into her office with a gesture. I grabbed some tea and joined her.

"I'm getting calls from the media," she said.

I boggled, then understood. "Because she worked here."

Kris nodded. "Do you want to be interviewed?"

"No!" I put my cup and saucer on Kris's desk and pressed my hands to my eyes.

If my friend Gina had been there, she'd have told me I was crazy. Passing up a chance to get the tearoom mentioned on state-wide TV?

Except we already had more business than we could handle. And I couldn't—I just couldn't face reporters right now.

I took a deep breath, picked up my cup, and swallowed some tea.

"Shall I prepare a statement to give them?" Kris said.

"Yes. That's a great idea. We should say how saddened we are, how much we'll miss Vi...are they saying she's dead? Do they know it's her?"

"I don't think the police have confirmed it, but it sounds like someone has been counting heads and come up with Vi as the one who's missing."

"All right—let's do two statements. One that's non-committal and says we love Vi, and the other expressing our sadness, our shock..."

"I'll bring you a draft of each."

"Thank you. Anything else?"

She tilted her head. "How do you know it's Vi?"

I closed my eyes briefly. "I glimpsed the body. The clothes were black and violet. And Tony Aragón confirmed it was Vi last night, but I don't think we should spread the word on that."

Kris nodded.

"When you have time, would you look into getting a grief counselor to come in and be available to the staff tomorrow? Say, from ten to two?"

"I'll make some calls."

"Thanks, Kris." I stood, picked up my tea, and headed for my office.

"Hey, Ellen?"

I turned in the doorway. Kris's hands were clasped in front of her on her desk.

"Just wanted to tell you I'm sorry. I know you really liked Vi."

"Thank you. I'd be sad to lose anyone—you're all very important to me, as friends, not just as staff."

She smiled briefly, then turned to her computer. I returned to my desk, feeling low. I could hear the quiet murmur of Kris's voice as she spoke on the phone. I brought up some classical music on web-based radio to give myself some separation.

I glanced through my stack of "later" messages, but wasn't up to making calls just then. I started sorting out the "delegate" slips, making notes on each one for the lucky person who was going to get to deal with it. Mostly that was Kris, but some were going to Julio and a couple to Dee, who had been handling a lot of the purchasing for the gift shop.

Eleven o'clock came and went; the tearoom was open. I stayed upstairs, which was chickening out in a way, but I was feeling fragile. If there was an emergency downstairs I'd hear about it. Nat would come fetch me if anyone melted down.

I didn't answer my own phone, though I kept an eye on it in case Tony called. It didn't surprise me that he didn't. He now had two murder cases to cope with, and was probably going nuts trying to figure out how they were connected.

I didn't think for a minute that they weren't, or that Vi's death wasn't murder. I hoped Tony was finding helpful evidence.

When Kris brought me her drafts of the two statements about Vi—both tastefully written—I offered to take the deposit to the bank. She looked truly grateful as she accepted.

"Is the phone going non-stop?" I asked.

"Pretty much, and I'm hoping we'll hear from Sandra Usher."

"Don't expect it today. She's probably just getting the news."

Kris shrugged. "If she does call, I want to be available."

I picked up the bank bag and my phone. "Any other errands while I'm out?"

"Not that I can think of."

I fetched my purse from my suite and headed downstairs. Before going out I checked on the staff. They all seemed to be doing all right, though Julio looked tight-lipped and kind of tense. Iz was silent and rather stern, though she smiled when I greeted her.

Nat was ringing up a purchase for a customer when I looked into the gift shop. "Going out? Good. Don't hurry back, we're doing fine."

That was the moment for me to say something teasing in

return, but I couldn't think of anything. I headed to my car, thankful that there were no emergencies.

The day was beautiful. Sunny but not too hot, with clouds creating some shade and promising a chance of more rain. My visit to the bank was uneventful. I was on my way back when I thought of Vi's mother.

I was at a stop light. I gripped the wheel, wondering if I should run to the nearest florist and place an order. Then I knew that I had to do better than that. I wasn't close to Rhonda, but I had been close to Vi. I owed Vi's mother a personal visit.

Their house was on the southeast side of town. I turned my car around and headed that way, remembering the times I'd dropped Vi off there when she hadn't driven to work. I stopped at a florist shop that I liked and picked out one of their ready-made arrangements, and drove on, trying to decide what I should say.

It wasn't easy. I knew that Rhonda would be broken-hearted, and that whatever I said wouldn't truly make it better. The only thing that would make her life better right now would be if it wasn't true that Vi was dead.

But it was true. And Rhonda would be in terrible pain. And I couldn't fix that. All I could do was let her know she wasn't alone.

There were two cars in her driveway. I considered going away, but that would be cowardly. I was here, I had flowers. I didn't have to stay long.

The house was an older one, stuccoed in the ubiquitous adobe brown that was seen all over Santa Fe. Walking up to the door with my offering held carefully before me, I couldn't help thinking of Vi. Her laughter, and more recently her tears. The stress she'd been feeling, stress she didn't want to burden her mother with.

A man answered the door.

"Is Rhonda awake?" I asked, offering him a polite way to refuse me. "I'm Ellen Rosings. Vi worked at my tearoom."

"I'm Bill Southerton, Rhonda's brother."

"Ellen?" Rhonda's voice, from inside the house.

Mr. Southerton—who had Rhonda's coloring, I realized belatedly—opened the door to let me in. The house was quiet; no radio, no music.

Rhonda met me at the entrance to her living room. She looked haggard, which was no surprise. She stopped, her gaze fixed on the flowers in my hands.

"How did you know?"

"I heard from Detective Aragón. And I'm afraid the news stations have been speculating."

She closed her eyes. I set the flowers down on an end table by a cream-colored sofa.

"I'm so sorry, Rhonda. Please let me know if there's anything I can do for you."

She pulled herself together and looked at me with a feeble smile. "Thanks."

I could tell she was on the edge of tears. I put a hand on her shoulder, just lightly, but it was enough. It was permission. She clung to me and cried, and I cried too.

We sat on the sofa and talked a little and held hands. I told her about Vi's singing the shepherd-boy; Rhonda hadn't been there that night.

Her brother came quietly in with a tray of coffee. I accepted some, and as soon as I had drunk it I rose to go, feeling I'd been there long enough. Rhonda thanked me for coming but didn't ask me to stay.

I said goodbye, repeating my condolences and my offer of help. Rhonda's brother saw me out, and at the door he quietly thanked me for stopping by.

"She's still in shock," he said.

I nodded. "I know what that's like. You're good to stay with her."

I said goodbye and went back to my car, resolving to bring a casserole by in the next couple of days. And I'd write Rhonda a letter of condolence. That was pretty much all I could do.

I drove back to the tearoom, feeling pretty calm. Visiting

Rhonda had done me good. I hoped it had done her a little good, too.

I parked and went in the back door, pausing to look into the kitchen. Julio was sitting at the break table, frowning at the floor. Ramon, rolling out dough for scones, looked up, glanced toward Julio, then looked back at me with eyes that silently asked for help.

I took a steadying breath, then walked over and sat across from Julio. He didn't move at first. I just waited, and finally he slowly raised his head and met my gaze, dark eyes full of pain.

"Why?" he said in a thick voice.

"I don't know."

"Somebody killed her. Didn't they?"

"I don't know, Julio. Maybe."

He closed his eyes and whispered something in Spanish. I didn't quite catch it.

"Would you like me to take you home?" I said after a moment.

He didn't answer. Just opened his eyes and stared off at nothing again.

"You've been working awfully hard, and this has been a shock. Why don't you call it a day?"

He looked toward the work tables. "I have to finish the...the ..."

I followed his gaze and saw what he'd been working on. Aria Cakes. His creation for Vi.

"I'll finish this batch," I said.

He dropped his face into his hands, but almost immediately straightened, wiping his cheeks. "No, I can do it."

"May I help?"

He gave me a long look, then nodded. I stood.

"I'll just take this upstairs," I said, lifting the bank bag. "Be right back."

I gave Kris the bag, left my purse in my suite and changed into comfortable shoes, then went back to the kitchen and put on an apron. Julio handed me the job of making the almond buttercream icing while he tended a pot of syrup on the stove. We worked in silence, assembling the long cakes, trimming and cutting them, and decorating them with toasted almond slices and the last of my candied violets. There weren't quite enough of those, so we had to break into the commercial ones, which weren't quite as delicate, to finish the batch.

Ramon put a tray of scones into the freezer just as Dee and Mick came in. From the look on Dee's face, they'd heard the news. I asked them both to step into the butler's pantry, not wanting to discuss Vi in front of Julio.

"Is it true?" Dee asked me. "Is it Vi? That's what the news is saying, but—"

"The police haven't announced it yet, but yes. Detective Aragón told me it's been confirmed."

Dee started crying. I offered to let her go home, but she shook her head.

"Why don't you go upstairs for a few minutes," I said. "Sit by the window. I'll bring you some tea."

She agreed, and headed upstairs escorted by her brother. I started a pot of tea, then checked with Rosa and Iz, who had everything under control, though they looked a little harried. I poked my head in the gift shop, where Nat was just saying goodbye to some customers.

"Shoo," she said to me. "You don't want to be up front. There's a news van camped out on the street."

"Crap." I glanced toward the front windows, but the wisteria vines obscured the street. "You OK here for now? Dee just came in and she needs a little support."

"Yes. Go."

"I owe you a huge margarita, Nat."

"Make it a Doña Tules."

"Yikes."

I went back to the kitchen, where Ramon met me at the door. "We're going home," he said, glancing toward Julio.

"OK. You driving?"

He nodded. He hadn't known Vi—I was pretty sure he hadn't

even met her—but he was obviously concerned about his cousin.

"Thanks, Ramon. See you tomorrow." I included Julio in that last. He looked tired, but nodded. I watched them get into Ramon's car, then put together my tea tray and took it upstairs.

Dee and Mick were up front by the window, two blonde heads together as they talked quietly. I joined them, gave them tea, listened to what they knew and confirmed what I could. I was getting numb from having to support my staff, but they had taken up the slack when I was out of it the previous day, so I owed them. Mick was mostly concerned, but Dee was quite upset. She, Vi, and Iz had been my original servers.

"I'm sorry we missed the meeting," Dee said.

"Yes—I wanted to have it early, because the news was talking about it."

She nodded. "The radio said she might have fallen."

I closed my eyes briefly. A fall from the ground level into the elevator pit probably wouldn't have killed her. A fall from the top of the stage...

My mind flashed to the end of *Tosca*, when Tosca threw herself off the balcony. That moment had given me a stab of fear, and I now realized why: I knew that the height from the top of the stage to the ground level was dangerous. Usher must have had something to land on, but if Vi had fallen from that spot accidentally...or been pushed....

She wouldn't have landed in the elevator pit, but if the B-lift had been down, that was a height of twenty feet or more. I began to wonder if she had fallen first, and then been placed in the pit.

I shook myself out of my reverie. These were thoughts I couldn't share with Dee.

"We'll have to wait for more information," I said.

"Detective Aragón didn't tell you?"

"No."

Kris came out of her office. "Ellen? Got a minute?"

I glanced at Dee, who was looking somewhat calmer. "Will you excuse me?"

Dee nodded with a small smile. Mick took her hand as I

stood.

When I stepped into Kris's office, she handed me some message slips. "I'm going, but I'll be in early tomorrow. I've forwarded the phone to your desk, if you don't mind watching it until six."

"OK. No word from Usher?"

She shook her head. "Channel seven is pushing hard for an interview. I told them absolutely not today."

"Let me guess. They're the ones camped out front."

"Are they? I'm not surprised. I gave them the non-committal statement, but they're going to want more."

I sighed. "As soon as the police confirm Vi's identity, give out the second statement."

"Will do. Have a peaceful night."

She left, and I went back to Dee and Mick, who were now sufficiently composed to go to work. I went downstairs with them to double-check that everyone else was all right (Iz stoutly refused to go home early), then returned to my office to work on my messages.

The stack Kris had handed me included a confirmation of the massage reservation that Nat had made for me, and the first three calls of condolence. I sighed, knowing there would be many more. I couldn't face talking on the phone about Vi, so I set them aside.

I monitored the phone calls. If Sandra Usher called, I'd pick up, but everyone else was getting voicemail, thank you. I had reason to be glad of this decision when I noted the first of several calls from news media.

The day crawled to a close. Iz and Rosa went home, then Nat, and finally Dee and Mick.

I was long past weary. I changed out of my dress and into some comfy clothes, and went to my kitchenette. In the fridge: yesterday's sandwiches and fruit. I decided I'd rather cook.

Chicken and risotto would be good. The risotto would take a little while, but I actually liked stirring it and watching it come together. And, my favorite recipe required some white wine, so

I'd have to open a bottle. Gee whiz.

I poured myself a glass of sauvignon blanc, started some chicken defrosting in the microwave, and put some broth on the stove to warm up. I didn't have a whole lot of supplies in the kitchenette, but there were onions and some slightly tired spinach that would be OK braised in butter. While the onions were sautéing, I went out into the hall and peeked out through the sheers over the front window.

The news van was still parked at the curb.

I went back to the stove and got the risotto started, wondering why they were bothering. They should be camped at the Opera, not here.

I heard muffled strains of Mozart: my phone. Still in my purse from earlier. I dug it out and saw that the call was from Gina. I answered as I headed back to the stove.

"Hi, girlfriend," I said.

"Dude, you're on the news!"

10

Huh? I haven't talked to anyone." I frowned, wondering if the news van was broadcasting an image of my front door.

"They're showing footage from when Sylvia was murdered, and saying you said Vi Benning was an exemplary employee. Were you really at the Opera when they found the body?"

I dropped my spoon in the risotto. "They're saying that?"

"Yeah. Is it true?"

I refrained from cursing, and used a fork to fish out the spoon. "Yeah, it's true. I was taking the backstage tour. There were maybe a dozen of us, and we all saw."

"Really? The reporter is making it out like it was just you."

I gritted my teeth. "Probably because I'm the only one who knew Vi."

"Are you a suspect?"

"No. Geez, Gina, I called it in!"

I hoped I wasn't a suspect. How could I be? I hadn't been near the opera until I went there with the tour.

Was there something Tony wasn't telling me?

"So they're saying this might be related to the murder of that opera singer last week."

I put the chicken in with the onions, splashed some wine over them, and topped up my glass. "Are they?"

"You're not going to share with me?"

"There's nothing to share, Gina. You know about as much as I do."

"I doubt that, with Detective Arrogant on the case."

So the media were hassling Tony, too? "Don't call him that, Gina. He doesn't deserve it."

"If you say so. You came up with it, remember."

"That was before I got to know him."

"How's that going, anyway? That dating the cop thing?"

I drank a swig of wine. "Right now neither of us has time. How's *your* love life?"

She chattered about her latest. I listened, adding more broth to the risotto, stirring, being Zen. Eventually she went back to the news media.

"You should give them an interview," she said.

"Not if they're painting me as a suspect."

"You can clear your name. And it would be great exposure for the tearoom."

"To be honest, we don't need it right now. Thanks to some word of mouth at the opera, we're booked solid for the next week."

"That's great! There's nothing like having to turn away business! This could make the tearoom the latest hot spot in Santa Fe. Just do one little interview—pick your favorite station."

Sometimes Gina could be a little too profit-focused for me. "Maybe in a day or two," I said. "I'm not up to it right now."

"Oh, of course. She was your friend. I'm sorry, Ellen."

"Thanks."

Stirring. Adding broth. Stirring.

"You're mad," Gina said.

"I'm tired. We're crazy busy. I've hired a new assistant chef, I'm hiring two more servers, and I might still need more help."

"Wow! Sounds like you need a drink! Want me to come pick you up?"

"No, thanks. I'm making dinner."

"How about tomorrow night? We can paint the town."

"Sorry, I've got an appointment for a massage. Nat's idea."

"Nat's smart. OK, girlfriend, I'll call you again on Sunday, how's that?"

I smiled. "OK."

"Love you gobs."

"Back at you. Bye."

The spinach and the chicken were done. I added the last bit of broth to the risotto, ground some pepper over it, dash of salt and a handful of grated Romano. Stirred it all together, then plated up my dinner and ate it slowly, in solitary state, at my petite dining table.

I was already feeling the wine, but I topped up my glass once more before putting the bottle in the fridge. I'd killed a little over half of it, but that included what went into the risotto.

I cleaned up the dishes, put away leftovers, and tidied the kitchenette, then went back to my wine. I grabbed my phone again and checked for anything from Tony. Nothing, so I sent him a short text asking if there was any news.

Stupid. He'd have contacted me if there was. I was just feeling lonely.

I carried my wine out into the hall. News van still out front. I went downstairs, leaving the lights off.

Outside it was dusk, so the parlors were filled with twilight. I went into the main parlor, closed the pocket doors between the piano and the front window, and sat down to play.

My music was packed away somewhere, so I played from memory. Bach, Satie, and some Elizabethan ayres I'd been fond of in high school. My technique was rusty to say the least, but the only one listening was Captain Dusenberry, and I believed he wasn't one to voice his opinions.

He was a music lover. Probably uncritical. I could almost imagine him sitting in one of the wing chairs, teacup on his knee, smiling as he listened.

By the time I'd played through all I could remember, it was getting too dark to see the keys. I closed the piano, feeling a little better, and took another swig from my wine glass. The wine was getting warm.

I stood, gazing around the dusky parlor, feeling a little lost. Drifting out into the hall, I was surprised by a sudden intense light coming through the lights that surrounded the front door.

I tiptoed back into the main parlor and gently opened the pocket door, edging toward the front window but keeping out of sight. The sheers were closed, though the drapes were open. I moved as close as I dared to the window, and peered through a gap in the sheers.

A guy came up the front walk carrying a big black case. The news van was still at the curb, its side doors open. A crew was setting up for a broadcast, probably the nine o'clock news. On my doorstep.

My first instinct was to open the front door and yell at them. Bad idea.

Second thought: call the cops.

Also a bad idea. The media would just report my recalcitrance and make it a part of their story. No, best course of action was to ignore them.

Annoyed, I went through the gift shop and back to Marigold, the most remote of my parlor seatings. Its window on the south side, overlooking the rose garden, was not in line of sight from the front door, but I closed the drapes anyway. I turned on a little lamp on a side table and made myself at home, curling up in a wing chair with my feet tucked beneath me.

This was where I'd had tea with Vi the previous Sunday. It seemed forever ago. Remembering her laughter and the pleasure we had shared mellowed my mood. Hard to believe she was gone.

Shying away from that thought, I looked around at the décor. It was mostly gold, with brown touches and small hints of orange. Not my favorite colors at all. They reflected the name, was all. I loved the space—it was probably my favorite seating, just because of its situation, but I'd never liked the colors.

Well, maybe it was time for a change.

I finished my wine. I didn't need to redecorate Marigold. Better to put the money toward paying down my mortgage.

Besides, I'd have to come up with a different flower name if I wanted something other than yellow or orange. I'd already used a lot of my favorite flowers. What was left? Honeysuckle? Morning glory? Lilac?

Violet.

A shiver went through me. Yes, of course. I'd do it.

A tribute to Vi.

A few tears came. I wiped them away, thinking of how the room would look done in shades of violet.

Yes. It would be lovely.

Oh, Vi.

A thump from the front *portal*, and voices. The news crew intruded.

I picked up my wine glass and turned off the lamp. Did they even realize that I lived here?

It didn't matter. They didn't know I was there, and that was fine with me. In my best ghost-like manner, I slipped out into the hall and up the stairs.

Friday morning found me dragging. It was not because of the wine, but because I'd slept poorly. Troubled dreams, too vague to remember, had denied me rest. I wanted to stay in bed, but I couldn't let my staff down, so I dragged myself into the kitchenette and started a kettle.

Two more days, Friday and Saturday, and then I could collapse.

I looked in the refrigerator and found the fruit that Julio had cut up for me two days before. It was a little tired, but still edible. I had it for breakfast while my tea brewed. My phone was by my chair, and I discovered that Tony had sent me a text at a horrid hour when he should have been asleep:

NOTHING IN POOL.

Disappointing, but not surprising. I was just glad I hadn't been awakened by it.

I turned my thoughts to what I should wear that day. The news of Vi's death would soon be official, if it wasn't already. I'd worn gray the day before, but I was feeling more depressed now, and it was more likely that people would notice what I chose to wear.

I had a mid-length navy dress that was very plain, which I often wore to funerals. That would do. No jewelry. Hair up in a simple bun. I'd look like a stereotypical schoolteacher, but that didn't matter. What mattered was that people who were close to

Vi would see that I acknowledged her loss as something real and serious.

Fortified by two cups of tea, I ventured across the hall. Kris was at her desk, though it wasn't yet nine. She had on a fairly conservative, for her, black dress and a necklace of plain jet beads. If I knew Kris, it was Victorian mourning jewelry.

"You're early," I said, stepping into her office. "Want some tea?"

"I've got coffee, thanks." She indicated a travel mug on her desk. Black, with a red hourglass à la black widow. "We've got another server candidate. I scheduled her for two on Monday, if that's OK. You won't need more than an hour between appointments, will you?"

"I doubt it. This another friend of a friend?"

"Another friend of Ramon's."

"We don't need all three, do we?"

"See what you think of them."

"All right."

"Oh, and a counselor from the Hospice Center is coming in at noon."

"Excellent. Thank you. They can use my office."

Kris nodded as she answered the phone. I checked my desk, glanced through my messages, decided they could all wait, and went down to the kitchen.

Julio's chef pants, muscle shirt, and hat were solid black. If we'd had any black aprons, he'd have put one on, no doubt. Other than this overt expression of mourning he seemed all right, and promised me five minutes to talk after he had the current batch of shortbread in the oven.

I went up front, just to see if the news crew had done any damage on the *portal*. Before approaching the door, where I'd be visible through the surrounding lights, I stepped into the parlor and peeked out the window. The van was gone.

I went outside, taking a deep breath of the morning air. Other than the disarrangement of a few tables and chairs, nothing was amiss. I straightened the furniture and went back inside to start some tea.

Julio poked his head in the pantry just as I was setting a pot to brew. "Done with the shortbread."

"I'll be right there."

I set a timer, then put it and the teapot on a tray and carried it into the kitchen. Sitting at the break table, I gestured for Julio to join me.

"You, too, Ramon. This is a kitchen conference."

They both came over and sat across from me. Ramon seemed fine. It was hard to recall how defiant he'd been when we'd first met; he was now deferential to both me and Julio, and I'd seen enough of him to know that his manners were excellent. I could only assume that he liked the job and was eager to keep it.

"First of all," I said, "do either of you have any concerns?"

They traded a glance. "Not really," said Ramon. "It's been busy, but you warned us it would be."

"You've been helping with the food more than I thought you would be, Ramon. Is that OK with you?"

"Sure. It's fun. Julio's teaching me stuff."

"Are you having any trouble keeping up with the dishes on top of that?"

"Not so far." He looked at Julio, who was staring at the table top. "I could probably help Julio more if I didn't have the dishwashing, too."

"Would you prefer that? Helping with the cooking?"

He hesitated. "It's not what you hired me for."

"That wasn't the question. Which would you rather be doing?"

"Cooking's fun."

"OK. I may look for another part-time dishwasher, then. Julio, are you OK with having Ramon help you, or do you need someone with more experience? No offense, Ramon," I added.

He shook his head, shrugging it off. We both looked at Julio.

"I hadn't thought about it," he said. "It's good to have help, since we're this busy. I don't mind showing Ramon how to do stuff. Long as he takes orders, eh primo?"

"Si, jefe."

"Ellen's the jefe," Julio said.

"You're the jefe in the kitchen," I told him. "I concede the title. Anything else either of you would like to talk about?"

Julio's expression went somber. "What about Vi?"

"I haven't heard anything more," I said.

"Will there be a service?"

"I'm sure there will. As soon as I hear, I'll let you know. As long as it doesn't interfere with next Wednesday's private party, you can have time off to attend."

"Thanks, but that's not what I meant. I meant here. Are we going to do something to remember her?"

There was pain in Julio's eyes and in his voice. It made me want to gather him up and hold him, but he probably wouldn't like that.

"I have some thoughts," I said, "but they're more long-term. What do you think we should do?"

"Something here. Just for us. Where we can all talk about it. We're so busy...." He swallowed. "Can we just do something after hours? It doesn't have to be fancy."

I nodded. He was right; we were all stressed, and hadn't really had time to properly acknowledge that we, as a group, had suffered a terrible loss.

"How about tomorrow evening?" I said. "Potluck supper, here, after we close?"

Julio nodded. "That would be good."

"Um," said Ramon, "I could bring my guitar."

"That would be wonderful, Ramon. Thank you." I looked up at the whiteboard, stood, erased my previous message about the staff meeting and wrote: POTLUCK 7:30 p.m. SATURDAY, MAIN PARLOR, TO REMEMBER VI.

"How's that?"

"Good," Julio said.

"Should I invite Vi's mom?" I asked, thinking it might do Rhonda some good.

"Sure, I guess."

"We'll also have a counselor here this afternoon, if you feel like talking to someone in the meantime."

Julio pressed his lips together. "We'll see. Got a lot to get done today."

"Then I'll let you get started. If I have time I'll come and help. Thank you both—you're doing a fantastic job."

I went upstairs, told Kris about the potluck, and sent a text to the staff about it for good measure. Then I called Rhonda's number and got her brother. I told him about our gathering and said they were both welcome to come if Rhonda felt up to it. He was non committal. No surprise.

Before I hung up, Kris was in the doorway, eyes gleaming with excitement. I said goodbye to Sam and looked at her.

"Usher called. The party's on."

"Oh."

"She wants a talk about Captain Dusenberry. Should I call Willow Lane?"

Did I want to deliver a talk about my ghost? "Yes, call her. The fee will cover it, right?"

"Oh, Usher's paying for any extras. We're talking string quartet at the moment, and ten cases of Gruet."

I blinked. "We don't have a liquor license!"

"The Opera can get a picnic license. They'll send a couple of their bartenders to serve."

"You told Ms. Usher about our occupancy limit, right?"

"Right, but there's also the *portal*. That gives us seating for an additional twenty, and we could put tables in the garden, with umbrellas for shade."

"Let's not," I said. "We don't want to disrupt the neighborhood."

Kind of a lame objection, since my neighbors were also businesses, but I didn't want this affair to turn into a block party. Not classy.

Kris drew herself up. She didn't quite pout, but she was disappointed.

"Don't worry, Ellen. I won't let it get out of hand."

"Occupancy plus twenty. That's the limit," I said.

"OK."

She went back into her office. I looked at my chaise longue, where my unfinished novel beckoned to me. Couldn't justify it, not when my staff were busting their behinds.

My phone buzzed with an incoming text. I glanced at it and saw that it was from Tony.

NEED MORE STEAK. PICK U UP @ 7?

I smiled in spite of myself.

NOT TONIGHT – GETTING A MASSAGE.

TOMORROW?

Too complex for texting. I dialed Tony's number. He picked up on the second ring.

"We're having a potluck after work tomorrow," I said. "The staff wants to remember Vi."

"Can I come?"

"Ah...well, I'm worried that would make them uncomfortable."

"I won't ask any questions. I'll just be a fly on the wall."

"Or in the ointment."

"You really think I'd bother them?"

I rubbed my forehead. "I don't know...I guess I'm feeling protective. If it looks like anyone's upset, will you make yourself scarce?"

"You bet. Kick me out whenever you want."

"Then all right. Seven-thirty."

"Can I buy you a drink after your massage? I need to consult with you."

"New developments?"

"Sort of."

"After my massage I'm going to pour myself into bed."

Silence never made me blush before.

I cleared my throat. "We could meet for breakfast."

"Tecolote?"

"Too far. La Fonda?"

"Pricey."

"My treat. It's my turn, and I don't have time to make you that dinner right now."

"We'll see. What time?"

"Eight. Meet you there?"

"You got it."

Dead line.

I wondered, not for the first time, if I could get Tony to read Miss Manners. He would probably equate it to torture, I suspected.

I worked my way through most of my neglected messages. Just when I was starting to think about lunch, Kris buzzed me.

"I have Willow Lane on the line. She wants to talk to you."

"All right."

She put the call through and I picked up. "Hello, Willow."

"Hi, Ellen. Your manager asked if I could talk about Captain Dusenberry at this private party next week. I'll have to reschedule a tour, but I think I can swing it."

"OK."

"What I wanted to ask you is whether your friend could do his demonstration again—of Captain Dusenberry's uniform and weapons."

She meant Tony. He'd done that for the Goth group—Ramon's friends—when I'd given a night-time tea for them in the dining parlor to get them to stop trespassing with their ghost hunts.

"Ah...I'm pretty sure he's not available, but he might be able to get someone else."

"OK. Could you let me know, or put me in touch with him?"

"I'll find out who to call and get back to you."

"Great. Thanks, Ellen. And thanks again for providing iced tea for my groups."

"Least I can do while we're so busy. Sorry you can't bring them in."

"That's all right. I'm telling them that we're planning tea/tour combos in the fall."

An idea we'd talked about. It had never quite come together, but fall would be a good time.

"After Fiesta," I said.

"Definitely. Maybe not until October, but I think it would be very popular that month."

Oy. Halloween. Yeah, it would.

"I think you're right. Let's connect in a couple of weeks."

"Sounds good. Thank you, Ellen."

We said goodbye and I made a note to ask Tony if one of his reenactor friends might be available for Usher's party.

Come to think of it...Tony might want to do it himself. Observing the opera crowd at play....

Maybe not. I'd tell him about it and see what he said.

My stomach growled. I went across to my suite, taking my phone with me, to look for lunch.

Two-day-old sandwiches: no. Carton of yogurt? I didn't have much else.

What the heck. It was Friday, almost the end of a long week. I called in an order for three pizzas and a giant salad to be delivered to the back door. On my way downstairs, I met Rosa on the landing, escorting a tall, slender man with pale blond hair, dressed casually and carrying a small folio.

"Ellen, this is Mr. Jackson."

"Loren," he said, nodding. His eyes were brilliant blue and friendly. "I'm from the Hospice Center."

I liked that he didn't offer to shake hands. A small detail of old-fashioned courtesy, but rare these days.

"Thank you for coming," I said. "I'm Ellen Rosings."

And I initiated the handshake. He smiled. His hand was warm, like his voice.

"I hope I can help," he said.

"Come on up and meet my manager. I thought you could use my office, if you'd like."

"I'm going back," said Rosa.

"Yes, thank you, Rosa. I'll be down shortly." I led Mr. Jackson the rest of the way up. "We're rather busy this week, which is adding to everyone's stress."

"What a wonderful space!"

He stepped forward, gazing at the front window where the sheers were glowing with light. I joined him.

"Thank you. It was sort of wasted, so I turned it into a sitting area."

He turned to me with a smile. "Not wasted at all. It must be a great place to rest and regroup. So light and airy. It makes one think of heaven."

"Are you religious, Mr. Jackson?"

"Please call me Loren, if you don't mind. I'm not evangelical, if that concerns you. I have to be open-minded about people's beliefs. But almost everyone has some concept of heaven, even if it's abstract."

His voice was gentle, and his face had a peaceful quality that I found set me at ease. Combined with his fair looks, it made him seem a little angelic. I could see why he'd make an effective counselor.

"Would it be all right if I used this area to meet with your staff?" he asked.

"Wherever you're comfortable. Have a look at my office, and then you can decide."

I stepped to the doorway and looked in at Kris. She was typing away, but looked up.

"Kris, this is Loren Jackson from the Hospice Center. My office manager, Kris Overland."

Loren nodded. "I think we talked on the phone yesterday. Nice to meet you."

"Hi," Kris said, watching him with a wary eye.

"This side is my office," I said, inviting Loren to follow me. I tucked the few message slips on my desk into a drawer.

He stood near the entrance, gazing around the room. "Interesting, how the roof impacts the space. This is an old building."

"1865. Are you an architect?"

"I was going to be. Two years toward a degree, but I wound

up changing directions."

I knew what that was like. I wondered if some personal tragedy had inspired him to become a counselor. None of my business, of course.

"If you don't mind, I think I'd rather use that sitting area," he said.

"Not at all. Anything you need? Paper and pen?"

He lifted his folio. "I think I have everything here."

"Would you like some tea? I'm afraid we don't serve coffee."

"Tea would be nice. Thanks."

We went back out to the hall. It was warm, so I cracked open the window while he made himself at home. "When the sun gets around to the west, you can close the drapes if it's too hot."

"OK. May I ask you a couple of questions?"

"Sure." I took a seat.

"Your manager—Kris?"

I nodded.

"She told me that one of your employees passed away this week, and that it's been in the news."

"Yes. Violetta Benning. She was an apprentice at the Santa Fe Opera, and..." I found my throat tightening. "Well, perhaps you've heard about it on the news."

He nodded, looking serious. "Yes. A tragedy to lose someone so young."

I took a steadying breath. "She was one of my first employees. Vi and Iz Naranjo and Dee Gallagher were the servers when we opened."

"I see. Are Iz and Dee here today?"

"Yes. Well, Dee will be in this afternoon—she might be here by now."

He made a note on a pad from his folio. "Is there anyone else Vi was close to?"

"Julio, my chef. I don't know if he'll want to talk...."

"If he doesn't it's all right, but please let them all know I'm here."

"What's the best way...should we have a sign-up sheet?"

"Probably not necessary. They'd each take a break, normally, right?"

"Usually."

"Then you might suggest they come up during their breaks if they'd like to talk, or have any questions. I have some information sheets. I'll leave some of those with you in case anyone's curious but shy."

"OK."

"Do you have any questions?"

I looked at him, then my gaze landed on his notepad. I didn't have a question, but my mind had jumped to the backstage tour.

"I understand you were at the opera when she was found," he said gently.

"Yes." I straightened in my chair. "I called the police. I know a detective. He's working on the Victor Solano case."

"Ah."

"Vi knew Mr. Solano quite well. She was very upset by his death."

"Upset enough to—"

"No. Vi wouldn't do that."

He gazed at me for a long moment, then wrote something on his pad.

I suddenly felt like I was being interrogated. I took a deep breath and stood.

"I should get downstairs. Is there anything else you need?"

"No, thank you. Just let your people know I'm here."

I nodded, then went down to the pantry and started a kettle. Rosa came in with a ravaged tea tray, which she took through to the kitchen. When she came back I asked her to take some cups and saucers upstairs, and told her about Loren. I set a large pot of Keemun brewing, then stepped into the kitchen.

Julio was breaking eggs into a bowl. Ramon was measuring flour into another. He looked up with a quick smile.

"I ordered pizza for everyone," I said.

That got Julio to look up. "I could have made pizza."

"You're busy. Yes, I know yours would be better."

That got a reluctant smile out of him. I proceeded to tell them about Loren, and suggested they go up and say hello to him on their breaks. Then I left them to consider that and went back to the pantry, where the tea had just finished brewing. I put the pot on a small tray along with milk and sugar, and carried it upstairs.

Rosa was sitting with Loren. They both glanced up as I set the tea on the table before them, next to the tray of cups that Rosa had brought up. I left again immediately, in case they were having a productive discussion, and went back downstairs to encourage Iz to see Loren on her break.

Nat was in command in the gift shop. I wasn't worried about her emotional state, but for the sake of thoroughness I told her about Loren, and also about the pizza.

"That all sounds excellent," she said. "I like the potluck, too."

"Julio's idea."

"OK if I come?"

"You look like staff to me."

She smiled as a customer came up to the register with some leaf tea to purchase. "This week, anyway."

I went back to the pantry, made a round of the parlors with a pot of tea, and checked on the outdoor tables. By then, Rosa had come downstairs and the pizza had arrived. I ate lunch at the staff table, then went upstairs to check my phone.

Iz was sitting with Loren, talking in a low, intense voice. I went into my office, checked the phone and a couple of slips Kris had left on my desk, returned a call and then stepped into Kris's office.

"There's pizza downstairs."

"Thanks. I was just about to go to the bank."

"Want me to go?"

"No, I need a break, but thanks."

We went downstairs together and I donned an apron and presented myself to Julio. He put me to work on sandwiches. Ramon was cutting out scones on the other table, and Julio was doing something at the stove.

After half an hour or so, I heard Iz and Rosa talking in the pantry. "I think Loren's free, if anyone's interested," I said.

Ramon glanced at me, then at Julio. Neither of them said anything.

Well, I couldn't force them.

I finished the sandwiches, covered them and slid them into the fridge. Julio gave me a batch of boiled eggs to peel.

My thoughts kept returning to Vi as I worked. I recalled our last two conversations, both here in the tearoom. Had she said anything that might give me a clue to who had attacked her?

The director of Cesar Chavez had yelled at her during rehearsal. Not necessarily a prelude to murder, but she had seemed surprised and confused by his wrath. Unless he had some connection to Victor Solano, though, he wasn't a very likely suspect.

I was, of course, assuming that the two murders were linked. It was possible they weren't, but my instinct told me they were. Vi had somehow presented a danger to the killer, and he had killed again to protect himself.

Or herself. Sandra Usher was a possibility.

I thought about Tony's sketch of the romantic involvements in the opera company. Usher was possibly sleeping with Neil Passaggio (that's why his wife had confronted her), but it looked like she wasn't sleeping with Ebinger, her onstage lover. Vi had said they didn't like each other.

Which made the comment Tony and I had overheard from the Brit make no sense. "Practically snogging him onstage." That could refer to Ebinger and Usher (but apparently didn't), or to Usher and Solano (but she didn't seem devastated by his death). Who else had practically been snogging onstage? I couldn't think of anyone. Tosca and her lover and Scarpia were the only romantic—or perhaps sexual was a better word—relationships in the opera.

There was one other romance that I knew of, between Carter and Harrison, but I couldn't recall a moment when they'd touched onstage. They apparently preferred to do their snogging in private.

Vi had said that everyone had been on edge since Solano's death. From what I'd chanced to observe, that had also been true on Friday night—a week ago, now—the night Solano was killed. Was it really a coincidence that the Passaggios had argued, and Mrs. Passaggio taken the rather extreme step of going backstage during a performance to chew out one of the artists, just before the murder?

And another unusual circumstance was the sudden withdrawal of the singer who should have performed the shepherd-boy, leading to Vi's singing the role. I hadn't even met the woman—Lydia, Vi had called her. I wondered if Tony had talked to her. I was curious why she had canceled.

I was out of eggs. I disposed of the eggshells and presented the bowl of peeled eggs to Julio.

"Deviled, or egg salad?"

"Deviled."

Julio pushed a recipe card across the table to me. I took it and the eggs back to my station and collected everything I'd need: seasonings, mayonnaise, watercress for garnish, tray for the finished eggs. Julio's recipe was different from mine, but he was the jefe. I did it his way.

I was just piping filling into the last row of egg halves when Nat came in. "There you are. That nice young man said to tell you he's got time to talk to a couple more, if anyone wants to go up."

"Did Dee get to see him?" I asked.

"Yes."

"Does he need more tea?"

"I just set a fresh pot brewing for him."

"Thanks."

I stepped over to Ramon, who was wiping down his end of the work table. "Want to talk to the counselor? I think this is the last call."

He shrugged, then glanced at Julio, who was being deaf. I gave Ramon my best pleading-puppy look.

"OK, I'll go say hi. Need a break anyway."

"You can take the tea up with you," Nat said, leading Ramon into the pantry.

I glanced at Julio. Still deaf. Writing something.

Resisting the urge to bug him, I garnished my eggs with watercress leaves, then covered them and put them in the fridge. Cleaned up my work area, then decided to check on the guests. Abandoning my apron, I went to the butler's pantry, armed myself with a fresh pot of tea, and sallied forth.

The parlors were filled with small groups enjoying their tea and conversation. Everyone seemed content, until I looked into Hyacinth and found a solitary gentleman there who looked rather forlorn. He was a few years older than I, very clean-cut with short dark hair and chiseled features. His face looked familiar.

I took a step into the room. "Good afternoon."

He had been staring vacantly at the empty fireplace, but looked up at me with questioning eyes. I was sure I had seen him before.

"I'm Ellen Rosings, the owner. May I warm up your cup?"

He proffered his empty cup. As I filled it, I noticed a slice of Aria Cake, untouched, on his plate.

I don't know why, but that clicked a memory into place for me. "You're Mr. Ebinger, aren't you?"

He nodded, his gaze drifting back to the fireplace.

"I was at the Opera last Friday. You sang magnificently."

"Thank you."

"I'm so sorry about Mr. Solano."

A frown pinched his brow. "Thank you," he said again, barely above a whisper, then looked up at me with a gaze that was suddenly sharp and sent my mind back to Tosca: his character's torment, anger and grief.

"Victor asked me to make this reservation. We were going to come together. I almost canceled, but I decided...because he wanted me to come here...."

This was not a man who had killed. This was a man in pain.

"I understand he recommended us to a number of people," I said gently. "It was very kind of him."

"Yes. He was kind."

"Is there anything I can do for you?"

I meant more than tea and sandwiches. I was tempted to invite him to talk to the counselor upstairs, but that would probably be too forward.

"No, thank you," he said. "I'm all right."

"Well, let us know if you need anything."

He surprised me with a stunning smile, then subsided into reverie once more. I left him to his solitude, wishing I could do more and knowing I couldn't. Maybe I would slip him one of Mr. Jackson's cards before he left.

I returned to the kitchen, where I found Julio making a list. He looked up at me, then tore the page off the pad and handed it to me.

"Gonna need some groceries for tomorrow."

"OK. You need more help here, or should I go get this now?"

"We're caught up, pretty much. Think I'll go home, if you don't mind. Tomorrow's going to be a long day."

I glanced at the clock. Past three-thirty.

"Sure. Thanks, Julio."

I looked over the list and surreptitiously watched him get ready to leave. He always patrolled the whole kitchen before he clocked out. He traded a nod with Mick as he passed the dishwashing station. That little gesture made me feel better about Julio's state of mind.

Macho kid. Didn't want to talk to the counselor, though he probably needed it more than any of us.

Well, at least Loren's time hadn't been wasted. He'd probably done Iz and Dee some good.

I headed upstairs to get my purse. The drapes were partway drawn over the front window, and even so it was warm. The swamp cooler was humming away, though with the humidity outside it wasn't very efficient.

Ramon stood by the window, hands in pockets, Facing Loren.

He gave me a sharp look, which I answered with a smile as I nabbed one of Loren's cards from the table, then went into my suite.

Armed with purse and phone, I stepped across to ask Kris if she needed anything and tell her where I was going, then headed downstairs again. Julio was gone. Dee and Iz were setting up tea trays in the pantry, raiding the sandwiches and eggs I'd labored over. I spoke with them briefly and was glad to find them both in even spirits. They assured me everything was under control and I was safe to go shopping.

I'd have preferred a nap, actually, but oh well.

I looked in on Mr. Ebinger and found him signing a credit card slip for his bill. Wishing I'd thought to make his tea complimentary, I handed him Loren's card.

"Mr. Jackson has been very helpful to us. You might wish to give him a call."

He glanced at it, then at me. "Thanks."

"Thank you for coming."

He sighed. "I'm glad I did."

Closure. I smiled, understanding, and quietly left.

Julio's list was fairly short, mostly staples. Despite bumping our grocery orders on Monday, we hadn't quite had enough to get us through Saturday. I drove to the nearby shopping center on the north side of town and hit the grocery store there, picking up some sodas for the potluck while I was there, and was back at the tearoom in less than an hour.

Ramon had left. Except for Mick washing dishes, the kitchen was quiet. I put away the groceries and took the receipt up to Kris. To my surprise, Loren was in her office, sitting in her visitor's chair. He looked around at me and smiled.

"Groceries," I said to Kris, handing her the receipt. She nodded, her face neutral.

I turned to Loren. "Thank you for coming. I think you've helped quite a bit."

"I hope so. I'm sorry I didn't get to speak with your chef."

"He wasn't ready. He and Vi were close friends."

He nodded. "I've left a few of my cards on the table out where I was sitting, and a couple of handouts. Anyone is welcome to call me any time."

"Thank you."

He stood, stepping out from under the sloping roof until he could stand straight. "I guess I'll be going, unless you'd like to talk a bit."

God, his eyes were blue.

"Thanks," I said. "Maybe later. I'm still processing."

He nodded and headed for the hall. I walked out with him and he turned to me with an inquiring look. "You've done this before," he said.

"Not this exactly. My parents are both gone."

"And there have been some deaths in the building."

That surprised a laugh out of me. "Well, yes. It's an old building."

He smiled. "I've learned a few interesting things about it today."

"I'm sure you have."

"You're doing wonderfully, all things considered."

This was getting close to stuff I didn't want to discuss, so I just nodded. Loren looked around the hall once more.

"You've created a peaceful atmosphere. Downstairs, too."

"That's the idea. This is a place for people to get away for a while."

"Much needed in the modern world." He smiled. "I'm glad to have met you."

"Thanks."

"Please call me any time. About anything."

He held out a card. I took it, not quite sure to interpret that last. He smiled again, and headed down the stairs.

I allowed myself a sigh, since I was alone. I was so ready for this day to be over.

I put my purse in my suite, checked my desk (nothing on fire), and poked my head in Kris's office. "Everything good?"

"Yes."

"Hope I didn't interrupt an important conversation."

"With that Loren guy? No."

"He's pretty good, I think."

"I thought he was kind of pushy."

"Maybe a little."

Ever the cool and collected Goth, my Kris. It occurred to me that I didn't know whether she and Vi had been close. I suspected not; their personalities were rather different, and Kris was a couple of years older.

I went down to the gift shop to talk with Nat. She and Dee were discussing where to display some new tea accessories that had arrived that day. The shop was already crammed with infusers, tea cozies, teapots, and tea-themed knick-knacks.

Eventually I might have to give up Poppy, or even Poppy and Hyacinth, in order to expand the gift shop. I'd have to ask Kris to estimate how much income we'd gain from retail sales as opposed to how much we'd lose without those two seating areas.

I would never give up Marigold, soon to become Violet, or its neighbor, Dahlia. Both areas shared a fireplace, and were large enough for parties of four.

"Nat, when you have a minute, I'd like to bend your ear."

"Of course, sweetie. Dee, I think you're right. Go ahead and move the note cards to the shelf and put the infusers on the table with the teapots."

Brushing her hands, Nat came up to me with a smile. I invited her to walk in the garden with me and we went out the front, past a couple of parties enjoying tea on the portal.

The roses were happily baking in the sunshine. A warm breeze wafted different scents to us as we walked between the bushes and around the south side of the house.

"Remember your massage tonight," Nat said.

"Oh, I haven't forgotten. I'm counting the minutes." I pulled the petals off a faded rose and held them to my face for the scent. "You going to Mr. Ingraham's?"

"Yes."

"Give him my best."

"I will. You all right, Ellen? You didn't get a chance to talk with the counselor."

"I have his number. That's not why I asked you to come out here." I paused outside Marigold's window. "I'm planning on making a change, and I'll need your help. Remember how you never liked the color of the chairs in Marigold?"

She nodded. "They're too brown."

"Well, I've decided to redecorate that whole area and change its name."

"Really?"

"To Violet."

She glanced toward the window. "Oh, Ellen. That's a lovely idea."

I smiled, blinking, caught off guard by the sudden tightening of my throat. Nat gathered me into a hug.

"You poor dear. You miss her terribly, don't you?"

I nodded. "I've missed her since she went to the Opera, but I always thought she'd be back."

"Oh, honey."

I stepped back and rubbed at my eyes, annoyed with myself. "Anyway, I want the chairs and the loveseat to be violet, but I can't decide if I should have them reupholstered or just get new ones."

"Reupholstering takes forever, and costs almost as much as new furniture. I'd say just get new ones. We could put the old ones in the front hall for people who are waiting to be seated."

"That's a good idea. Will you help me pick out the fabric for new drapes? And new decorations."

"I'd be honored."

"I don't know when we'll have time..."

"We'll make time. This is important."

She'd confirmed what I'd been thinking but trying to logic myself out of. She was right, though. This was important and it couldn't wait. Or not long, anyway. It would have to wait until after Wednesday.

"Thanks, Nat," I said. "You're the best aunt in the world."

"And you're the best niece. Now, it's—" She checked her watch. "—just after five. You're done for today." She took my arm and started back toward the front door. "Go up and change, grab your swimsuit, and go on up to Ten Thousand Waves."

"It's too early!"

"Soak in the hot tub until it's time for your massage. I'll close up the tearoom."

"But you'll be late for the dinner party."

"No, I won't. It's cocktails until seven-thirty. Don't fret. Have a relaxing evening, and I'll see you tomorrow."

"Well...yes, ma'am!"

We stepped through the front door and she smooched my cheek. "Go on, scoot."

I followed my orders. Kris passed me on the stairs and we said goodnight, see you tomorrow. I changed into jeans and a caftan top, grabbed a sweater in case it got cold later, and snuck out the back door of the tearoom.

Ten Thousand Waves is one of my favorite places on earth. I've been going there since I was a teen. It started out as a Japanese spa with a handful of hot tubs. It has grown to include rooms for overnight guests, a fabulous gift shop, and a full-service spa with amazing treatments and fascinating Japanese plumbing.

One of the best things about 10k Waves is its location, only a few minutes from the Plaza on the road to the ski basin, but set apart in a beautiful piñon forest with gorgeous Japanese-style landscaping. The walk up the path from the parking lot is a journey from modern mundanity to peaceful sanctuary. The door to the spa is next to an indoor waterfall, the sound of which follows the visitor up the short staircase to the lobby/gift shop.

Though I'd brought along a suit as Nat suggested, I opted to hang out in the women's tub rather than the communal tub. I was tired, and I didn't want to have to watch how I sat or keep an eye on who was looking at me. I wore the suit anyway, more as a sign that I wanted privacy than from any concern about nudity. As it happened, there were only two other women there, one of whom appeared to be asleep on a lounge chair. The other was in the pool. I gave her a cursory glance as I joined her, noting dark hair up in a bun, skin a shade too tan, and tension lines around her mouth.

As I entered the tub, I breathed a sigh of relief. River stones provided a variety of smooth shapes underfoot, and the hot water made my muscles very happy. The tub was long and oval-shaped. I moved to the far end, leaned back, and looked up through pine boughs to the sky.

The sun hadn't set, but it was obscured by the trees and by hills to the west. A warm twilight filled the space under the canopy, with just an occasional breeze to stir the branches. I let go of all my worries—or rather I pushed them away—and concentrated on appreciating my surroundings.

The smell of the pine trees. Bird song. The endless motion of the water, ripples reflecting fragments of sky on the pool's surface, stirred by the tiniest movement from myself or the other woman.

Water.

That little message had been a dead end. Poor Willow.

I looked up at the sky again, noting clouds above the pines. I wasn't here to worry about Willow.

A splash made me glance up; the other woman was heading for the cold plunge in the corner. I didn't need that kind of stimulation, but after a while I did get up and go inside to the sauna. I took a paper cup of water in with me and drank it while I sweated, then took a quick shower rinse and returned to the tub.

I stared at the shards of light dancing on the water. Shards, not knives. Not as sharp.

Where was the knife, if not in the water?

In some landfill or arroyo miles away. Or not. By now, the police might have given up on finding it.

Find the weapon, find the killer. But maybe that was only true on TV.

As a detective, I was pretty sure I sucked.

11

When my fingertips started to look like prunes, I got out and went back to the dressing room, showered, donned my complimentary kimono and went to report for my massage. I was a few minutes early, so I sat in the waiting room and sipped more water, and watched the beautiful people go by.

There were always beautiful people at 10k Waves. I sometimes wondered if the communal tub was a pickup rendezvous, but it hadn't ever felt like that to me. Just a place where beautiful people liked to lie around being beautiful, admiring themselves and each other.

"Ellen?"

I looked up and saw the hostess standing at the reservations podium. I went to report to her and was introduced to my massage therapist, a tall, lean, and glowing woman named Naomi. She led me to a private room and proceeded to turn my tense muscles into melted goo.

I nearly fell asleep on the massage table. Stray thoughts ping-ponged around in my head, but I was too busy appreciating the massage to give them much attention.

I was just wondering if it would ever end, when it did. So of course, I immediately wished for more. I thanked Naomi profusely, left her a whopping tip, and oozed back to the dressing room for a long, hot shower.

Back in the lobby, I surrendered my kimono and splurged on a bottle of house-brand yuzu lotion. I kept yawning on the drive home, and when I got there I went straight to bed, expecting to fall into deep, untroubled sleep.

Instead, I dreamed.

I was at the Opera, performing the role of Tosca. Victor Solano was Scarpia, but he kept paying more attention to

Cavaradossi than to me, which pissed me off. The scene where Scarpia tormented Cavaradossi went on forever, with Scarpia gloating and caressing him in almost an obscene manner while I watched from upstage, with the wind blowing my long black hair around me through the open back of the stage. I got madder and madder, and started trying to plan how to swap my stage knife for a real one in Act Three, but the real knife was in the water and I couldn't fish it out during the performance.

Then Tony showed up and halted the opera in mid-aria. Solano was angry and started arguing with him, and Tony put him in handcuffs to march him away, but he wrestled free, ran up to the top platform where I was standing, threw me a look that said "This is all your fault," and jumped off the back of the stage.

I sat up with a gasp.

In my bed. Safe. Dark. Oh, crap.

I turned on my bedside lamp. My limbs were tingling with adrenaline-spiked fear. The room felt stuffy and warm.

The clock said three-thirty.

Knowing I wouldn't get back to sleep right away, I put on a light robe and slippers, opened the window a crack to let some fresh air in, and shuffled to the bathroom. The image of Solano falling away from me kept returning, his mournful expression burned into my brain.

Hot milk. Cure for all ills.

I put some milk in a pan on the stove and wandered over to the window. All quiet outside; no rain, no wind. The streetlight on the corner cast shadows across the neighboring business and my garden.

What a wretched dream. It had all kinds of hits to my self-esteem: performance anxiety, rejection (in favor of a homosexual relationship, no less), guilt...

Wait a second.

Practically snogging him onstage.

Holy crap!

Scarpio and Cavaradossi. Their scene together had been

almost caressing, in creepy juxtaposition to the torture. It had bothered me when I saw it.

Solano and Ebinger. Could they have been having an affair?

I wondered if Tony still had his chart.

A warning hiss sent me back to the stove just in time to rescue the milk from boiling over. I poured it into a mug, sprinkled a dash of nutmeg on top, and curled up with it in my favorite chair.

I tried to recall my brief conversation with Ebinger that afternoon. He had plainly been upset by Solano's death, but I hadn't thought that unusual. They were colleagues, working closely together. Now, as I thought back, it seemed obvious to me that Ebinger had been grieving. I'd even given him Mr. Jackson's card, so I'd known it, on some level.

And Solano had apparently made a pass at Julio. So he might be gay or bisexual.

Who was it who had objected to the onstage snogging? I frowned, thinking back.

Neil. Neil Passaggio.

But why? Wasn't he supposed to be sleeping with Sandra Usher?

My brain hurt.

I was also out of milk. I cleaned up the kitchenette and went back to bed, still trying to puzzle out the connection between Passaggio and Solano and/or Ebinger.

I woke to the thump of a car door closing outside. Turned my head to look at the clock: 6:30. Had to be Julio.

I groaned and rolled over, but I was awake and the snogging dream came back to pester me. I got up and found a notepad, scribbled down the details before I could forget them, then got dressed. Black broomstick skirt and lavender blouse. I wasn't feeling creative.

I had time to make some tea before heading to La Fonda to meet Tony. I drank it at my desk, sorting through messages and making notes on things I wanted to talk to Tony about: Lydia something, Ebinger, snogging. When the tea was gone, I tucked all my notes into my purse and headed downstairs.

Julio and Ramon were both there. They must be carpooling, I decided. Julio looked moody but all right. He even offered me some of his coffee.

"No, thanks. I'm on my way to breakfast. I'll be back by ten."

"'Kay."

I walked to the Plaza and across it to La Fonda. Despite the early hour there were plenty of tourists wandering around. It was peak tourist season, and coming up on the Spanish and Indian Markets. I had a hazy idea that one of them was the next weekend; I'd have to check my calendar.

La Fonda was full of even more tourists than the Plaza, many of them waiting for tables at the restaurant. I bit my lip, thinking we'd probably end up in the French Pastry Shop, which I hoped Tony wouldn't mind. I couldn't spend all morning waiting for a table.

As I approached La Plazuela, Tony rose from an armchair to meet me. He'd made an effort: black dress shirt tucked into his jeans, nice belt with a silver buckle.

"Hi," I said. "I should have remembered it would be crowded."

He picked up his motorcycle helmet from the floor beside his chair. "I made us a reservation."

"You're a genius!"

We were seated immediately and waited on promptly. Tony ordered huevos rancheros and I chose a spinach and mushroom omelet. When we had our coffee, he took out his pocket notepad.

"Remember your oath of secrecy," he said, looking up at me under dark eyebrows.

I crossed my heart and held two fingers in the air.

"We found the Brit," Tony said. "Name's Richard Whitby. The people he was talking about were—"

"Solano and Ebinger."

He gave me a grouchy look. "You knew?"

"I figured it out last night. Go on—what else did he say?"

Tony grimaced. "A lot of stuff that wasn't to the point. This guy was flaming."

"Oh."

"But what was to the point was that he implied—didn't say, mind you, but implied—that Neil Passaggio was pissed off because of jealousy."

"Jealousy of Solano and Ebinger."

"Yeah."

"Because...?"

"He wouldn't say. Claimed he didn't know, but I think he was scared of retaliation. My guess is that Passaggio was porking one of them. Sorry."

He gave me a swift glance. I waved it away, but frowned.

"Everything I found about Passaggio online was about him and women," I said.

"Yeah. That's his public face."

"And his wife was jealous of him and Usher."

"Uh-huh."

"So if he was—involved—with Ebinger or Solano, why wasn't there any gossip about it?"

"Because he didn't want it public."

I sipped my coffee. "Why? What harm could it do? He's in the performing arts. Not exactly a conservative industry."

"His wife comes from a conservative family."

"Oh? Pardon me, but from what little I've seen and heard, I don't think he would care much about what his wife thinks."

"Oh, yes he does. She pays the bills."

I put down my cup. "The trophy wife?"

Tony grinned. "She's from big oil money. Went to Yale. It's more like he's a trophy husband."

"They don't seem very happy together."

Tony tore open a packet of sugar and dumped it in his coffee. "Well, no surprise, if he's been sleeping around."

"And she thought it was with Sandra Usher, and even yelled at her backstage! Jeez!"

"He's been sleeping with Usher, too."

"What?!"

Our breakfasts arrived. We were silent until the waiter had arranged everything on the table, asked if we needed anything else, and departed.

"Are you serious?" I said softly.

He already had a mouthful of huevos. "Mm-hm."

"Did someone tell you that, or is it just rumor?"

He washed down his food with a swig of coffee. "Usher told me."

"Let me guess. You charmed it out of her."

"Hell, no. She's a bitch on wheels. She couldn't wait to brag about it."

I poked at my omelet, though I'd pretty much lost my appetite. This description of my most extravagant customer made me uncomfortable. I was still wondering whether I should defend Usher when Tony went on.

"She'd been sleeping with Solano, too."

I put down my fork. "Do you still have that chart you made?"

"It's up on the whiteboard at the station. You should see it now. It's like a diagram of the solar system on crack."

I took a swallow of coffee. "Did you ever talk to the singer Vi took over for? Lydia..."

"Taylor. Yeah, I talked to her. She called in sick because Passaggio had made a pass at her the day before at a rehearsal. She was still upset."

"Jeez, who does he think he is? Casanova?"

Tony made no comment.

I thought back to my conversation with David Ebinger. I was reluctant to discuss his grief with Tony, but felt I should at least inquire where he stood.

"What about Ebinger?" I said, stirring my coffee. "Did you talk to him?"

"Guy's an oyster. He's not giving anything up. But he was onstage during Act Three except at the very beginning, so he's got an alibi."

"So he's not a suspect?"

Tony's eyes narrowed as he chewed another bite of food. He

swallowed and stabbed a papita.

"I'm pretty sure Passaggio's our guy. Trouble is, his wife is providing him with an alibi. I think she's lying, but I can't prove anything. We still don't have the murder weapon."

I sipped my coffee. "What about Vi? Do you think he...."

"Yeah. I think she knew something, or found out something, that made her a threat. So he killed her."

I closed my eyes. I ought to ask about the autopsy results, but I was becoming overwhelmed by sadness.

"She was dead before she went in the pit," Tony said.

I looked at him, swallowing the tightness in my throat.

"Sorry if that's too abrupt. I just wanted you to know she didn't suffer. She was killed by a fall from a height. We suspect from the top of the stage, after which she was placed in the pit. Should I stop?"

I shook my head and sipped more coffee. I had to hold the cup with both hands.

"The evidence team found some of her DNA on top of the lift platform. We think the lift was down when she fell, then someone raised it enough to push her into the pit, then lowered it again."

I winced.

"I'll stop."

I traded the coffee for my water glass. "Who knew how to raise and lower the B-lift?"

"It's not rocket science. There are two buttons, 'up' and 'down'."

"No safety lock or anything? No key?"

"Nope."

I frowned. Something was niggling at the back of my mind.

"I want to see it," I said.

"What, the B-lift?"

"Yes. I...want to look at it from the stage. Can you get me in?"

"They won't be happy. Every time I go back there I get sour looks."

"You can do it, though, right?"

He tilted his head. "There's nothing to see. There wasn't much even when the techs were processing it, and it's been cleaned up since then."

"I'm not looking for evidence. That's your job."

"What, then?"

"I'm not sure."

I couldn't put my feeling into words, or at least not words that would make sense to Tony. If I told him about my dream he'd dismiss it. But I had the feeling there was something to see, as strongly as I'd had when I'd signed up for the tour to check the water in the pool.

Bad example, Rosings. You didn't find anything then.

But as a result of that hunch, I'd been present when Vi's body was found.

A cold shiver went through me.

Tony glanced up from mopping up chile sauce with a tortilla. I realized he'd been silent for a couple of minutes. Letting me think things through.

"Vi told me she was distracted by something she saw from the upstage platform," I said. "She got in trouble for missing a cue."

Tony's brows drew together. "When?"

"It would have been...Monday afternoon, during rehearsal. Probably late afternoon."

"And she died Tuesday night."

"It might not be related..."

"At this point I don't care. The Solano murder's already getting cold. If we can solve Vi's murder we might kill two birds with one stone."

"I don't know if this will solve her murder."

"It's worth a shot, right? You want to go now, or wait until afternoon?"

I put down my glass. The conditions under which Vi was distracted wouldn't occur until afternoon, but it would be harder to get onto the stage then. They'd be preparing for the evening's performance.

Also, it would be harder for me to get away from the tearoom then.

"Let's go now."

"You're not finished."

"Not hungry." I swallowed the last of my coffee and looked around for the waiter.

Tony paid the bill, forestalling my argument by saying there wasn't time. "Did you drive?"

"No, I walked."

"We'll go on my bike, then."

"I'm in a skirt!"

"It's full, right?"

"It could get caught in your wheels!"

"Not if you wrap it around your butt." He grinned as he stood and picked up his helmet. "I'll help."

He led me out of the hotel to a side street where he'd parked his bike. I thought about suggesting that we go to my place and get my car, but that would just take extra time, which neither of us could afford. Plus, he would think I was chicken.

Which maybe I was.

I don't much like motorcycles. I don't like the noise and the vibration, even when I'm not on one.

I was at a loss for how to mount a motorcycle gracefully in a skirt. Miss Manners had not covered that, so far as I knew.

Tony got on his bike and sat grinning at me. I pulled the skirt to my left while I swung my right leg over. The skirt hiked up above my right knee.

"Good," Tony said. "Now wrap the extra fabric across your lap and sit on it."

I did so. Now both my legs were on display.

"Is it going to stay?" he asked.

I tugged at the skirt. "I think so."

"Put this on." He handed me the helmet. I strapped it on, then wrapped my arms around his waist.

"Hold tight," he said, and started the engine.

He glided away from the curb and into traffic. Maybe he was

humoring me, but it seemed gentler than the last time I'd ridden with him. I dreaded getting on the highway, though.

He turned onto Paseo de Peralta heading north. I caught myself holding my breath and deliberately inhaled. To my surprise, Tony took a left turn and drove to the tearoom, pulling up beside my car in the back.

"Change your mind?" I said, my voice muffled by the helmet.

"Safer."

Unspeakably relieved, I got off the bike and gave him back his helmet, shook my skirt down around my legs, then took out my keys and unlocked my car. Tony went around to the passenger side and deposited the helmet on the back seat. I drove out of town and got on the highway to the Opera.

"You just wanted me to show you my knees," I said, when I was sufficiently composed.

He grinned. "I wanted to see if you'd do it."

"You know I dislike motorcycles."

"Uh-huh."

I shot him a dirty look and devoted my attention to driving.

Despite the early hour, there was already an attendant in the Opera's parking lot. He waved us toward a specific space in the lot that was empty except for three other cars. I humored him and parked where he indicated. We walked down to the entrance, where a flash of Tony's badge and a few words of explanation got us past the gate.

My heart was thumping. Maybe it was leftover reaction from the bike ride. I felt nervous and unsteady, and was tempted to slide my hand through Tony's elbow. It would cramp his cop style, though, so I didn't.

We walked around the south side of the house. I hadn't been back since the backstage tour, of course. Memories of that awful morning increased my anxiety.

The stage was set with a collection of gray, geometric platforms of varying heights, connected here and there by small sets of stairs. Looked like an uncomfortable set. At the back of the top platform was a railing that appeared to have been made out of metal pipe. I wondered if it was part of the set or if it was a safety precaution.

This must be the set for *Cesar Chavez;* the premiere had been the previous night. They'd be switching to *Tosca* soon, unless there was a rehearsal for something else in the afternoon.

A stage hand came out onto the platforms and knelt down at a corner where two of them joined. A couple of thumps, and he moved to another spot.

Tony led me to the stage door. I glanced at the unhelpful reflecting pool while he knocked. It took a few tries before someone answered.

"We could go around," I said, just as the door was opened by a skinny, shaggy-bearded guy in baggy jeans and a long-sleeved tee-shirt.

Tony showed his badge. "Detective Aragón. We need to look around the stage."

"We're changing scenery."

"We'll keep out of your way."

Tony moved a half-step forward. It worked; the guy backed up and Tony stepped in. I followed him through the door and past the wings, out onto the stage.

Out of curiosity, I glanced toward the audience. The house seemed smaller from this angle. The pool glinted in a ray of sunlight reflected off of something outside.

The stage hand was working on a platform stage right. Tony led me up the set of steps farthest to the left. Stepping from platform to platform, we worked our way up and back until we were beside the pipe railing. We had to be at least twelve feet above the stage floor.

I looked out the back at the landscape behind the theatre. The roof cut off my view of the mountains; all I could see were the back deck, the hillside beyond it, and the rainwater collection tanks. I searched in vain for a glint of distracting light. Whatever had caught Vi's eye wasn't noticeable now.

Disappointed, I looked down. The B-lift was down, its surface level with the back deck. Certainly a dangerous fall. I instinctively stepped back and felt Tony's arm come up behind me.

"Careful," he said.

I glanced around and saw that I was close to the front edge of the platform. A much shorter fall, but still not fun. I moved to the center of the platform and slowly turned completely around.

There had to be something here. I was sure there must be.

I peered into the wings, out at the seats and the mezzanine, down at the orchestra pit and the pool. I could see a glimpse of the stage manager's console, and part of the railing on the stairs backstage left.

What could have distracted Vi?

I faced upstage again. She had said she was looking out the back of the stage when she missed her cue. I stared at the back deck, and the hillside beyond it. Nothing.

A heavy tread shook the platform where we stood and made hollow, drum-like thumps. I looked around and saw a man in black shirt and jeans, with a black ball cap pulled over sandy curls, approaching us from the stage.

"I'm sorry, you can't be up here."

Tony showed his badge. "SFPD. Just checking something."

"We have to take down this platform."

The guy sounded cranky. I cast one more glance at the hillside out back, then turned to Tony.

"Let's walk out onto the deck."

"Who is this?" demanded the guy in black.

"Consultant," Tony said, stepping past him to the stairs.

I followed him down and into the wings. The guy in black followed me. I headed for the stairs to the deck, and Tony came with me.

My heart started to thump as we descended. The whir of the B-lift starting up didn't help. I kept my gaze away from the pit and walked straight out onto the back deck, toward the hillside.

"Did you see something?" Tony asked.

"No."

I walked along the edge of the deck toward the north. Now I

could see the mountains, deep shades of blue against the brighter blue of the sky, but I gave them only a brief glance. I peered over the railing at the hillside, which was quite a drop from where I stood. I was looking for something on the ground. Something shiny.

A knife? Come on, Rosings, they must have searched all around here.

"We've been over this," Tony said quietly, echoing my thoughts.

I reached the northern edge of the deck. The scene shop was there; closed. I went back the other way, and down the stairs to the level below, where the scenery storage was. Outside there, we were closer to the hillside. I peered at the ground and under the bushes, until we reached the water tanks.

"Babe..."

Water.

I took a sharp breath and looked up at the tanks. There was no ladder that I could see, not from this side anyway.

I had been able to see the top of the tanks from the upstage platform. Something on top of the tanks could have glinted, catching Vi's eye. The angle of the sun would be different in the afternoon, when she was rehearsing.

I glanced around and saw that the guy in black was watching us from the foot of the stairs. I turned away from him, facing the water tanks.

"Tony, did you search on top of these?"

He looked at me, then his gaze rose to the top of the tank, probably twenty feet high, as his eyes widened.

"Shhhit," he said.

He hopped over the railing onto the hillside and strode to the south side of the southern tank, setting up puffs of dust from the dry soil. A ladder was mounted on the side of the tank, and Tony was up it in seconds.

"Hey!"

I turned to face the guy in black, ready to do my feeble best to fend him off.

"You can't go up there!" he said, coming toward us.

"We have a warrant that says he can," I said, hoping it was true.

The guy in back apparently believed me, because he slowed down and just frowned up at Tony. Tony walked around on top of the tank, then bent down out of sight. There was a moment's silence.

"Hey, Ellen, what time is it?"

I checked my watch. "Nine-forty-seven."

"We'd better get going, then."

He came back down, traded a suspicious glance with the guy in black, and walked south toward the parking lot, where he climbed onto the pavement. He led me past the rehearsal hall, up a set of stairs to the theatre, then up more stairs toward the main parking lot. I had to hustle to keep up with him.

"What's the hurry?"

"You open at ten, right?"

"Eleven."

"But you said you had to be back at ten."

"Ideally, but nothing will explode if I'm not. Tony—"

"Let's get to the car."

I saved my breath for brisk walking. My shoes were reasonably comfortable but not intended for track and field. Between Tony's stride and the many steps up to the parking lot, I was slightly winded by the time we reached the car.

I unlocked it and Tony got in, taking his cell phone out as I joined him.

"Did you find something?" I asked.

He glanced at me, then toward the theatre. No menacing figures were coming toward us.

He reached into his jacket and took out a clear plastic bag, which he laid on the console between us. The date and "9:47" were written on it in black marker, along with Tony's initials.

Inside it was a small, brass, folded knife.

12

I drove while Tony called the police lab. He'd be bringing in a new piece of evidence, how fast could they process it? Yes, it was freaking important.

I wanted a better look at the knife. It looked odd, and also somehow familiar, but unlike any pocket knife I'd ever seen. It was smaller than a Swiss army knife, and much thinner. It probably only had one blade. Very simple.

I parked and Tony was out of the car immediately, grabbing his helmet from the back seat.

"Tony, may I see it? Just for a moment?"

He gave me a hard look, then handed me the bag. "Don't open it."

I turned the bag over in my hands, peering at the knife. Yes, very small. It looked like there was something engraved on one end, at the base. I smoothed the plastic and caught my breath.

"Did you see this?"

He frowned and took the bag, holding it closer and squinting. A second later his face lit with a smile of triumph.

"I owe you the biggest steak in town. Hell, I owe you a whole cow!"

I laughed. Engraved on the base of the knife was the letter "P."

Tony caught me by the shoulders and kissed me. Surprised, I gasped and stared at him. Heat lit in his eyes and bloomed in my cheeks.

"I have to go," he said in a raw voice.

I nodded. "Go."

"I'll call you."

He stuffed the bag back in his jacket and put on his helmet, then practically vaulted onto his bike. He didn't bother wheeling it to the street before starting the engine. In fact, he kind of roared out of the parking lot.

I forgave him.

When he was out of sight, I went inside. The smell of baking scones brought me up short.

Welcome back to a different reality. Soft music played on the stereo: Chopin, a nocturne. Iz and Rosa were setting up trays in the pantry. I peeked into the kitchen.

Julio glanced up. "How was breakfast?"

"Um, fine. Do you need me?"

"No, we're good."

"Then I'll be upstairs."

Kris wasn't in yet. I made myself a pot of tea and carried it to my office, then sat at my desk.

What if the knife we'd found wasn't the murder weapon? What if it was just a random thing?

No, the engraved initial was too much a coincidence. "P" for Passaggio.

He must have thrown it on top of the water tanks, maybe accidentally. Maybe he was trying to throw it out onto the hillside. It didn't matter; Tony had it now.

What now? I felt oddly adrift. We knew who the murderer was, but was the evidence enough to convict him?

If there were fingerprints on the knife, probably. If not...

There would be traces of blood, maybe, even if the knife had been wiped. But all that would prove was that the knife was the murder weapon, not who had wielded it.

I shook my head to rid it of mental cobwebs. This was Tony's problem now; there was no more I could do to help. I had my own problems to manage. A whole stack of them.

I went through my messages, dealt with the easy ones, then made a trip downstairs to say hello to Nat. Neatly attired in a dark green cotton dress, she greeted me with a smile from the register in the gift shop.

"Everything going all right?" I asked.

"Fine. I think we're getting used to this pace."

That led me to several different thoughts, some of which I didn't want to examine. Couldn't stop myself from wondering what would happen if the current pace was our new "normal."

"Thomas gave me your tray to bring back. I put it in the kitchen."

"Oh, thanks!" I'd forgotten the tray that I'd used to take Aria Cakes to the Opera. It seemed ages ago.

"I thought about bringing some Doña Tules for tonight," Nat said, "but I wasn't sure if all the staff are over twenty-one."

"Um, they aren't. Thanks, but we'll be all right. I picked up some sodas."

The front door opened and we both turned, ready to welcome customers. I froze when I saw who it was: a couple, fortyish, middle-height man with curly dark hair and silk suit, petite woman with ice pale hair up in an elegant coiffure and a cobalt sleeveless dress. Neither smiling.

Nat, who *was* smiling, said, "Welcome to the Wisteria Tearoom! Is this your first visit?"

"Yes, we'd like a table for two, please," said the man.

I'd heard the voice before, at a distance. Up close it was a bit forceful.

"Do you have a reservation?" Nat said, glancing at the list.

The woman shot the man a look. They had apparently discussed that question, perhaps without reaching an agreement.

"No, but you've got some tables outside. We don't mind sitting out there." Now he smiled; the smile of one accustomed to being obeyed.

"Well, let's see," said Nat, running her finger down the list. "Yes, I think we can squeeze you in."

She shot me a glance, but I didn't dare speak. The only thing I could think of to say was that we didn't cater to murderers.

Nat guided the Passaggios out to the *portal*, and I was able to breathe again.

I wanted to call Tony and demand that the police remove that man from my property. This, I knew, was impractical, but I enjoyed imagining it.

He had killed a brilliant artist at the peak of his career, and a dear friend of mine at the beginning of hers, and I resented being obliged to offer him my hospitality.

I needed to calm down. I left the gift shop and headed upstairs. Kris glanced up as I stepped through the doorway to our offices.

"Who fed you a lemon?"

I waved my hand, still unable to speak. I poured myself some tea and sat at my desk, nursing it.

Why had he come? It must have been his wife's idea; everything I knew about Passaggio implied that he was not an afternoon tea sort of person.

Maybe she had heard the word going around the opera crowd about the tearoom and demanded a visit. That I could believe.

I tried to put them out of my mind, but I was seething.

Rise up, furies, from horrid abysses...

I hoped Julio wouldn't see the Passaggios. But then, Julio didn't know. No one knew, except Tony, and maybe some others at the police department by now.

My indignation prompted me to send Tony a text:

WANT TO ARREST P? HE'S HERE.

That made me feel a little better. I got up to get more tea, and by the time I returned my phone was buzzing.

NOT YET.

Sighing, I picked up my messages and looked through them, though I really didn't have the patience at the moment. My phone buzzed again.

STAY AWAY FROM HIM.

No problem. The last thing I wanted to do was talk to him.

Too restless to stay at my desk, I went back downstairs. Julio and Ramon were turning out shortbread and sandwiches.

"We're fine," Julio said before I could speak. "Got it covered."

Denied kitchen-therapy, I went back to the pantry for my standby: an empty vase and my garden shears. I put a little water in the bottom of the vase and stepped out the back door.

The lilacs were done, alas, but some poppies and larkspur were blooming. I cut a few, then headed around the back of the kitchen to the south side of the building. I needed roses.

I took my time, smelling blooms from each bush, cutting one now and then to add to my vase. The fragrance calmed me, and inhaling deeply didn't do me any harm. I began to feel more balanced.

I worked my way toward the front of the tearoom. When I heard Passaggio's voice I held still for a moment. My intention was to pretend he didn't exist, but I indulged in a glance.

They were seated at the south end of the *portal*, and didn't look any happier than they had before. All the savories were gone from their tiered tea tray, and one of the scones, but the sweets were untouched.

I was about to turn away when a glint of metal caught my eye. Passaggio had taken something out of his pocket that looked like a miniature guillotine. As I watched, he took out a cigar and used the guillotine to chop the end off it.

My mind flashed to the courtyard at the Opera. Passaggio lighting a cigar, except that then he had used a knife to cut it.

A small, brass knife.

I became aware of his attention, and looked up to meet his gaze. I don't know what my expression told him, but his eyes narrowed.

I swallowed and stepped forward. "I'm very sorry, but we don't allow smoking on the *portal*. It's too close to the entrance."

He stared hard at me for a full ten seconds, then silently put the cigar and the guillotine back in his pocket.

"Thank you," I said, and proceeded toward the front door.

I felt his gaze on me the whole way. My skin crawled. I took a firm grip on my shears, and held my head high as I walked up the steps and through the front door.

I closed it and leaned against it, slightly dizzy. Nat stepped out of the gift shop.

"Are you all right?"

I nodded. "I will be. It's...a little warm out."

I went straight up to my office and left the vase and shears on my credenza. No new texts, so I sent one.

I SAW HIM USE THE KNIFE AT THE OPERA. JUST REMEMBERED.

I waited impatiently for an answer. Kris came in and looked at me.

"Going to the bank. Need anything?"

I shook my head. "Thanks."

She looked bemused. As I listened to her footsteps going down the stairs, my phone buzzed. I pounced on it.

WTF??

HE USED IT TO CUT A CIGAR.

I waited. Finally, when I was about to send a new text, it rang.

"You're sure?" Tony said.

"Pretty sure." I lowered my voice, just out of paranoia. "Small brass folding knife."

"Did anyone else see it?"

"The man he was talking to. I think it was the Opera's Director."

"He might be a friend. Anyone else?"

I closed my eyes, thinking back. "Thomas Ingraham was standing with me."

"I'll call you back."

Dead line.

Feeling useless, I took my flowers across to my suite and tidied them up, then went downstairs to put away my shears. I carried my phone, not wanting to miss a call from Tony.

As I came out of the pantry I nearly collided with Mrs. Passaggio, who was emerging from the restroom. I stepped back.

"Oh, I beg your pardon!"

She paused and gave me a thoughtful look. "Have we met?"

"I don't believe so," I said. We had passed at the opera, but that's not meeting. "I hope you enjoyed your tea," I added, to fill the silence.

She favored me with a frosty smile. "It was very nice. This house is quite charming."

"Thank you."

She turned away and I felt a moment's pity for her. Maybe she wasn't very pleasant herself, but that didn't mean she deserved to be married to a faithless man who was also a vicious killer.

I ducked through the pantry to the kitchen, not wanting to risk encountering the Passaggios again in the hall or the gift shop. Julio was at the counter writing on a notepad, and Ramon was assembling deviled eggs. I snitched one. Lunch.

"There's some soup left," Julio said. "Want me to warm it up?"

I swallowed. "Yes, please. Or I can. I have a few minutes."

"It's in the fridge door."

Ramon waggled a scolding finger at me. I stuck my nose in the air and he grinned.

I found the soup, put some in a bowl, and stuck it in the microwave. When it was hot, I took it out onto the back *portal*, where I had a small patio table and a couple of chairs, shaded now that the sun was past its zenith. I sat and sipped soup and tried to relax.

I was *hungry*, having failed to eat most of my lovely and expensive breakfast. I made myself eat slowly, though Julio's soup had only improved over time.

I gazed at my back garden, enjoying the green and the shelter of the shade. The day was pleasantly warm. Traffic hummed along, slightly muted by distance. Birds fussed in the bushes, and hummingbirds flitted around the feeder hanging outside the kitchen window. Someone had filled it; I hadn't had time.

My phone was annoyingly silent.

Julio came out with his notepad and a small plate holding two tea sandwiches and two shortbread cookies. He set this beside me.

"Got a minute?"

I picked up a sandwich. "Sure. And thanks."

He pulled up a chair and laid the notepad in front of me. "This is the menu for Usher's party."

I glanced through it and whistled. Lobster canapés, roast beef sandwiches, pâté, crab salad, champagne sorbet.

"Will the fee she's paying cover everything?"

"Oh, yeah. You'll turn a nice profit."

"And this won't be too stressful?"

"We're closed all day Tuesday, right? So I'll have the morning for the fragile stuff. Ramon and I can come in Monday, probably just half a day, to prep the rest. Should be fine."

"OK, then."

"I'd like to put in our grocery orders today, so we'll have everything by Monday afternoon."

"Sure, go ahead. Or do you need me to do it?"

"Nah. We're caught up. Ramon's a fast learner."

"I'm glad he's working out well."

Julio smiled. "He's a big help. We're keeping him, right?"

"As long as we need to. But he said he's going back to UNM in the fall."

"We've been talking about that. He might take some classes online and drop back to part-time at the tearoom. If that's OK with you."

"Sure. Better than looking for someone new."

He nodded, then fell silent, hands clasped on the table in front of him. I ate the other sandwich.

"Been thinking about Vi," Julio said.

I waited, watching his face. The frown he'd been wearing lately was there, but softened now. There was sadness in the lines around his mouth, and bewilderment in his eyes.

"I hope they get the bastard that killed her," he said.

I took a slow breath. "Me, too."

He shook his head. "Such a waste."

We were silent for a minute.

"I'm going to change Marigold to Violet," I said. "For her."

He turned a surprised gaze on me, then nodded. "Good.

That's a good..."

His voice had gone tight. I put my hand over his, watched him blink furiously. After a minute he stood, sliding his hands out from under mine.

"Better call this in," he said, picking up the notepad.

He went inside, leaving me alone with the hummingbirds and two pieces of shortbread. I ate one, musing on the myriad forms and expressions of grief.

The rest of the day was uneventful. The tearoom was busy but not crazy; though we were booked full, the staff handled everything smoothly. I lent a hand here and there, but never felt like I was putting out fires.

My phone, though I kept it with me through the afternoon, didn't ring or buzz once. Tony was busy. I imagined him lining up evidence against Passaggio, perhaps talking with the District Attorney, trying to decide if their case was strong enough.

I sure hoped it was. I couldn't bear to think of that horrible man going free.

As the day drew to a close, the staff began to depart. Julio, Ramon, Rosa, Kris, and Nat all took off, promising to be back for the potluck. I took over in the gift shop while Dee and Iz looked after the last few guests. Mick was in the kitchen keeping up with the dishes.

By 6:45 the last customers had departed, and I locked up and sent the staff home. I put the sodas in the downstairs fridge to chill and took the receipts upstairs to lock them in Kris's desk. The warmth in the upper hallway drew me back out.

The drapes were still closed, though a ray of sunlight fell through a gap, spilling golden across the oriental rug. I stepped to the window and opened the drapes, basking in the late sunlight.

Vi had stood here, just before her event in the parlor below. My heart ached at the memory of that day; her excitement, all the promise of her summer as an apprentice.

Vi would haunt me always, not in the way that Captain Dusenberry did, but as a dear friend lost to a terrible tragedy.

No, a crime. Tragedy could be accidental. The loss was tragic, but the cause was a crime, the deliberate action of a criminal.

I had dark feelings about that man, and I didn't want to be sucked into them. I sat in an armchair and gazed at the sheers glowing with light, trying to imagine Vi in a place of beauty, free from pain and worry.

The sun was too bright for my eyes, even through the sheers. Blinking, I looked away, and my gaze fell to the low table before me, where a couple of pieces of paper and a small stack of business cards lay.

Loren's cards. I picked one up.

I should probably call him. Talking through some of this would do me good. I'd have to wait, though—there were some things Tony might not want me to mention. I'd need to check with him first.

I gathered up the papers—handouts about grief—and the cards, and took them down to the dining parlor. I'd mention them and remind the staff that Loren was available.

The dining parlor was big enough for all of us, and any spills would be easier to clean up there than in the main parlor. Besides, the main parlor was rather full of memories.

I cleared off the sideboard and put out some paper plates, cups, and napkins. As I headed to the closet to get out the extra leaves for the dining table, the floorboard creaked beneath my foot.

Maria Hidalgo's letters. I still needed to follow up on that.

Suddenly I felt very tired.

I stood still, thinking about Maria and Captain Dusenberry. How sad that their love had never been realized. If he hadn't been killed they would have married; I was certain of it.

I would find out who had murdered him. What I would do with that knowledge I had no idea, but I still felt compelled to search until I had solved the problem.

I heard a car pull up out back. Glancing through the French doors, I saw that it was Nat's. She got out and took a huge pan covered in foil from the passenger seat. I hurried to open the back door for her.

"What did you bring? An elephant?"

She chuckled. "Smoked brisket."

"Oh my...I owe Manny a pie."

"Cake, dear. He adores cake."

"Cake it is, then. Go ahead and put it on the sideboard."

Nat helped me put the leaves in the table and cover everything with sturdy tablecloths. The lace was put away; this was not a dainty occasion. I set out a bowl of ice and the drinks, and soon the staff started arriving.

Rosa and Ramon brought a huge tray of enchiladas from El Vaquero. Dee brought a big salad, and Mick brought a dozen doughnuts. Iz brought fresh-baked horno bread with butter. Kris brought a slow-cooker full of baked beans. I couldn't have planned a better comfort meal.

We all loaded our plates and sat around the table. When everyone was seated I held up my cup of ginger ale.

"I just want to thank you all for taking the time to gather tonight and remember Vi. Thank you, Julio, for suggesting that we do this. It's been a hard week and I'm grateful to all of you for holding the tearoom together."

Everyone was silent. Some traded glances. Afraid I'd put a damper on things right from the start, I decided I'd better try to lift everyone's mood a bit.

"I've decided to change Marigold to Violet in her honor. If any of you have suggestions for the decorations, please let me know."

"That's a wonderful idea!" Dee said. "Can there be a portrait of her?"

I nodded. "Good thought, Dee. I can ask her mother for a copy of a photograph."

"It should be a painting," Julio said in a rather fierce voice. "I'll do it."

"You paint, too?" Nat said.

He nodded. "I was going to go to art school, then I switched to culinary."

I hadn't heard about that. "Why did you change?" I asked.

"Chefs have a better chance of making a living."

That explained a lot, I thought.

The staff continued to brainstorm about how to redecorate Marigold while we ate. I mostly listened, thinking that we'd need twice the available space to implement all the ideas. It didn't matter; this was helping us remember Vi, and honor her, in a happy way.

Gradually the conversation shifted to stories about Vi. Everyone had a fond memory of her to share, even Ramon, who hadn't met her. He had come to her event earlier in the summer, and been wowed by her voice. I hadn't remembered seeing him there, but I had been pretty busy.

The only one who remained silent was Kris. I watched her surreptitiously, wondering how she felt about Vi.

We had pretty much run out of stories, and room for food, by the time the daylight outside started fading. I was about to get up and turn on the chandelier when it came on by itself.

Everyone looked up, and a couple of people gasped. I helped myself to a doughnut and returned to my place.

"You've all seen that before by now, right? Maybe not you, Ramon."

He answered slowly, eyes on the chandelier. "Actually, I was coming out of the bathroom once when the hall light came on. There was nobody there but me. Julio was in the kitchen."

"Maybe you should have someone do a sing," Iz said quietly.

I thought a moment, then shook my head. "He's never done anything belligerent. I don't think he means any harm."

"But he's not at peace," Rosa said.

"I'm working on that."

That got me a couple of curious looks. I ate another bite of doughnut. I wasn't ready to talk about the letters yet.

The sound of a motorcycle made everyone look out the windows. I swallowed the last of my doughnut hastily.

The back door was open, and Tony must have seen us through the windows. He let himself in and came to the door of the dining room.

"I'm not going to stay," he said, helmet in hand, "but I wanted to let you all know that the D.A. has asked for a warrant. We'll be making an arrest tonight."

Everyone exclaimed. Over the hubbub of questions, Tony met my gaze. He wasn't smiling—it wasn't something to smile about—but the triumph in his eyes matched what was in my heart.

He raised his hands. "Can't give you any details, sorry. But we're pretty sure we've got Vi's killer. I thought you'd want to know."

Julio got up and gave him a fist bump. "Thank you, man."

I carried my plate to the kitchen and came back with a tall wastebasket. The potluck was breaking up; people stood around the table, talking, nibbling doughnuts, finishing drinks. Tony extricated himself and headed for the back door, and I followed him out.

"Thank you," I said. "This meant a lot to us."

He paused, standing by his bike, staring at me in the light spilling through the windows. "I have to go back."

"I know. Lock that man up, please."

"That's the plan."

I stepped toward him, and before I could chicken out, planted a kiss on his cheek. He caught me around the waist with one arm and demanded a real kiss.

A chorus of cat-calls and applause arose from the *portal*. I pulled away, blushing hard, heart pounding.

"Movie," Tony said, and put on his helmet. "Soon."

"Yes."

I watched him ride away, then turned back to the tearoom.

I never saw so many grinning faces.

Aria Cake

Lighter than an Opera Cake, this dessert blends almond and tea flavors in a cake that is both airy and rich. This recipe makes eight cakes. It can be doubled (but you'll need two jelly-roll pans).

Tea Syrup

Assam tea brews quickly and has a robust flavor, but other varieties of tea may be substituted (they may have to be brewed longer; about three times the usual steeping time).

> 3 T Assam tea leaves
> ½ c granulated sugar
> ¾ c boiling water

Place tea leaves in glass or ceramic measuring cup or bowl. Pour boiling water over them. Let steep for 3 minutes. Strain into small saucepan, add sugar. Stir over medium heat until sugar is dissolved, then simmer for 5 minutes. Set aside to cool.

Cake

This is an almond sponge cake (joconde). Our version is less sweet than usual, to counter the sweetness of the other components.

Important: Measure out all your ingredients before you begin, including cracking the whole eggs into a bowl. Cut two sheets of parchment paper to fit inside the bottom of the cake pan. Make sure your counter top is clean.

> 3 room-temperature egg whites
> ½ c almond meal flour

½ c powdered sugar, sifted
3 large eggs
2 t flour
4 T butter

Preheat oven to 425° F. Melt butter in microwave; let stand while preparing the pan. Spray or grease the sides of a 10"x15" sheet pan (jelly roll pan), then line bottom with one sheet of parchment cut to fit. Skim the butter solids off the melted butter and onto the parchment, setting the rest of the butter aside. Brush butter solids over the whole parchment.

In medium bowl, beat the egg whites to stiff peaks. Set aside. In large bowl, beat almond flour, powdered sugar, and eggs on medium until light and fluffy, 3-4 minutes. Add the flour and blend on low speed until just incorporated. Gently fold in the egg whites by hand. When mostly combined, fold in the melted butter.

Pour batter into pan, spreading to edges. Bake 7-9 minutes until lightly browned. Remove and place on range top. Check edges; if they are sticking to the sides of the pan, gently loosen with a knife.

Lay second sheet of parchment over cake, then turn out onto clean counter. Gently remove the top parchment, turn it over, and lay it on top of the cake. Let stand until cool. (Can be refrigerated for one day or frozen for up to a month.)

Toasted Almonds

Spread ¼ c sliced almonds in cast-iron or other heavy frying pan. Toast over medium heat, stirring occasionally, for five minutes. Remove from heat and set aside to cool.

Almond Buttercream Icing

10 T unsalted butter, softened
1 ¼ c confectioners' sugar, sifted
pinch or three of salt
½ t vanilla extract
1 t almond extract
1 T whipping cream

Beat butter until smooth, about 30 seconds. Add sugar and salt, beat on medium until blended. Scrape sides of bowl, add vanilla, almond, and cream, and beat at medium until blended, then beat on high until fluffy, about 4 minutes.

Assembling the Aria Cake

Remove covering parchment sheet from cake and fold it in half (roughly square). Lay onto one side of cake to measure, and cut cake in half along edge of folded parchment. Fold parchment in half again, cut each half of cake in half using parchment to measure. You now have four rectangles of cake.

Lay fresh parchment over a cutting board, cake board, or flat plate for cake assembly. Using icing spatula or long knife, transfer one rectangle of cake onto the parchment, turning it over as you do so (the bottom is more absorbent than the top). Align as you wish on the parchment.

Brush cake generously with tea syrup. Allow to soak in for two minutes, then spread icing over cake, no more than 1/8 inch thick. Move another rectangle on top of the first, turning it over. Brush with syrup and ice with buttercream as before. Repeat with third and fourth layer.

Trim edges of cake. (Keep the trimmings – they're your reward!)

Refrigerate cake for 1 hour or more. Cut into eight pieces: long slices, triangles, or squares. Garnish each piece with toasted almonds and a candied violet.

Doña Tules

The flavor of this drink will vary depending on the liquors used, as well as whether the cranberry juice is sweetened. The salt, if used, tends to bring out the tequila.

Ingredients (for one large or two small cocktails):

> turbinado sugar
> table salt (optional)
> 2 limes
> cranberry juice
> tequila
> vodka
> orange liqueur

Squeeze both limes, saving husks. If desired, strain lime juice.

Place sugar on flat plate or in wide, shallow bowl. Optional: sprinkle a little table salt over the sugar (don't use margarita salt–too coarse). Use the pulp side of a husk to moisten the rim of a champagne glass or martini glass. Press into sugar to coat rim.

Put crushed ice in shaker, rinse with cold water to melt tiny chips. Strain water out, then pour in:

> ½ shot lime juice
> ½ shot tequila
> 1 shot cranberry juice
> 1 shot vodka
> 1 shot orange liqueur

Shake gently, then strain into sugared glass.

About the Author

Patrice Greenwood was born and raised in New Mexico, and remembers when dusty dogs rolled in the Santa Fe plaza. She has been writing fiction for over twenty years (no, not just these books–she's not the fastest writer around, but she's not *that* slow).

She loves afternoon tea, old buildings, gourmet tailgating at the opera, and solving puzzles. Her popular Wisteria Tearoom Mysteries are informed by many of these interests. She is presently collapsed on her chaise longue, planning the next book in the series.

Wisteria Tearoom Mysteries

A Fatal Twist of Lemon
A Sprig of Blossomed Thorn
An Aria of Omens

Made in the USA
San Bernardino, CA
15 December 2015